JOHN L. FRENCH'S
PARADISE DENIED
Stories of Fantasy, Mayhem and the Undead

BOOKS of the DEAD

BOOKS of the DEAD

BEST NEW ZOMBIE TALES (Vol. 1)
BEST NEW ZOMBIE TALES (Vol. 2)
BEST NEW ZOMBIE TALES (Vol. 3)
BEST NEW ZOMBIE TALES TRILOGY
BEST NEW WEREWOLF TALES (VOL. 1)
BEST NEW VAMPIRE TALES (Vol. 1)
CLASSIC VAMPIRE TALES
GARY BRANDNER - THE HOWLING
GARY BRANDNER - THE HOWLING II
GARY BRANDNER - THE HOWLING III
GARY BRANDNER - THE HOWLING TRILOGY
JAMES ROY DALEY - INTO HELL
JAMES ROY DALEY - TERROR TOWN
JAMES ROY DALEY - 13 DROPS OF BLOOD
JAMES ROY DALEY - THE DEAD PARADE
JAMES ROY DALEY - ZOMBIE KONG
JOHN F.D. TAFF - LITTLE DEATHS
TONIA BROWN - BADASS ZOMBIE ROAD TRIP
JOHN L. FRENCH - PARADISE DENIED
MATT HULTS - ANYTHING CAN BE DANGEROUS
MATT HULTS - HUSK
TIM LEBBON - BERSERK
PAUL KANE - PAIN CAGES
ZOMBIE KONG ANTHOLOGY

Table of Contents

Foreword: Write What You Know	9
A Word From The Author	12
FAST EDDIE'S BIG NIGHT OUT	13
A NEW HOUSE	25
PARADISE DENIED	27
THE BEST SOLUTION	43
EFFECT AND CAUSE	55
PI IN THE SKY	61
THE RIGHT BETRAYAL	76
A SECOND AWAY	90
NOT WRONG AT ALL	95
SO MANY DEATHS, SO MANY LIES	102
SURPRISE PACKAGE	115
THE LAST CONVENTION	126
TISSUE OF LIES	139
CONFIDENTIAL INFORMATION	146
CAIN	151
HERO	162
WHAT GOES AROUND	170
Publication History	183
About the Author	184

BOOKS of the DEAD

This book is a work of fiction. All characters, events, dialog, and situations in this book are fictitious and any resemblance to real people or events is purely coincidental.

All rights reserved.

No part of this book may be used or reproduced in any manner without written permission except in the case of reprinted excerpts for the purpose of reviews.

Cover Art by Diego Candia
Book Design by James Roy Daley
Graphic Design by Derek Daley
Edited by Ashley Davis

PARADISE DENIED

Collection Copyright 2012 by John L. French

For more information, contact: Besthorror@gmail.com
Visit us at: Booksofthedeadpress.com

This one's for Patrick Thomas.
Friend, writer and creator of the best bar
that never was but certainly should have been.

WRITE WHAT YOU KNOW

That old adage, "write what you know," is not so much advice as it is a warning. You see, you really can't write that which you do not know. You can try, but you will fail. And trust me, readers can tell when an author is out of their depth – the guys who have never been in a fight attempting to write about combat, the folks who have never known love tossing out clichés because movies TV are all they really know about heartache.

Everything about a writer fuels their work. Where they grew up. Where they went to school. What kind of family they were a part of – single mom, grandparents living in the house, only child, et cetera. What kind of pets they had, grades they earned, summer jobs they held, television shows they watched –

Were they the guy who hid from the bully or flattened them (writers seldom seem to ever have been the bully)? Did they marry their one true love or run through a series of disastrous relationships? Meat eaters or vegans? Boozers or social drinkers? Gamers? Skiers? Card sharks? Horticulturalists?

Well, you get the point. Like any gadget, authors are ultimately the sum of their parts. Which makes me wonder ... what are the parts that make up the writing machine known as John L. French?

I would not presume to guess. Not only would it be the height of hubris, it's unimportant. Whether he was raised Catholic or had three brothers or grew to love the smell of steel being sharpened during his days as a Heidelberg fencing master does not matter. These are the kinds of details quested after by those who are always despairing that they cannot find the doughnut's center.

Who cares why John French writes as he does? What matters is that he does write as he does.

French is a master of the bare bones approach. Now, this is not an insult. I'm not asking you to think of a skeleton to lament how much more his work could hold. No. I'm asking you to remember the opening of the film 2001, where a single bone was capable of revolutionizing an entire planet.

French's stories are clean – devoid of extra verbiage, annoying chatter, the extra nonsense of so many authors. He does not attempt to brag to the reader by showing off his knowledge at the expense of a story. Is he well-read and well-traveled – absolutely. Does he have a variety of skills and abilities upon which he can call – you bet. Would he ever slow down a tale he was writing to slip in some hint that he thought was nifty?

Not on your life.

John French is a writer's writer. He comes to the table to tell tales and tell them well. There is no extra meat hanging on the bones he provides – all the rotting musculature and decaying cartilage which litter the works of lesser talents are trimmed neatly away long before his stories reach the public ... if they are ever even present in the first place. His work is clean, logical, and direct.

The kind of stuff writers like to read.

You, dear reader, are in for a treat. You will not be thrilled beyond your endurance, dazzled by the non-stop adrenaline rush of his words, or any other Hollywood infused nonsense. No. Here, with this guy, what you get is good, solid work. The kind that creeps up on you. The kind you can curl up with and read and simply enjoy. It's the kind of stuff that can't knock you over the head because it's too busy simply doing what literature is supposed to do.

You are about to be entertained. The old fashion way. No tricks, no gimmicks, no attempts to pull the rug out from under you. This book is filled with stories that are constructed methodically, one brick at a time, until they not only can stand on their own, but until they can stand the test of time. When the dust of centuries settle, John L. French is one of the names that will remain when the pan-flashes have long fizzled.

This book is jam-packed with stories that will leave you nodding. Not falling asleep, but subconsciously nodding your head in agreement. Try it. Right now. Nod your head two or three times. That's what we do, you know, when something is just right. When it fits perfect. And that's what this book is filled with – perfect little unassuming home runs. One leather-covered spheroid after another knocked out into the parking lot by the guy we don't so much cheer for when his bat meets the ball because, well, we expect it do so. We know that ball is going to fly. And when it does, we just nod our heads in that time honored, satisfied manner.

I have little doubt you are about to enjoy yourself. Will every single story in this book be one of your favorites forever? No. Probably not. But, will one of them end up one of your top five favorite stories of all time? Yeah. That's quite possible. One of the stories in here is one of my top three favorites of all time.

That's just the way it is when you read the work of an author who writes what he knows.

CJ Henderson/2012

C.J. Henderson is the creator of at least a dozen different series, including PI Jack Hagee, supernatural investigator Piers Knight, the team of Blakely and Boles, the wacky cast of Challenge of the Unknown and the Teddy London series. He has written some seventy books, hundreds and hundreds of short stories and graphic novels, thousands upon thousands of non-fiction pieces as well as the hilariously disturbing children's book, BABY'S FIRST MYTHOS.

He invites you over to www.cjhenderson.com to read and comment on his work.

A brief word from the author

What you are about to read is a collection of mostly unrelated stories written over the twenty years I've been a writer. Some were written at the request of editors; some because an idea came to me and just would not go away and others just for fun. I hope you enjoy reading them.

John L. French

My first zombie story, and second horror story. It was published in Vince Sneed's zombie collection "The Dead Walk Again." I liked the medical examiner so much that I use him as a reoccurring character in my Bianca Jones series.

FAST EDDIE'S BIG NIGHT OUT

Safe: that's what he felt like when he finally became aware of himself. Safe and warm. He hadn't felt like this since...since—he didn't know. It didn't matter. Wherever he was, he was at peace.

* * *

He called himself "Fast Eddie". It wasn't his real name. That was Wallace—Wallace Cromwell. He'd hated that name. Hated being called Wallace. Hated "Wally" more. Hated being asked how the Beaver was. Then one night he saw a movie on late night TV about some guys shooting pool, with Paul Newman and a fat guy. Newman's name was Fast Eddie. He liked that and started using it as his own name.

By then he was mostly on his own. He still lived in his mother's house, but his bedroom was in the basement. He came and went as he pleased. Mostly he went home to eat, sleep, and get clean laundry. Some days he didn't go home at all. There was too much happening on the street—people to see, stuff to do.

Some of the stuff involved drinking—beer, wine, whatever he could get. And some of it involved girls—the ones who gave it away, the ones who traded it. And some of it involved drugs—reefer, crack, whatever made him feel good and forget the boredom that was at the foundation of his life. And all of it involved money. Money he usually didn't have, and always needed. Money his mother had stopped giving him. Money he had to get from somewhere no matter what.

He tried street jobs, but that was low percentage. The guy you robbed might not have any more than you. Or he might be armed, and your payoff a knife in the side or a nine in the head. It was better to B&E. Less chance of getting caught, and VCRs, DVDs and computers always brought him enough to get by.

He went home less and less. One night he went back and didn't have his key. Hadn't had it for a long time. How long, he didn't know. He pounded on the front door. No answer. He went around and pounded on the back. Still nothing. He broke the glass pane of the basement door, reached in, and unlocked it.

Things were changed. None of his stuff was there. He didn't know the man standing in the basement. He did know that the man had a gun. And he knew that the sirens in the distance were coming for him.

Nobody believed that he thought it was still his house. His mother hadn't lived there for months. What had happened to her, he never found out. Without money for bail, he sat in the Baltimore Detention Center for six months, awaiting trial. In that time his prints came back on six other burglaries. He got three on top of the half he had already served. Overcrowding forced him back on the street inside the year.

When Eddie came out he went back to the B&E, back to yoking tourists who went down the wrong street, back to jacking cars from the fools who came down from PA looking to buy drugs. He had to. Inside he had picked up the habit, and now it needed to be fed every day.

He went inside the second time because he got stung. The guy in the Honda looking to buy turned out to be a cop. When Eddie pulled his piece, the cop pulled a bigger one. Without turning around, Eddie knew that there were two more big guns pointing at the back of his head.

Two years this time. Eddie's cellmate was a no-parole lifer who had found Jesus. Or was it Allah? Whoever It was, the lifer always talked to Eddie about a 'better way'. With nothing else to do, Eddie listened.

It didn't make sense until three months after Eddie was out. Out in the cold and rain, huddling in a doorway, the 'better way' that the con had talked about seemed very good to Eddie. He'd change, Eddie told himself. He'd find a program and get clean, give up this half a life, and start living again.

Getting clean was harder than scoring without cash. All the programs were full. The drug treatment centers had waiting lists. Despite his wanting it, no one was offering any help. Desperate, and willing to do anything to escape the limbo he was in, Eddie did the one thing he never expected to do. He called a cop.

* * *

"Yeah, I'm interested…Thought there might be, how much? . . . Oh! That might take some doing…No, didn't say it couldn't be done, have to pull in a few, that's all…Give me your cell…Thought everybody did…Pager, then…Well then, call me back in two days…Yeah, this number. I'll work something out, get you clean." Detective Dante Amberson hung up the phone.

"Who was that?" Andy Russell asked his partner.

"Some stoner called Fast Eddie," Amberson replied, turning to his computer. He logged on to the Citynet and searched "drug treatment centers open beds." There weren't that many.

"I remember Eddie; we almost shot him, what, two years back?"

"That's why he called us—because we didn't shoot him when we could have. Thinks he can trust us." Amberson started copying names, numbers, and email addresses into a document, highlighting the ones he'd try first.

"What's he want?"

"To give us Santos."

Russell's eyes widened. Antoine Santos wasn't a major drug dealer, but he was big enough that once arrested, he could be squeezed until he gave up a few people who were. "How's Eddie know Santos?"

"Used to work for him, still does some running." Amberson hit print. Two lists came out of the printer.

"And for Santos he gets...?"

"Placement in a drug treatment center. He wants out of the life."

"That's it, no money?" Russell was amazed; everybody wanted money.

"He wouldn't turn it down, but without treatment, no Santos."

"We better make some calls."

Amberson handed Russell one of the lists. "Tell me about it. Start calling, partner."

Two days later, Eddie called back.

"All arranged, my man," Amberson told him. "Got a room at the McCulloh Treatment Facility with your name on it...That's right, where Church Home Hospital used to be...You're getting the works—detoxification, blood cleaning, counseling, job placement, everything. You be there tomorrow morning, eleven sharp. We'll get you settled, then you give us what we need on Santos...What's that?"

Eddie had stopped talking to Amberson. The detective heard him say something to somebody, his voice low, as if turned away from the phone. There was a muffled reply, then three loud *pops*.

"Oh shit! Eddie! Eddie!" Amberson yelled into the receiver. To his partner, "Andy, call 2284. Get this line traced. Get an ambo started. Eddie!" he yelled again. No answer.

"Got it," Russell said calmly. "Units and medics are rolling. Anything on your end?" Amberson shook his head. "Damn. Well, let's get out there." Amberson looked at the admissions folder they'd gotten from McCulloh. "Damn," he said again, "and after all our hard work."

When the two detectives rolled up on the scene, they saw the ambulance pulling away.

"Follow that," Amberson told his partner. "Let the district guys and the Lab worry about witnesses and spent casings. If Eddie's still alive, we'll get his statement."

Russell followed the ambulance down Wolfe Street. He groaned when it turned right, bypassing Johns Hopkins.

"Taking him right to Shock Trauma," he said. "Must be bad."

Madison to Central. Central to Fayette. From Fayette straight to Shock Trauma, and the best emergency care available. Russell knew the way—every detective did—and he stayed close to the wagon. He wanted to be there when Eddie was pulled out, to hear him say who shot him, hoping the name would be 'Santos'.

Lights flashing and siren screaming, the ambulance raced down Central. But when it turned on Fayette, it went silent and dark as its emergency system shut down. It slowed, now keeping pace with traffic rather than weaving in and out.

There could only be one reason for the sudden lack of urgency. "Damn." Amberson's fist hit the dash. "They lost him."

Still, Russell followed. From Fayette Street the wagon turned on to Penn Street, and from there down the ramp that led to the Medical Examiner's Office.

Russell parked alongside the ambulance. The detectives caught up to the paramedics just as they were wheeling Eddie into the receiving area.

"He say anything?" Amberson shouted as soon as he got into the room.

"Like?" asked the medic. He was on the twelfth hour of a sixteen-hour day. He'd had two "breaks." Once he stopped for a coffee and doughnut at a convenience store, both of which he gulped down as he rushed to yet another overdose call. An hour later at Hopkins, he had stopped briefly to call his wife and use the bathroom. Somehow he couldn't bring himself to get as excited about this dead junkie as the detective was.

"Like did he say who shot him?"

The medic shrugged. "Maybe. I wasn't listening." In fact, the medic had stopped listening a year ago. He'd heard a dying declaration from a gunshot victim, reported it to the police. That lead to his going to court several times, spending hours waiting in a cold, dark hallway, only to be told the case was once again postponed. When he finally did get to testify, he was on the stand for three hours as a team of defense attorneys challenged his competency, questioned his hearing, and subtly suggested that he'd let the victim die so that declaration could be used in court. When a "not guilty" verdict came back, the medic decided that from then on, he'd be deaf to anything not directly related to treating his patient.

* * *

Like a baby, Eddie felt himself being cradled in someone's arms. There was a gentle, rocking motion. Gradually, the arms became a hand, with Eddie cupped in its palm as if being weighed. He became aware of all the decisions, good or bad, he'd ever made in his life. He saw, too, all the decisions he'd failed to make. Every path his life could have taken was revealed to him. Some were worse than the one he had lived. Most were better.

From somewhere, there was a voice. "A life mostly wasted. An effort at redemption towards the end." A light appeared—a golden light. Eddie was drawn toward it. But he knew without the voice telling him that despite his yearning, he'd get no closer to the light than where he was now.

* * *

"Can you make the ID?" the attending examiner asked Amberson and Russell.

The detectives looked down at the body. There wasn't much to see—a body ravaged by drugs, thin and dirty from too many months on the street.

"Yeah," Russell answered. "For your records, I identify this body as one Wallace Cromwell, aka Fast Eddie."

"And do you agree, sir?" the examiner asked Amberson. There was the slight lilt of the Caribbean in his voice.

Amberson nodded. "Well, Eddie," he said to the corpse, "I guess you won't be needing that treatment now. I just wish you'd held on long enough to give us Santos."

Now would be a good time, the examiner thought. In his six months in this country, five months doing this job, he'd seen too much of this tragedy, too many wasted lives. It was time to do something about it, if these men were willing.

"He still could."

Both detectives looked at the examiner, who had finished weighing the body and was now filling out a toe tag.

"Excuse me, Mister...?" Amberson asked

"Jones—Dominic Jones. I said that maybe he still could."

"And how, Mister Jones, could he do that?"

"I am from the Dominican Republic. My country, as you may or may not know, shares its island with Haiti. When I was in medical school, it was close enough to Haiti that, occasionally, myself and other students would slip across the border to study, shall we say, comparative medicine and religion."

"Voodoo," Amberson said softly.

"*Vodou*," Jones corrected, giving the word a slightly different pronunciation.

"Wait a minute," Russell said, almost shouting, "you're saying you can bring this guy back from the dead?"

Jones smiled. "Not exactly. Rather, it may be possible to awaken a soul, as if from sleep, before it passes on. If so, one can ask what questions one needs to before the soul is called away forever."

Russell gave a derisive laugh. Amberson, however, asked, "And you can do this?"

"I have seen it done. An old man, called back to tell where he had hidden his wealth. A woman, dead after childbirth, summoned from the dark to say which man in the village had fathered her child. In each case, the priest performed the ritual. In each case, an answer came from the corpse."

Russell interrupted. "And there are guys in Vegas who stick their hands up dummies' butts who can do the same thing."

"Ventriloquism, Detective? Maybe. But the money was found where the old man's ghost said it would be. And the child grew up in the image of his announced father."

"Do you know the ceremony?" Amberson asked suddenly.

"This is crazy!"

At his partner's exclamation, Amberson said, "And we haven't seen crazy before? Besides, it's not like we got anything to lose. Unless you've got a better idea?"

"I can do it, Detective. I have watched the priests and studied with them. One thing about this place. It's got everything I need, except…do you know where we can get a live chicken?"

* * *

Eddie drifted. Try as he might, he couldn't move closer to the glow. Then he felt himself being pulled away. He thought he heard someone calling his name. And then—something else. There was something else he had to do. The golden light got fainter, smaller. Like the dot on an old TV, it faded away.

* * *

"Eddie, Eddie, can you hear me?" Amberson shouted, shaking the corpse. "Come back, Eddie! Give us Santos!"

"It's no good, partner." Russell drew Amberson away. "It was dumb idea to begin with."

"It should have worked," a despondent Jones said. He looked at the bodies of the dead pigeons in the biohazard waste bin. "We should have used chickens."

"Yeah," Russell turned on him, "and maybe I should run us all up to Mercy for an emergency commitment. Me searching the parking garage for those birds—catching them, yet. I have to be crazy."

"The only other choice was regular or extra crispy," Amberson said. "Come on, we've already wasted two hours. Let's get some papers signed and get back to work. Mr. Jones, thanks for your effort, but let's not mention this to anyone."

"Agreed, Detective. Now if you two will step into my office, we can get the paperwork out of the way."

It took Jones about ten minutes to find and fill out the forms. Amberson signed them and gave them back. Jones was just putting them into a folder when an alarm sounded.

"What's that?" Russell asked.

"The door to our vehicle bay," Jones explained. "Someone's coming in."

They went out into the receiving area to see who it was. Russell was the first to notice the empty gurney where Eddie's body had been lying. "Or someone left."

Beside him, Amberson swore quietly.

"You know," Jones said, staring at the empty place where Fast Eddie had been, "when you use a chicken, they don't get up and leave."

* * *

Eddie woke up, sort of. Light and sound rushed back in. His chest hurt. He felt the cold steel of the gurney beneath him. Not knowing where he was or how he had gotten there, Eddie got up and walked toward the door. It opened automatically, as did the gate of the vehicle bay when Eddie crossed the electric eye. Driven by a need he didn't understand, Fast Eddie walked out into the night.

He was confused. Memories of a warm, safe place where he was loved conflicted with other thoughts. He was talking to someone, someone who was helping him. He heard a noise. He turned. Talking, then more noise—louder this time. Pain. Eddie looked down at his chest. His shirt was open. He could see the holes that the loud noise had put there. A clear liquid was seeping from them.

Eddie was still looking at the bullet wounds when he wandered into the street. There was a screeching of wheels, then Eddie was struck by steel, glass, and steel again as he went up and over the car that hit him. Eddie stood up and, ignoring the curses of the driver, slowly walked away.

* * *

"Now what do we do?" Amberson asked no one in particular.

"I don't know about you two, but if he's not back by six a.m., I'm shredding everything, and he was never here."

"We'll find him, Jones,"

"We will?" asked Russell.

"Of course," Amberson assured him. "How far can a dead guy go?"

The detectives left the ME's and walked out on to an accident scene. A late-model sedan with pedestrian damage to the hood, windshield, and roof. Two patrol cars blocking the street. A uniformed officer taking a statement from a distraught driver. No victim, no ambo.

"What happened?" Russell asked one of the officers standing by.

"Damnedest thing," came the reply. "Driver here says some junkie walked out in front of him. He couldn't stop in time and the guy went up and over. Says he came down hard, then got up and walked away."

"Driver didn't try to stop him?" Amberson asked.

"Would you?" The officer shook his head. "You'd think the guy would be dead, wouldn't you?"

Amberson looked at Russell. Russell looked back. Neither said a word.

* * *

Eddie wandered, his thoughts a jumble. He sensed a need, but for what? Dimly he recalled the taste of food, of strong drink. He vaguely remembered the touch of a woman and how that had made him feel. Then there was the needle, the high that had made him float and forget. It had taken the place of the others, but it was still not enough, not now, not tonight.

Brightness blinded him. His wanderings had taken him out of the dark streets and alleys and now he found himself on Greene Street. Streetlights, stoplights, neon, and the glow of the not so distant Oriole Park hit his too sensitive eyes all at once. It came back—he needed the light, the golden light he'd been denied earlier. But no, that light was gone; it had been taken from him when he was called back. Its absence left a yearning, a hole to be filled. Instinct turned Eddie to the east, towards the one man who had always given him what he needed.

* * *

"We've been driving in circles for hours," Russell complained. "It's time to give it up."

"It's only been an hour, and we're not giving up," Amberson said in a flat, determined tone.

"Can't we at least put out a description?"

"And say what? Eastern CID looking for a walkaway from the Medical Examiner's. Suspect's a light-skinned black male, about five-nine, and believed to be dead?"

"That would do it," Russell said after some thought. "Look, Danny, we are never going to find him this way. We turn right, he goes left, and we miss him. We drive straight, he turns down an alley, he's gone."

"So we quit?"

"No, we start thinking like cops looking for a suspect. Eddie never was that bright, and I'm betting that whatever smarts he had died when he did, and didn't come back. He's down to memory and habit. Let's hit the Eastside, check out his haunts. See if anybody saw a zombie tonight."

Nobody had. Russell and Amberson hit all the corners where Eddie hung out. They questioned some of the girls he saw when he had the stuff to trade for their favors. They braced the low-level dealers Eddie knew. Everywhere was the same story.

"Nope, ain't seen him."

"Guess you ain't heard, Eddie bought one tonight."

"Hasn't been around."

"Eddie gone, some fool done kilt him over a phone call."

"Eddie got wasted."

"I want a lawyer. This is police harassment."

"Fast Eddie who?"

"You guys don't talk to each other, do you?"

"Eddie wouldn't get off the phone. Junkie wouldn't wait. Blew him away."

"You 5-0, I don't talk to 5-0."

"Thought I saw him. But he be dead, so it wasn't him."

The two detectives questioned this last one more thoroughly. "Where'd you see him? Which way was he going? How long ago?" For answers, they got: "Around, down there, don't know."

"The good news," Russell said as Amberson turned down yet another side street, "is that he's here somewhere."

"So says one lowlife out of ten. And what's the bad news? Other than we haven't found him yet."

"Who says there's bad news?"

"There's good news, gotta be bad news."

Russell thought for a moment. "I guess the bad news is that Santos didn't kill him. Just some crack head who thought Eddie was taking too long on 'his' phone."

Amberson gave a rueful smile. "Yeah, it would have been nice to pin this one on Santos. Murder one, killing a witness—you get the needle for that."

"Damn shame," agreed Russell. "Santos would have sung just to do twenty to life. Actually would have worked out better than if Eddie have stayed alive to give him up."

Amberson stopped the car and looked at his partner, an idea forming in his mind.

* * *

I got a good life, Antoine Santos told himself. *Not great, but good. A decent house, plenty of food, a nice ride, women when I want them. It's not a mansion in Guilford, steak every night, a Mercedes, and Playmates, but it's better than what the slobs I deal with have.*

Unlike his clients—the ones who bought and resold his product—Santos lived outside the drug area. His house was on the east end of Federal; close enough to the Eastern District police station that it was in a safer neighborhood than most. That's why he bought it, for the security. He also liked the idea of the police helping to keep him safe, that the same cops trying to put him away were, by their very presence protecting him. *Irony*, he thought, remembering an old English lesson. It was what Miss Helens back in high school would have called irony.

And was how it ended with that Fast Eddie guy irony, he wondered. Word from the street was that Eddie was shopping him to the cops, that he'd worked some kind of deal to trade what he knew about the organization for cash and a ticket out. Santos was going to have the boy hit, then he'd found out tonight that he wouldn't have to. Poor Eddie, guess he forgot that you didn't use the holy phone whenever St. Kevin was around. Hell, everybody knew that. Kevin thought that that phone was his direct line to God, that one day the Savior would call him up and invite him to Heaven. He got very upset if anyone used it. God might call, and what if He got a busy signal? And who would have thought that Kevin had a gun?

As Santos contemplated his life, he heard a pounding on his front door. *Who the hell is that*, he wondered. Wasn't cops; they'd have broken down the door. Can't be clients; they knew he didn't sell direct. And his boys had the word not to come to the house. Always some fool didn't get the message. *Well, he'd get the message tonight*, Santos decided. Find out who that fool is, then fire him or cut him off. He'll be flipping burgers for his cash and going to the Westside for his stuff.

Santos moved to go downstairs. The banging got louder. Then there was a crashing of glass. Santos paused, got his nine from under the bed, made sure the clip was good and the chamber was hot. He tucked it in his dip, just in case.

More banging, more glass breaking. Santos got to his door just as the invader came through. "What the..." he started as he saw who it was.

Fast Eddie stood in his doorway, his shirt bloody, clear fluid leaking from the wounds on his chest. His face and arms had a death pallor, and he moved with the stiffness of the rigor that had come over him.

"Saanntoooosss," Eddie's voice creaked as he raised his pale hands towards the drug dealer. "I neeeedddd..."

Santos reached into his dip, pulled out his nine. "You're dead," he cried, recognizing the absurdity of his statement while realizing at the same time that it was true.

Eddie ignored the gun, kept coming one step at a time. Santos fired—once, twice, a third time. Eddie's body jerked with each impact, but he kept coming. Backing up, Santos emptied the clip. Eddie slowed, stopped, fell.

Relief washed over Santos. He had stopped the Eddie-thing. Then, as he wondered what to do next, Eddie's left hand twitched, then clawed at the carpet. His right hand moved, fingers clutched the carpet and pulled his body forward. Slowly, Eddie crawled toward Santos.

Russell and Amberson were just pulling onto Federal Street when they heard the shots. They looked at each other. "I got the back," Russell said as they both bailed out of the unmarked car. Amberson gave his partner time to get around back before going through the open front door.

Russell got to the rear of the house just in time to see Santos run out the kitchen door. Both men had their guns out. Santos saw Russell, made him for a cop, and dropped his piece. A good thing. A second later, Russell would have done Santos like the dealer had tried to do Eddie.

"You okay?" Russell heard his partner call from inside the house.

"Okay," Russell confirmed, snapping the cuffs on Santos. "You secure?"

"Under control. Come on in."

"Let's go," Russell urged Santos forward. The dealer balked.

"Not going back in there. Don't take me back," Santos pleaded.

Russell shoved the dealer into the doorframe—hard. "Walk or get dragged. Either way, you're going in."

Amberson looked up as Russell came in from the back, pushing Santos ahead of him. "Found him," he said, indicating the mostly lifeless body on the floor.

Eddie was still trying to get to Santos, his hands and knees weakly moving him along. Hearing the detective's voice, a distant memory came back. He turned towards Amberson, raised an arm, and pointed it towards the dealer. "Saanntooooosss," he croaked out. Then, his appointed task done, Fast Eddie collapsed and was finally still.

The detectives were quick to seize the situation.

"Doesn't look good, Antoine. Dead man in your house, your bullets in him," Amberson told Santos.

"Why'd you steal him from the morgue? Going to dig the bullets out?" continued Russell.

"No, no," Santos protested. "He was dead when he came in and..."

"And nobody's going to believe that, Antoine." Amberson interrupted. "Except maybe me and my partner." The sound of sirens in the distant, getting closer. "You gonna deal, deal now; else you get you a manslaughter charge."

Men in blue uniforms rushed the house from front and back. Amberson and Russell, weapons holstered, held up their hands and badges to stem the charge. "I'm yours," Santos shouted over the initial confusion of men and voices. District detectives then homicide men arrived as Amberson and Russell held tight to their charge.

By the time morning came, Santos had given up his entire network, from suppliers down to runners. In exchange, he was charged as an accessory after the fact in the death of Wallace Cromwell, aka "Fast Eddie," with minimum sentencing guaranteed.

As for how the theft of Eddie's body was explained, Amberson and Cromwell referred anyone who asked to Dominic Jones. Jones, in turn, told the questioner to ask Santos. Santos, whose reputation was only enhanced by the belief that he had committed such an audacious crime, always denied it, but always in such a way as to assure his listener that he had done the deed. The Medical Examiner's Office did get a new, state-of-the art security system to keep whatever had happened from happening again.

With no one to claim it, Fast Eddie's body was turned over to the Anatomy Board. Unusually well preserved for an unembalmed corpse, it was used for three weeks before it was cremated and the ashes disposed of.

* * *

Safe and warm, Eddie again felt the warm embrace of loving arms. He floated, bathing in the warmth of the golden light. It was not for him, not this time. He'd been judged and he acknowledged that the judgment was fair and just. He felt a tug; somewhere a new life was being created. Consciousness faded as the soul that had once been Fast Eddie Cromwell sped off towards another chance at doing things right.

I started out writing crime fiction. I guess that's why I have a different take on vampires, zombies, and the like. In this story, a vampire finds that moving into a new house can bring unexpected problems.

A NEW HOUSE

It is a fine house, thought the vampire, *well suited to my purpose.* He had searched for months for just the right dwelling, similar to that in which he had lived in Europe. He did not require a mansion or any kind of luxury. He was beyond that. He needed a house that no one else wanted, one that would not be disturbed in any way. He did not want trespassers stumbling over his resting place, or vagrants starting fires that he could not put out. Trespassers and vagrants had their uses, but suspicions were aroused when too many disappeared from the same area. He would not make that mistake again.

But the house could not be too derelict. Then the authorities would come and tear it down, exposing his secrets. He needed a place that people shunned, where no one wanted to go.

He had briefly tried living among his prey, renting a house in a residential neighborhood, keeping to himself, attracting no attention. The needs of this kind of "life" proved too demanding. He had to create documents to show to landlords, arrange for utilities that he did not need, hire people to maintain the exterior of his dwelling. He also had to show himself to his neighbors on occasion, just to avoid being thought of as "different". It was too much; too many people became aware of his existence. No; better to live alone, away from the cattle.

Finally, during his nightly forays through the city, he had learned of a house that fit his needs. There had been a tragedy, a death of some sort. It had stood vacant for over a year. No one wanted it.

The vampire learned more. There had been a burglary. The owner had confronted the thief, and had shot and killed him as he attempted to flee through a window. Despite his pleas of self-defense, the owner was imprisoned for manslaughter and should be another two years in jail. The rest of his family moved away. Unable to sell it, they abandoned the house. The homeless and drug addicted made use of it for a while, but even they had given it up, moving on to less visible haunts. The house was his to take.

He waited for the conditions to be right, and created a fog that covered his movements. He placed his box of earth in the basement, in a corner away from the windows. His trunks of personal possessions he also put in convenient—yet secluded—spots. As an additional precaution, he drove heavy nails into the rear basement door and silently collapsed the stairs to the first floor. Even should someone enter, they would not be likely to disturb his rest by coming into the basement.

His efforts had tired him. He would not hunt this night. He sought his coffin for an early rest.

The noise woke him—the breaking of glass, the raising of a sash.

Why tonight? he asked himself. *I watched this house for a week and no one even glanced at it. Some even avoided it, crossing the street to keep from passing it. And now, on my first night, someone breaks into my home.*

He considered ignoring the intruder, trusting in his precautions. But in the end, anger at the invasion and a hunger from his previous exertions caused him to mist and rise to the first floor. Reforming, he saw the broken window in what had been the kitchen. He turned and saw the young boy creeping around the living room.

Don't they ever learn? he thought as his fangs descended. *Well, this one never will.*

He stalked the boy as at the same time he considered what to do with the body. Just as he struck, his quarry turned, staring through him. His fangs entered the boy's neck and he began to feed.

Too late he realized the nature of his prey. A cold burning pain raced through him. He had never felt agony like this, not even at his conversion. As the boy stepped away from him, he was flooded with the youth's last living memories.

Through the boy's mind, the vampire remembered approaching the house, sure that no one was home. Again, there was the breaking of glass and the raising of the window. He got as far as the living room when there was the man with the gun. He fled past the man, but too slowly. There was a gunshot, a sharp pain in his back, and then darkness. Coming back to his own mind, the vampire collapsed on the floor.

Unlike the warmth he received from blood, the chill he had gotten from the boy did not diminish. Rather, the pain intensified, until it was all he could feel. The ghost watched him for a time and then slowly faded, taking the pain with him. Again, there was darkness.

The vampire found himself reforming on the first floor. He saw the broken kitchen window. Turning, he saw the young boy in the living room. Trapped now in the cycle of the haunting, he forever stalked his prey.

My second zombie story, this one saw print first in Vince Sneed's classic, "The Dead Walk". Like so many of my stories, I got the idea for this one while talking to my daughter at the dinner table.

PARADISE DENIED

The Apocalypse was a big disappointment. No trumpets, no Second Coming. Maybe somewhere the Forces of Good were preparing to do battle with the armies of Satan, but not in Baltimore.

All the signs had been there. Astronomers were suddenly unable to find stars that had always been in the sky. And some quasar that had been 40 million light years away was now only 39.9 million light years from us. The scientists tried to explain it away by talking of dark matter and refinements in measurements. But the next month, that quasar was just a little bit closer, and more stars were gone.

And then the Righteous disappeared.

It wasn't like the Fundamentalists had predicted. Planes didn't fall from the sky, and cars didn't crash into buildings when their operators suddenly vanished. It was more gradual. One by one, a few more each day, people just disappeared. A husband and wife would fall asleep together. One would wake up to find only the pajamas the other had slept in. A family out camping would go for a hike. They'd come to a bend in the trail with the children out of sight for just a second. The parents would be left alone. Or a man would leave his house, go back in for his umbrella, and would not be seen again.

Police Missing Persons Units were so busy that they stopped taking reports. Terrorists were blamed, then aliens. The religious right had an answer, but no one listened to them. That is, not until all the children disappeared.

By the time everybody figured out just what was going on, the world's population had been reduced by twenty percent, and all children who had not yet reached puberty were gone. The Pope, the Archbishop of Canterbury, and the Chief Rabbi of Jerusalem (all three newly elected) made a joint announcement declaring that The End of Days was upon us.

What surprised most people was not that Judgment had occurred, but that so many had been Taken. Twenty percent? Who would have thought there were that many truly good people in the world? And they were from all walks of life, though there was a sudden and acute shortage of nurses, teachers, and religious ministers. Yeah, I know, the last surprised me, too. Maybe dedicating your life to God and the service of others pays off.

More poor people were taken than rich. I guess having money gives you more time and opportunity to commit the really big sins. Prisons were emptier by about ten percent. Says something about the legal system.

Who stayed behind? Well, let's just say there weren't that many special elections on local, state, or federal levels. And those groups that had preached about and looked forward to the Rapture were more than a bit disheartened that no more of them got taken up than anybody else.

After the initial shock went away, a feeling of despair swept through the survivors. We had fought the good fight, we had run the race, and we had lost. Our souls had been weighed and found wanting. We were just not good enough.

Church attendance fell. For who could trust a minister whom God had rejected? Crime rates went up as the police slacked off. Why bother arresting some when all had been judged guilty? And charities collapsed as donations dried up and most of the remaining do-gooders left to do something for themselves.

The party started shortly after that, one big party that lasted for weeks. When you know that Heaven has been denied you, when there is no hope of a reward after death, why not grab all the pleasure you can? Drugs, alcohol, sex—why abstain? Adultery, theft, even murder—if you wanted to, why not? 'Do What Thou Will' became the first and only commandment for far too many people.

Gradually, though, some sanity returned. A general religious council was called. All were invited—Catholic, Protestant, Jew, Muslim, Hindu, whatever; it didn't matter—every denomination, every faith was invited. There was a God, and He didn't play favorites. By mutual consent, it was held in Jerusalem. There, Hope was again found at the bottom of the chest.

God had not abandoned us, it was decided. Those that had been taken were the ones who, at that time, had found favor with Him. And they had been taken for a purpose—to warn the rest of us that the end of the world was approaching. It was a test, to see if we could overcome our faults and weakness, to see if we could make ourselves worthy of Heaven.

We had not gotten off to a very good start. But slowly, things got better. Churches filled up again, and charities found even more donors and volunteers. And people went back to work mindful of the fact that each word said in anger, each lie told about a co-worker, each customer cheated, was a step away from Paradise.

That didn't last, either. Humanity being what it is, things soon leveled off. There were good people, better people, worse people. Mostly, there were just average people, content to live out the days they had left. With all the children gone, and no babies being born, the story of humanity was coming to a close.

Then the dead returned.

We were ready for them. With the Taken gone and the universe growing a bit smaller every time we looked up, it didn't take a divinity degree to figure out what was going to happen next. So when the first of the undead crawled out of their graves, there were people there to meet them.

Granted, some of those people had flamethrowers, just in case. No one knew just what we'd be dealing with. Too many late night movies had everyone thinking "flesh-eating zombies."

No one got napalmed. The dead who emerged were more like frightened children—unsure of what was going on, unable to remember what just happened, and willing to go anywhere and do anything they were told.

Camps had been set up, and those who returned were led to them. There they were photographed and fingerprinted, their identities checked against the names on the graves out of which they had crawled.

One thing we didn't know was how many would return. Would all of the dead rise, or just some? Would there be centurions wandering Europe, wondering just what the hell had happened to their perfect world and the *Pax Romana*? Would legions of soldiers rise up and resume fighting the wars that had killed them?

It turned out that not everyone came back, just those who had died in the past ten years or so. When a final count was finally made, about the same number returned as had been taken. Some kind of balance had been made.

It was commonly believed that the recent dead who didn't return were those who, if they'd been alive, would have been among the Taken. The ones who returned hadn't earned Heaven in their lifetime, and were sent back to try again.

One thing that no one had thought of was the legal issue. What rights did the Returned have? I guess that's why so many lawyers were left behind, to argue that point. In the end, a heavily conservative Supreme Court ruled that precedent held: that most rights of citizens ended at death, and unless Congress acted, it didn't matter if the dead had come back or not.

Congress didn't act. Mindful of the fact that their living constituents, the survivors, and (more importantly) heirs of the deceased could vote and those who had Returned could not (except in Chicago, where the dead had been voting for over a century), the House and Senate did nothing.

The camps closed. Most of the Returned were taken in by family. Some just wandered from place to place. Still others found their way into the cities, where they took shelter in the poorest of dwellings and did the work no one else wanted to do.

All this had been a year ago. Back then I was cop, a good cop. At least, I thought I'd been a good cop. I guess I was, by the standards of the day. Sure, I'd planted evidence, but only when I knew my guy was guilty. And maybe at times a suspect got roughed up, but he wouldn't have talked any other way. And if somebody ran from me and I caught up to him, well, he had to get a beat down, just to teach him some respect. But I did my job—catching the bad guys and protecting the average citizen. And I never took more than I deserved, and even then only when it was offered.

It was back when the big party ended. A lot of people started taking a good long look at themselves, trying to figure out why others had left and they had stayed behind. I was one of them. I remember sitting at home alone. My wife and I had split and my son, well, he would have been eight that year. I remember looking at my badge and for the first time seeing the tarnish on it.

I almost quit. For a long time I wondered if the kind of cop I was could give way to the kind of man I had to become. What could I do—go private? Same job, same environment, less pay, and no pension. I could give it all up and do the 9-5 bit, but that would leave me with too much free time to find trouble and get in it. So I'd kept the badge and did what I could to polish it up.

The first thing was to get out of Narcotics and Vice. Too much temptation. My record was good, so I was able to wrangle a transfer to the Northeast Station as a district investigator. It wasn't a high crime area. A few shootings a week in the trouble spots, the occasional B&E in the residential areas, and hold-ups along the Belair Road and Harford Road corridors.

The District Investigation Section office was set up in the old courtroom. When they moved the district courts to a central location, the judge's box and prisoner benches went with them, leaving a large empty space to fill. Some cheap drywall and spackle, second hand desks and chairs from city surplus, and a few computers with obsolete operating systems, and it was office space.

Being the new guy, I got the desk closest to the door. That meant I'd be the person anyone coming in looking for help would see. I got the cranks, the complainers, and the kooks. I also got the people who came in with real problems, the ones who had no one else to turn to, the ones I needed to help.

I was reading reports about a B&E suspect called 'The Spider' for his ability to get into otherwise inaccessible second floor windows, when I heard laughter out in the hall. It wasn't the hale and hearty kind that comes from a shared joke told well, but rather the hard-edged laughter that comes at someone's expense. Then I heard, "Dead man walking." More laughter. After it died down, a slow, deliberate voice asked something. "Through that door, freak," the desk sergeant answered. "Office on your left. And don't touch anything. Hey, somebody hold the door for this corpse." Funny that, fear of contamination leading to a basic human courtesy.

I turned in my chair and watched as the zombie came in. He had the same deliberate gait they all had, moving a limb at a time as his conscious mind gave the orders that once came automatically. They might be up and about, but fully alive, they weren't.

I stood up and waited while he shuffled over. As he did, I took mental notes. He dressed well, a suit with a clean, white shirt and a knotted tie. That must have taken some time, given the undead's usual lack of hand-eye coordination. He carried a briefcase, and if it weren't for his shambling walk and grey-on-white pallor, he could have been any businessman coming in to file a complaint.

When he finally got close enough, I held out my hand in greeting. His face showed what little surprise it could, then he brought up his hand and we shook, me trying not to flinch at the touch of his cold grip, him pretending not to notice. Civilities over, I invited him to sit down with a wave of my hand.

"How can I help you, Mister…"

"Foreman," he said, his speech slow and deliberate as his mouth formed the word one syllable at a time. "Terry Foreman."

"I'm Detective John Scott. What can I do for you?"

"I would like you to investigate a murder."

I was ready for anything but that. Sometimes the undead would come in and try to file a theft or assault complaint. I'd have to explain to them that, being dead, they had no standing under the law, so technically, whatever anyone did to them was not considered a crime. Then I'd find out what happened and try to find a way to charge their assailants. Desecrating a corpse is a misdemeanor, so is robbing one. One of those charges generally sticks if brought before a liberal enough judge.

Murder was a different story, and I told Foreman that. "Not my division, Mr. Foreman. If you witnessed a murder or know of one that's been committed, I can call a Homicide detective for you."

He sat there unmoving, not saying a thing. Maybe he was forming his words. Maybe he was waiting to be told to leave.

"Give me the details," I finally said, breaking the uncomfortable silence. "I'll look into it and call Homicide myself. Now, whose murder are we talking about, Mr. Foreman?"

"Mine."

This was new. I'd talked to many a murder suspect, but never a victim. And it suddenly occurred to me that a lot of cold cases could be cleared up if we could only locate the victims and ask them what I was about to ask Foreman.

"Who killed you?"

He shook his head. "If I knew, I wouldn't be here."

I'd forgotten. In the post-resurrection interviews, it turned out many of the Returned didn't remember their deaths, especially the sudden or violent ones. And none of them remembered what happened between death and resurrection.

"What do you remember?"

"Not much of that last day. I know I had a meeting with my business partner. After that, a young National Guardsman with a nasty looking weapon was saying something about crispy critters."

I wanted to go further, but then I realized that I might be dealing with a closed case. His murder might already have been solved.

"Mr. Foreman, I am going to look into this, but first I'm going to have to pull the report. Give me your number and…"

While I was talking, he had reached into his briefcase and pulled out a folder. He handed it to me. It was a BPD case file, complaint number 06-4G97810. Under the number was the heading, "Homicide – Foreman, Terrence."

"Where did you get this?"

He smiled, "It's one of the few rights we have left."

Of course. The Victim's Rights Bill of '03. When the City Council had passed it, zombie rights weren't a consideration. The bill specified that crime *victims* had the right to review their case folders. And while Foreman might not be a citizen under the law, there was no doubt he was a victim.

I opened the case folder and took a quick glance. On the first page, stamped in red, was the word "Open." That meant it hadn't been solved or otherwise disposed of. I leafed through the rest of it—police and crime scene reports, lab results, witness interviews—it looked like it was all there. I put it on my desk to read later.

"Who wanted to kill you, Mr. Foreman?"

"I can't think of anyone."

The trouble with questioning zombies is that they show little emotion. Their faces generally don't move much unless they want them to. And with a near expressionless voice, it's hard to tell if one of them is lying. I fell back on one of the givens in detective work—everybody lies.

"Mr. Foreman, when I look through that folder I'm going to find two or three people with a reason to have wanted you dead. Why not save me the trouble and tell me yourself? Let's start with the obvious—wife, girlfriend?"

"Wife, we were married five years."

"And how did you two get along?"

"Fine."

The answer came too quickly. I started tapping the case folder with one finger. If he were telling me the truth, he'd see the tapping as a nervous gesture. If not…

"She'd been having an affair." Something showed on his face that time, a sorrow so deep it had to come out. A sadness that death couldn't ease.

"When did you find out?"

"A few days before I…you know."

"Who wanted the divorce, you or her?"

"No, we were trying to work things out."

That could be true or not. Either way, his wife was now suspect number one.

"You mentioned a meeting with your partner. How was business?" I started tapping again.

"Not good—bad, actually. I'd gotten the result of an independent audit and…"

"Your partner was cheating you."

Foreman nodded. Suspect number two.

"Your partner and your wife, were they…together?"

"No, it wasn't him. She wouldn't tell me who, but it wasn't him, I'm sure."

Unknown boyfriend, number three.

I stood up with the folder and made copies. When I came back he was standing. He took his originals with his left hand and offered me his right. I took it, asking, "Your wife, ex-wife, is she…" I fumbled for the right term. Words like "alive" and "dead" were losing their meaning.

Foreman forced a smile. "She's alive, not a zombie like me."

My face must have shown my surprise—the undead don't usually use the Z-word. Foreman kept his smile. "I am what I am, Detective. Thank you for your help."

I walked him out, hoping my presence would prevent any more harassment from the desk sergeant.

It did, sort of. The uniformed Buddha behind the desk saved his comments for me.

"You were with that cadav a mighty long time, Scott. What are you, some kinda necro or somethin'?"

There was a lot I could have said back. Comments about his large size, small IQ, or doubtful parentage came to mind. I even thought about the ever popular 'He wanted directions to your mother's house. I told him to expect at least an hour's wait and have his two dollars ready.' Instead I turned the other cheek, took the laughter that came my way, and went back to my desk.

I called Homicide and told them what I had.

"Foreman, Foreman," muttered the harried detective as he searched through a year's worth of computer entries. "Oh yeah, here it is. It's been dropped into the Cold Case bin. No one's really working it right now, but if you want to bring him down, I can see him…" I heard him paging through a calendar, "…Tuesday, a week."

"So soon?" I asked, not trying to disguise the sarcasm.

"Listen, Scott, I don't know what it's like up in the great Northeast, but down here in the real world we're swamped. The murder rate's been going up ever since the dead returned. Word on the street is that it ain't murder if they come back after you kill them. And you try getting a homicide conviction after the so-called victim walks into the courtroom. Baltimore juries never were the brightest, and there's always one of the twelve who can't tell the difference between alive and undead."

He rambled for another few minutes. When he paused to breathe, I made my offer. "Look, if it's that busy, how about I look into it? If I get anywhere, I'll give you a call, say, Tuesday next."

I got a, "Yeah, you do that," and then he hung up.

I slipped a CYA memo into the case folder noting the date and time that I had been given permission by the Homicide Unit to investigate one of their cold cases, then sat back and started reading reports.

Ten months and three days before the Righteous started leaving us, Terry Foreman was found dead in his car. The car was parked in his driveway, the motor running. Foreman was slumped over in the driver's seat, having died from a close-contact gunshot wound to the head.

Foreman's body was discovered by a curious neighbor, who had noticed the car idling for about twenty minutes before he went over to investigate. According to his wife, Debbie (neé Lochlear), Foreman had left the house forty minutes prior to the discovery of his body.

No gun, casings, or bullets were found on the scene. The Medical Examiner did recover a .38 bullet from the inside of Foreman's head. The bullet was suitable for comparison, should a suspect's weapon be recovered. The Crime Lab did a nice job of photographing and diagramming the scene. The lab techs also dusted Foreman's car, recovering quite a few latent prints, all of which were matched with Foreman, his wife, the neighbor, and the first officer on the scene.

The area was canvassed and, of course, no one had seen or heard anything. Foreman's wife and business partner were both questioned—routinely, it seemed—with no mention of either infidelity or embezzlement. But then, that's not the sort of thing one brags about to police investigating a murder.

Updates filed one, two, three, and six months after the murder reported little progress in the case. The last update listed solvability as "poor" and recommended that the case be placed in the Pending file to await further developments.

There were none—not until the dead returned and one of them walked into my office.

I started with the wife, the ex Mrs. Foreman, who was now just Debbie Lochlear. She'd moved out of the Hamilton duplex she'd shared with her husband and into a pricier Perry Hall condo. Perry Hall was in Baltimore County and out of the city's jurisdiction, but I was only going there to chat—this time, at least.

I'd called ahead and she was expecting me. So when I rang the bell, she buzzed me in right away.

"Ms. Lochlear," I said when she opened the apartment door, "I'm Detective Scott." She let me in and offered coffee. I took a cup and we sat at the kitchen table and talked.

"You said you had some information about my husband's death?"

"Yes, ma'am. I've been asked to reopen the case."

"By who?"

"Your husband."

"But I'm not married...Terry's back?"

She was genuinely surprised. I looked at her hard, trying to find some guilt or fear, but came up empty.

"He's back," I told her. "You didn't know?"

She shook her head. "I knew it was possible, but thought maybe he'd call. When he didn't, I thought that he'd been one of those that...didn't come back."

"How did you and Terry get along?"

It must have been the way I asked the question, because right away she said, "He told you, didn't he—about the affair?" I nodded and let her continue. "It was one of those things. Terry was a good man, the best. He loved me dearly, gave me everything. But he wasn't—exciting. One day I decided that I needed some excitement and went out and found it. Terry was never supposed to find out."

"But he did."

Her 'yeah' came out like a curse, and her words grew bitter as she came near tears. "Someone who knew us, a 'good friend' of ours, saw me with my boyfriend one day. I guess we were being a bit obvious. Anyway, he thought Terry should know, so he told him. That night when he came home, Terry asked me about it. I never was a good liar."

"How did he take it?"

"Sat there and cried like a baby. Blamed himself for not being what I needed. We talked and I said all the right things, the things he needed to hear. Told him I'd end the affair, that I'd make it right between us again."

I halfway believed her. She might have just been someone who had made a mistake. We all make them. But then she might just be telling me all the right things, too, hoping I'd believe her, like her husband had. "Did you make it right?" I asked.

"I would have tried, but Terry was killed a few days later."

We sipped our coffees for a few minutes, then Debbie asked, "When you talked to Terry, what did he say happened that night?"

"He doesn't remember." Did a look of relief pass across her face? It was time to play bad cop.

"Ms. Lochlear, what was your lover's name?"

"I don't think Frank had anything to do with it?"

"Frank?"

"Chavis." She gave me the address she had for him. "But he didn't do it."

"Why not? You were his. You might have told him you loved him. He didn't want to lose you. With Terry out of the way..." I let that hang in the air and changed direction. "When your husband died, you got the house, the bank account, everything. Right?"

"Yes, but..."

I interrupted. "And Terry was well insured, he was that kind of person, double indemnity for 'accidents' like murder."

She caught on. "I did not kill my husband." No tears now. The eyes that glared at me were clear and hard.

"Someone did. Somebody put a gun to his head and pulled the trigger. Why not you or Chavis? You both got something out of it. He got you and you got..." I looked around the room, "...a condo in Perry Hall."

She called me a name, one I'd been called before. "I did not kill my husband," she repeated. "You want someone with a reason to kill Terry, talk to his partner. Talk to Ronald Morrison. That bastard stole from Terry; he was going to leave the firm and take most of their clients with him. Terry was going to sue. He wanted to give Morrison one last chance to make it right. He had a meeting with him the night he died. He never got there. Go see Morrison, and get out of my house."

I thanked her for her time. On the way out I stopped at the door. "You never asked, you know."

"Asked what?" she said icily, wanting me gone.

"About Terry—how he was, what he was doing, that sort of thing."

For a moment she softened. "Terry's dead," she said quietly, then she closed the door without saying another word.

It was the weekend before I could do any follow-up work. A rash of B&E's in the Glenham area combined with a string of armed robberies along Harford Road kept us all busy. Then I got picked for a special detail.

Friday, City Hall. The first Zombie Rights Rally here in Baltimore. Anyone who didn't expect something like it sooner or later hadn't been paying attention to the last 100 years of American history.

I got volunteered as part of the security taskforce, to make sure the prominent undead brought here from other cities didn't end up dead—again. It had happened in other places: one speaker shot by a sniper, two more blown up in a car. It didn't stop the cause, only slowed it down while everyone waited for the deceased to come back from wherever the newly dead go these days. The terrorism backfired. Nothing feeds a cause like martyrs, and having living (sort of) martyrs makes the cause stronger still.

There was the usual rhetoric—Zombies should give up their old identities and adopt "post-existence" names. There was a call for a Zombie Nation, where the undead could dwell in peace. Even the name "Zombie" was attacked as insulting, a slur based on beliefs fostered by horror fiction and the movies. "Revenant" and "Non-breathing American" were the best replacements offered.

Scattered among the above were some ideas about basic human rights— freedom from harassment, fair housing and employment, the right to vote and own property. Petitions were passed around asking the State of Maryland to grant citizenship to the undead. I signed one. As one living speaker pointed out, zombie rights were in everyone's interest. You may not benefit now, but you will when you die and come back.

The rally broke up about eight. We were released at nine, after the last of the stragglers left City Hall Plaza and any threats of violence were reduced to the normal dangers a Baltimore night has to offer.

Since I was already downtown, I decided to do some work on the Foreman case. Debbie had given me an address for Frank Chavis. A phone call when I had gotten back to my desk on the day I talked to her had told me that Chavis had moved on. A few calls later, I had traced him to his last official place of residence—111 Penn Street: the City Morgue. He had died almost six months to the day after Foreman had passed on. Drinking had killed him. That, and the tree he hit doing sixty with a 0.24 blood alcohol content.

Chavis didn't have a fixed address. According to government records, he was among the last to leave the containment camps set up to welcome the dead back to this world. When no one came for him, they asked him his city of origin, and when he said 'Baltimore', they gave him twenty dollars and put him on a bus headed for the Trailways Travel Plaza. In life, Chavis had had a history of alcohol-related arrests and problems. Figuring that old habits die hard and that some come back with you, I decided to check out the zombie bars.

It says something about Baltimore that it's only a short walk from City Hall to the notorious Block. Back in the fifties and before, the Block was Baltimore's main tourist attraction, the only reason for a businessman to stop in the city on his way north or south. Back then, the Block was really three or four blocks long, and its strip joints and burlesque houses were famous nationwide. Blaze Starr's Two O'Clock Club was on the Block, and at the Gayety one could watch the legendary Ann Corio and Irma the Body take most of it off.

It changed in the sixties, with "free love" and increasing nudity in the movies. Fashion changed, too, and by the eighties one could see more female flesh on the beach at Ocean City than Miss Starr ever showed on stage. Videotapes and DVDs brought adult movies into the home, and camcorders let people make their own. By the nineties the Block matched its name, having being reduced to that size, the once proud theaters now cut up into liquor stores, small video shops, and strip clubs where under-aged girls danced listlessly on stage and middle-aged hookers hustled drinks to a tired disco beat.

Nothing happens in this world that someone doesn't try to make money from it. The Block had revived itself since the return of the dead. It was still the same size, but the entertainment had changed.

The strip clubs were still there, but now the banners out front proclaimed "Dead Girls Live!" and "The Naked and the Dead!" The bars were a mixed lot—some were for still breathing patrons who paid for the novelty of having shuffling dead men bring them their drinks. (And where every night some drunk loudly proclaimed, "Hey, I didn't order a Zombie," then laughed like he was the first to tell the joke.) Other bars catered to the undead crowd, where the Returned could be among their own kind. When one of the breathing mistakenly entered these places, they were stared at by pairs of cold, unblinking eyes until they felt uncomfortable and left. It was in one of these that I found Frank Chavis.

It was called The Horseshoe Lounge. If there was a reason for the name, it had been lost three owners ago. The bar wasn't on The Block proper, but rather halfway down Gay Street. It was the third place I tried that night. and I was tired. If Chavis wasn't there, I'd give it up and start again on Monday. I stood in the doorway to let my eyes adjust to the dim lighting, then walked over to the bar.

Unlike his customers, the bartender was still breathing. No surprise there. These days almost any skilled profession requires a license, one of the requirements for which is that you have to be alive.

"Beer, please," I ordered once he decided to pay me some attention.

"No beer," he replied mechanically, "Just the hard stuff."

"Ginger ale, then." I knew how hard they served it in these places.

He put a small glass in front of me. "Five bucks."

"For soda?"

"A drink's a drink, and drinks here are five bucks." I put a bill on the bar. "No tip?" he asked.

"Maybe later." I showed him a photo of Chavis. "Know this guy?"

He knew him. I could tell that by the look on his face as soon as he saw the picture. Would he tell me—that was the question.

"Maybe. Why should I tell you?"

I flashed my badge. "Because I said 'please'." I was hoping that the power of the badge would be enough. It was too late and I was too tired to think of any believable threats.

I didn't have to. He nodded toward a corner. "First booth. What about my tip?"

"Don't charge so much for drinks." I went over to where Chavis was sitting and stood by the booth until he looked up at me.

"Detective John Scott." I showed the badge. "Frank Chavis?"

"I used to be." He waved me to the opposite seat. "Chavis was my warm name. I'm Frank Thanos now. How can I help you, Officer?"

"I'm investigating the murder of Terry Foreman. I believe you knew his wife."

He filled a glass from a bottle of the hard stuff, then offered to cut my ginger ale. I declined. He took a drink, filling his mouth then pausing to swallow.

"Debbie," he said, putting his glass down. Whatever he thought of her was lost in the flatness of his voice. "They say you always remember your first. Debbie was my last. Not everything rises from the dead. I'm a stiff in every way but the one that matters." He looked down at the bottle. "The only vice I have left, and it has to be at least 180 proof before I feel any kick." He looked back up at me. "You think I killed Foreman?"

"Did you?" I asked. I had a feeling he'd tell me if he did. It wasn't like I could do anything about it. The courts had ruled that crimes committed before a person's death were not punishable if he or she returned.

Thanos gave me a slow shake of his head. "No, Debbie was a nice piece, but not worth killing over. When she told me it was over, it was over. Plenty more out there. Of course, after Foreman died, I did comfort her for a while. That ended about a week before I did."

"Debbie ever talk about it—say who might have wanted him dead?"

"Just that scum of a partner of his. Other than that, old Terry wasn't the type to have enemies. From what Debbie said afterwards, he was an all around nice guy, a church-going Christian sort. He'd have to be some kind of saint to take back a woman who did him wrong like she did."

"For the record, where were you when Foreman was killed?"

Thanos made the effort to shrug. "Nowhere near Debbie's place. Other than that, you find out, then we'll both know. There's parts of my warm life that just haven't come back yet. Anything else?"

I pointed to the bottle. "Just one: who's paying for that? You got a job?"

"Government handout; it's not much but all us cold ones get something to keep us out of trouble. Plus I got a few friends left."

"One of those friends named Debbie?"

He didn't answer, just stared straight ahead. When I got up he was still staring. I left him to his liquor and memories of warmer days.

Despite his denials, Thanos could still be the killer. He did wind up with Debbie. And she had wound up with a nice insurance settlement, some of which she could be sharing to keep him quiet. Or she could have killed Foreman herself, with Thanos knowing and not saying. I'd see about getting a court order to look into her financial records. Right after I got back from seeing Morrison on Tuesday.

"Everything I did was legal," Ronald Morrison told me once I finally got in to see him. He'd been tied up in a meeting, he said to explain the hour he had kept me waiting. That hour had given me time to review what I'd learned about Morrison & Associates.

The business grew from the remains of Foreman & Morrison. The two partners had run an advertising firm—not the biggest, but it had its share of regional and local accounts. Morrison was the idea man, the outgoing glad-hander who met and wooed the clients. Foreman worked behind the scenes, running the business end of things. It came apart when Morrison emptied the corporate account and filed to dissolve the partnership. He planned to start his own firm, taking most of F&M's clients with him, leaving Foreman broke and looking for a job.

"I wasn't my fault Terry made the mistake of trusting me. We each had equal access to the money. He could have cleaned me out first if he had thought of it."

"From what I heard, Foreman wasn't that kind of man."

Morrison let out a hearty laugh, the kind that comes from enjoying a good joke. "No, he wasn't. He was a good and decent fellow, the poor fool. Honest to a fault, considerate to the employees, fair with the clients. Definitely not meant for the business world."

"You used him," I said, my tone accusing him of a crime akin to murder, "to build the business, to get everything running smooth, then you screwed him over. The night he was killed he was coming to see you, to give you a chance to do the right thing."

"And I was waiting for him," Morrison said calmly. "Was surprised when he didn't show. Terry never, ever missed an appointment. Didn't hear about his death until the next day."

"Unless you arranged it."

Morrison took the accusation of murder lightly. "Detective Scott," he smiled, "I'll admit that over the last year of our partnership I slowly drained the corporate account. Terry kept the books and he wasn't a hard man to fool. However, according to my attorney, I had a legal right to do so. Terry's attorneys would no doubt have seen things differently, and he was free to sue me. He might even have won, if he had any money left to hire attorneys. So you see, I had no motive to want him dead. In fact, he had a better reason to kill me."

Morrison was so gleefully venal and proud of the way that he'd cheated Foreman that I doubted he'd killed the man. He'd want his victim alive. He would have gloated over the remains of Foreman's shattered career and then thrown the man a bone, offering him a job with the new firm. If he'd had no other prospects, Foreman may have swallowed his pride and taken it. I got the feeling that when the Lord called the next batch of us up, Morrison wasn't going to make the cut.

A week went by. In between doing the work the Department paid me to do, I managed to get Debbie Lochlear's bank statements. She showed a regular pattern of deposits from her job and withdrawals from both savings and checking. She could have been giving money to Thanos, but there was no way to be sure except to follow her. I also checked on the bullet that had been dug out of Foreman's head. It had yet to be matched to a gun, and the Firearms Unit's computer had not paired it to bullets recovered from other crime scenes.

There comes a time with some investigations when you look at what you've got and realize that you're not going to get any more. That's when you know it's time to close the case folder for good. I was at that point with the Foreman murder. I suspected that Debbie, Thanos, or both knew more than they were telling, but suspicions aren't the same thing as proof. Maybe it was time to admit defeat and call the real homicide detectives. I'd give them what I had and maybe they could close things out. For me, there were just too many questions I couldn't answer.

I was going over these questions yet again, looking for answers, not really wanting someone else to break this case, when I thought of the big question, the one nobody had asked. I signed out a car and drove to Perry Hall.

After the last time I didn't think Debbie would let me in, so I sat in my car and waited for someone else to enter and went in behind them.

I knocked on her apartment door. When Debbie answered and saw who it was, she tried to slam the door shut. I was a bit faster and had my foot and shoulder past the door before she could close it. "Get out," she told me, "I don't have to talk to you."

"Just one question," I said quietly, not wanting to rouse any helpful neighbors who might call the county police. "What did you do with the gun?"

"I didn't..." she started to deny it, then looked at my face. "You know, don't you?" I nodded and she let me in.

She gave it all up—what she did, what happened to the gun, all of it. "What happens now?" she asked when she was through.

"I honestly don't know," I told her before leaving.

Foreman lived with his sister in a housing development on 33rd Street, near where Memorial Stadium used to be before Baltimore's sports teams moved downtown. On the way there from the station, I stopped at Lake Montibello. *How*, I thought, looking at the placid waters of the lake, *did she get the gun past the police?* They would have searched her, the cars, the house. Where did she hide it? No matter, every house has a dozen hiding places known only to its occupants. It didn't matter that the gun was now resting somewhere at the bottom of the lake. Let it lay there. No one needed it.

Foreman was waiting for me. "You have news?" he asked, as excited as his kind can get.

"I know who killed you," I told him. We sat down. I took out a sealed envelope. "Before I give you this, what are you going to do after you open it?"

He thought a moment. "I—I don't know."

"No 'Revenge of the Zombie' plans?"

"No. I just want to know."

"Good, because there's nothing the Department can do."

"Statute of Limitations?" he asked.

"Something like that. Listen, Mr. Foreman, before you open that envelope, ask yourself how badly you need to know the name, and how willing you are to forgive the person who killed you."

I stood up and offered my hand. "Good luck to you," I said, meaning every word.

The big question in this case hadn't been who had killed Terry Foreman. It wasn't whether or not Debbie was paying for Thanos to keep his dead mouth shut. And it wasn't why she hadn't told the police about Morrison cheating her husband. No, it was more basic than that. This is a world where the sky is falling, where the truly good have been taken away, and the dead walk among us. So why, in this world, did Terry Foreman, a man who everyone agrees was a good man, return after death? Was it because he had some secret sin, some vice no one knew about? Or was it because, in a moment of weakness and despair, having lost his wife, job, and future, he got a gun, put it to his head, and pulled the trigger?

Debbie told me she had heard the shot and ran out to find Foreman slumped over in the front seat, gun near his hand. Even in her shock and grief, she realized that suicide cancelled Foreman's life insurance policy. So she took the gun, hid it well, and waited for the police to ring her doorbell. Later she dropped it in the lake. When the police decided it was probably a robbery gone bad, she let them think that, rather than telling the truth or trying to place the blame on Morrison.

I closed the case out as a suicide. One day someone might read the file and contact the insurance company. If so, Debbie might be in some trouble, but it's not likely.

I never saw Terry Foreman again, so I don't know if he ever opened the envelope. If he did, I hope he found the strength to forgive himself, to take the second chance we've all been given to make up for the weakness that had denied us Paradise.

My first vampire story. I had not been writing long when I was asked to write this horror story, but I knew enough to say, "Sure, I can do that". Then I had to make good on my boast. Anton Zarnak is a supernatural detective created by Lin Carter. Thanks to Robert M. Price for letting me reprint this story.

THE BEST SOLUTION
An Anton Zarnak Story

"You should have waited."

Sergeant Llewellyn sat back in his chair; a tired, beaten man. He had slept little in the past week. He had been busy defending himself to his superiors, explaining how and why he had led five men to their deaths. These same superiors left it to him to deal with the questions from the slain men's families, who found it difficult to accept their loved ones' deaths. Then, too, there were the reporters, hovering like vultures around any sensational death. They smelled scandal and whitewash behind the Captain's statement that the men had died in a gun battle with drug smugglers. Little information had trickled out of the guarded hospital ward where two injured men still remained. Shots had been fired on the scene, but what else had been reported had little to do with gunplay.

As their immediate supervisor, Llewellyn had been expected to organize the collection of funds for the support of those left widowed and orphaned. He also had to arrange funerals for the two men who had no family in New York, ship one body back home to Dublin, and find time to visit his wounded men. All this, and in his spare time try to track down the monster responsible for the massacre.

"There wasn't time."

Llewellyn's excuse sounded lame, even to him. Behind his desk, Anton Zarnak shook his head with disapproval. "There is always time to prepare properly. From what we have encountered in the past, you should know that."

"Lives were at stake; you were out of town. I thought I could handle it on my own." Zarnak's look reflected Llewellyn's own feeling of having been a major fool. The sergeant continued, trying for some understanding, some hint of absolution. "Look, it's not like this was the first time we've dealt with something like this."

"Yes, but that time I was there to help." Zarnak gestured toward the back of the room. "I'll have Ram Singh bring us something to drink, and then you can tell me exactly what happened. After that, we can decide just what to do about it."

While he waited for the Hindu servant to return, Sergeant Llewellyn allowed himself a small bit of hope. He thought back to the first time he had come to the door of Number Thirteen China Alley. Until then, he had put his faith in nothing but his badge and his gun. That was before there had been two murders on his beat, with all the evidence pointing to a man long dead. He had tried to ignore that evidence, but no other explanation offered itself. Then he remembered the advice his old instructor from the academy had given him.

"Son," Lieutenant Thorner had told him, "A word in your ear. Weird stuff happens, really weird crap that can't be explained by anything on this Earth. When it does, just remember that there's other Earths." He and Lieutenant Thorner were in the Emerald Lady tavern, and the Lieutenant had been drinking heavily. At the time, Llewellyn thought it was the drink talking.

The stories Thorner told that night went beyond anything that Llewellyn had ever experienced. The lieutenant talked of monsters and demons, of people getting lost in dreams and of paintings that killed.

"Sounds like you should be writing for the horror movies, Lieutenant."

"Go ahead and laugh, kid," Thorner said over his beer, "But one day you might run into a case that just doesn't make sense, where logic and reason just don't apply. When that happens—and after you've tried everything, and everyone else—" Thorner lowered his voice, as if passing on a great secret, "Go down to China Alley and see the doctor. Number Thirteen, and ask for Anton Zarnak. Tell the Hindu that I sent you, and those two will help you save the world."

Faced with a man who would not stay dead, Llewellyn finally took his old instructor's advice. He'd missed the door on his first trip, finding numbers Eleven and Fifteen, but no sign of any doctor's office between them.

But he remembered Thorner telling him, "You may have to try more than once. Sometimes the doctor's out of town." His old instructor had not explained any further, so the young patrolman paid another visit to China Alley, and this time Number Thirteen beckoned.

He was greeted by a tall, slender man, who would have appeared young but for a silver-grey streak that ran through his hair. Llewellyn took him for a servant and asked for Doctor Zarnak.

"I am Zarnak."

At the officer's puzzled look, the doctor added, "Is something wrong?"

"Sorry, sir, I was expecting someone older."

"Most people do."

Zarnak lead him into an elaborate office. Against the far wall was a desk piled high with books that had overflowed the many bookcases in the room. There may have been other objects in the room, but Llewellyn saw none of them. His whole attention was drawn to a hideous, three-eyed mask hanging just behind the desk.

"Fascinating, is it not?" Zarnak seated himself behind the desk. "Forgive my lack of hospitality, Officer, but my assistant had to remain out of town on business. He should be back sometime tonight, though."

Llewellyn heard none of this. He just stared at the devil face on the wall and finally asked, "What is that?"

Zarnak looked back at the mask. "*Yama*, a mostly dead god. I keep it there as a reminder."

"Of what?"

"Let us just say that it is a reminder of my own weakness. You may ask Lieutenant Thorner to tell you the story one day. That is who sent you, is it not?" At Llewellyn's nod he continued, "Well then, Officer, tell me your problem and I will see if I can help."

Doctor Zarnak did help. And together they stopped the murders and put a troubled soul to rest.

That was the first, but not the last time that Llewellyn had called on the doctor for help. Since then...

Llewellyn's reverie was broken by the arrival of Ram Singh, with drinks. The sergeant realized that he had almost fallen asleep.

"Sorry," he said sheepishly.

"Nonsense," said Zarnak. "You look as if you could use a few good nights of rest."

Llewellyn accepted his drink from Ram Singh. "I'll rest when this monster's caught and destroyed." He looked at Zarnak. At a nod from the doctor, he began his story.

* * *

It was just after you had left for San Francisco (Llewellyn began) that I got a call from Trapp at the morgue. Ever since he involved himself in that mess over in the Bronx, he's been getting all the bodies that look even the slightest bit strange. The other doctors are glad to be rid of them, and they'd rather Trapp be the one to explain a posting of "Death by internal insect infestation" to the Coroner.

Anyway, I was busy with that double murder I told you about just before you left. It was the brother-in-law, but I couldn't prove it right away. The press was making a big deal out of it, and the Captain was breathing down my neck, so I wasn't able to see Trapp as soon as I should have. Well, after I broke the guy's alibi, I went to see Trapp the first thing my next tour.

When I got there, Trapp was working on a body that had been fished out of the river. It had been there a while and was pretty much gone. Trapp looked up from his work as I walked in. "You're late."

"Trapp, it's eight in the morning; how early should I have been here?"

"Last Tuesday, but now that you've found the time, go look in the big box. They're against the far wall."

He grabbed for some kind of cutter and bent back over the body. I decided that I had been dismissed and went to see what he was talking about.

The 'big box' is the large freezer where the unclaimed bodies are kept. How long bodies are supposed to stay in there I don't know, but it wouldn't be the first time that Trapp had changed the date on a toe tag to keep something of interest from going to Potter's Field.

There were three of them. Even if Trapp hadn't told me which ones they were, I would have been able to guess. They were the only three in there whose heads had been turned around backwards.

I walked over and examined them. None of the three appeared to have been anyone who would have been missed. The victims were little more than skin over skeleton frames. Their appearance went beyond the ravages of hunger; they looked shrunken, reduced somehow. All were wearing the ragged clothes and multiple layers that mark the bums and derelicts the mayor keeps promising to get off of the streets. Somehow, I don't think this is what he had in mind.

I checked the tags, two John Does and one Jane Doe. The heads had all been twisted around to the point where the spinal cord would have snapped at the base of the neck. I'd only seen something like it once before, and I know you've seen it. It did not give me a good feeling, and I started to wish that I had let that double murder wait a while and that I had been there Tuesday when Trapp first called.

Twisted as they were, it was difficult to examine the necks for the wounds I knew would be there. Nevertheless, on each body I found what I was looking for: a straight tear just at the jugular. These three hadn't been shrunken; they'd been drained.

"Death by exsanguination, in case you weren't sure." Trapp came up behind me. "I thought the first one was just a routine exposure case, but the wound and the total lack of blood suggested that he had died of something more than cold and hunger. I called you right away. Since then, these other two have come in."

"What about the necks, were they found like that?"

"Oh no, I had Otto twist them around just in case. I don't really like it when my 'patients' get up and leave, and from the looks of things, we have one too many vampires walking the streets of New York as it is."

Vampires. Trapp had said it. I know we've faced these things—and worse—before, but it still seems strange to say the word and know that a creature like that is real. It still sounds like something out of the movies or Weird Tales.

I didn't bother telling Trapp that it takes more than just the draining of blood to turn a victim into the undead, that it takes a willful act on the part of the vampire, and most of them really don't want the competition. He had done what he thought was best, even risked his job in doing it, since that kind of mutilation is frowned upon, so I said nothing to him. Besides, I was more interested in where the bodies had been found. I had another killer to track down, and I wanted to get started as soon as I could.

The first thing I did after leaving the morgue was to come here. When I walked down China Alley and didn't see the door, I remembered that you had told me you would be going out of town. Thorner's retired, and not really up to fighting monsters anymore. So that left me—Thomas Llewellyn, NYPD Sergeant and fearless vampire hunter—to save the day.

Looking back, I don't know how I could have done it any differently. Three people dead in a week; how could I have waited? If I had known when you'd be back, maybe—I don't know. All I knew is that I couldn't stand by and let a monster hunt in my city without trying to stop it.

The first part was easy: finding the beast. You usually rely on me for that part anyway. The creature was either native or had come over from Europe. I put some of my men on checking undertakers, mortuaries, and casket makers for any thefts, missing bodies, or any strange or unusually large orders. The rest I sent to the docks to see if any shipments of coffins or large amounts of dirt had arrived just before last Tuesday.

Things went the way they should have. One of my men found a freighter that had brought over three boxes of dirt for a "Mr. Durant." This same Durant had a carter take these boxes to an address in Queens. We didn't have any luck with the casket makers and such, but another of my men was smart enough to start checking the cemeteries. One of them reported that a mausoleum had been broken into. The bodies had been dumped and the coffins taken.

The place in Queens was empty when we got there. It was a warehouse, and the new tenant had already moved in. We checked with the landlord, but Durant had moved out without notice or a forwarding address.

We finally found him after checking with realtors and rental agents. A Mr. Durant had just rented a house over in Brooklyn. The agent was glad to get rid of it and had let it cheap. It had been on the market for years, and was rather run down.

Okay, here's where I made my big mistake. If I had thought it out, I might have—*might* have, mind you—just watched the house and waited for you. But no, I was feeling cocky, and lucky, and wanted to get this creature before he killed anyone else. And, to be honest, I was a bit thrilled to be doing it alone, without help from you, Ram Singh, or Thorner. After all, it is my job to protect the citizens of New York, and I like to think I can do it without help.

I had a vision of sitting here, in your office, sipping brandy like we are now, but instead of telling you how I got my men killed, I'd just casually mention how, while you were gone, I'd tracked down and killed a vampire.

Looking back, yes, I should have waited, but we'd found him so easily. I thought we were dealing with a very new, or very stupid, vampire. Even the slowest crook down in the Kitchen knows that you don't keep using the same name if you don't want to get caught. It didn't occur to me that this monster might not care if we tracked him, might have wanted us to. I didn't think that he might even be laying a trap.

Trapp hadn't reported any more bodies, so I decided to go in.

We did it by the book. Your book, not the NYPD's. Just after sunrise we hit the house. We all had crosses and holy water, and me and one or two of the others had taken communion at an early mass. We went in, and the first thing we did was make sure that all the shades were open and sunlight was coming in through all the windows.

He wasn't on either the first or second floors, so that left the basement. We used axes to chop holes in the floors. We wanted to make sure that there was enough sunlight shining down there before going down. Everything was perfect, and that's when it all went to hell.

We had our stakes out and were ready to go when Thompson came flying down the steps from the second floor. He landed hard, and just from the way he laid there I could tell he was dead, and had been dead before he was thrown down the stairs. The way he was twisted, I knew that both his back and neck had been broken, and we hadn't heard a thing.

I froze for a second, just a second, maybe not even that long. I'd been up there and hadn't seen a thing. There certainly hadn't been anything up there that could have done that to Thompson. Before I could order my men back up, he came down.

Durant didn't look like a vampire. He was simply dressed in dark trousers and a white shirt that was open at the neck, as if he had been resting and we had disturbed him, which was the case. He was the smallest of all the men there, about five eight and one fifty. His face, though—it had a look of confidence, of superiority. I could tell that he regarded us as no more than a moment's diversion. He was our better, and we were no threat at all.

He smiled slightly as he came down the stairs. The steps had a slight turn just before the bottom, forming a small landing. There was a window at this landing, and the morning sun was streaming through. Durant briefly lost his smile as he passed through the light beam, but otherwise it did not seem to have affected him.

By this time we all had our crosses out. We'd planned for a confrontation, just in case. We'd use the crosses to force him into a corner, then douse him with holy water. In his weakened state, we'd be able to stake him.

Kenny was the first man he reached. Kenny stood his ground—I'll give him that. He held that cross out in a two handed firing stance, just waiting for

Durant to back off. By the time we all realized that Durant was not going to back off, it was too late. Durant took one look at Kenny's cross, gave a small laugh, then reached out and grabbed it.

I could smell the vampire's burning flesh as he crushed the cross. Then, as quick as thought, before Kenny could retreat, Durant reached over, grabbed Kenny, and ripped off his left arm.

That started it. I would have called for a withdrawal if I could. But Durant pushed Kenny on top of Thompson, then threw his arm into our midst like an ancient challenge. Then he stood there and waited, as if saying, "Come get me."

There was no stopping them—or me, either, to tell the truth. Two of our own were down with the killer in front of us. Ross and Martello were the first to act. They had their holy water out and splashed him with it. Again there was that burning smell, and you could see Durant's clothing and skin smoking. He ignored it and punched Ross through the chest, caving it in. Martello, he picked up and threw through the window.

O'Brien drew his revolver and emptied it into Durant. The bullets staggered him as they passed through, but that's all they did: pass through. One shot did ricochet and got Johnson in the leg, taking him out of the fight. Morgan and Patterson approached Durant, holding their stakes in front of them like short spears.

As Morgan and Patterson approached from either side, I came at him from the front. He left himself open and I threw my stake, hoping for a lucky hit, or at least to distract him and give the others a chance. He wasn't distracted, and they never really had a chance. He swerved to dodge my throw, then grabbed Morgan's stake and swung him around into Patterson, knocking both men down. He then reversed the stake and used it to pin them both to the floor. O'Brien picked up the stake I had thrown and charged Durant. He came close, but Durant stepped aside at the last moment, reached out, and snapped O'Brien's neck.

That left him and me. I didn't know what I could to do to stop him, but I was going to try. I took out my cross, reversed it, held it like a knife and waited for him to come.

"That just might work," he spoke for the first time. He had a middle-European accent and spoke like he'd been an important man when he was alive, or he wanted everyone to think so. "Yes, that might work, if it had a point and an edge."

We stood there for a time. I did not want to attack him, but I could not leave my men. The next move was his.

"You are their commander, are you not?" Durant did not wait for me to reply. "I will let you live, this time. There is an odor of sanctity about you—and him." He indicated Johnson in the corner, holding his wound and trying to keep from bleeding to death. "You both took His wafer this morning, and your blood is not now fit for drinking. Take him and go."

"Not without the others." Where I got the courage I don't know, but I gripped the cross tighter and readied myself for his charge.

"Oh—them. Return an hour after sundown. I shall be gone, and you can have what is left of them. Or you can die now."

If it had been just me, I might have gone after him. Ross was still alive—dying, yes, but right then he was still alive. I didn't want to leave him for Durant to feed on. But there was Johnson—him I could save—and maybe Martello outside. I helped Johnson up and started to walk out when his voice stopped me.

"One other thing, Officer. Do not hunt me again. You will only lose more men, and force me to turn my attentions to the more prominent members of this city. Leave me alone, and you and they will be safe."

With that, he was gone.

I got Johnson into one of the cars we had come in. Martello I found outside the window he had gone through. Even without knowing what they were, I could tell his injuries were serious. Somehow I got him in the car without doing much more damage. I drove us all to the hospital and then pretended to be in shock until it was safe to go back for the others. They were all still there, more or less as I had left them. Ross had been drained. I had Otto twist his neck just in case. There was no sign of Durant anywhere. I fired the house anyway. If he was in there, he'd be little more than ash, but the next day Trapp called and told me that two more bodies had shown up. He's still out there, Doctor, and I don't know if we can stop him.

* * *

Llewellyn ended his narrative by draining his glass of brandy. Without having to be asked, Ram Singh filled it again. Llewellyn took another healthy swallow and placed it on the side table.

Llewellyn had begun his report quite matter-of-factly, as if he were on the witness stand and was testifying against any common felon. He faltered a bit when he got to the morgue and the tracking of Durant. He was near tears and collapse as he described the brutal murders of his men. His voice stayed steady, but when he finished, he was almost as white as one of Durant's victims.

Zarnak remained silent to give the sergeant time to recover from the ordeal of his narrative. When the sergeant was at least somewhat composed, Zarnak leaned forward and granted him what absolution he could.

"You did as much, if not more, than any man could, Sergeant. Had I been with you, well, it might have been that Number Thirteen would now be waiting for a new tenant."

The telling of his tale—completely this time, without the omissions that he'd had to make for his official report, along with Zarnak's understanding—purged Llewellyn of the disgust he had felt for his actions so far. The guilt

Paradise Denied

was still there. It would be a long time fading, and would never leave him entirely, but he was whole again, ready to rejoin Zarnak in their fight against the dark things.

Zarnak reached into his vest pocket and checked the time. The time was late, and soon it would be growing dark.

"You need to rest," he said to Llewellyn in a tone that allowed for no argument. "You will spend the night here, and tomorrow we will begin the hunt anew. Ram Singh will show you to your room."

Dismissed by Zarnak, the sergeant allowed himself to be led out of the room and upstairs to bed. Once asleep, he had his first peaceful rest since his visit to the morgue.

Zarnak did not sleep, could not, as long as the problem lay before him.

What is this thing, he asked himself, *that resists both blessed water and sunlight? Might it be more then the undead?* He thought about this for a moment, then provided his own answer.

No, if it were something else, or from some other plane, it would not have reacted at all to the water or the cross. It is some form of nosferatu, *but what?* For the answer he turned to his books. Knowing what was contained in each one, his eyes searched the shelves for the one title that might help. He finally settled on Seward's *The Undead*.

There was little in the book that Zarnak did not already know. It did confirm, however, that in some circumstances, the undead could walk abroad in the daylight, although at some cost. Still, Seward had had only one encounter with such a beast, the rest of his volume being research conducted from behind the safety of library walls. And all of that research insisted on the power of Christian symbols.

"And what if the vampire was not a Christian?" Zarnak wondered. "If Ram Singh were so infected, would he flinch from the cross, and would the water burn like acid?"

Zarnak again checked Seward's book, but the author had apparently not considered that possibility, or had thought it not worth a mention.

It does not matter, Zarnak finally decided *The power of the symbols lies in the faith of those who use them, not in the past beliefs of the undead.*

Llewellyn had put his faith in those symbols and had been routed. Was his faith weak, or could it be that Durant's faith in himself was stronger? If so, how old must he be to overcome his natural fear of such items?

Zarnak realized that this creature would have to be very old, much older than Tepes and Ruthven, possibly by several hundred years. He would be one of the elders of the undead. A vampire that old might develop a tolerance for holy objects.

Zarnak spun in his chair, and studied the mask on the wall. "How do I fight this thing?" he asked it. "My traditional weapons will not work; it is effectively immune to the usual banes of vampires. If one were fast enough and could get close enough, a sword could take off its head. A crossbow with wooden quarrels might work, assuming we could hit his heart, but he is likely too fast for mortals. There must be a solution."

With that word came the answer. In reviewing his considerations of the night, Zarnak realized that he did indeed have the solution, or soon would have.

Zarnak summoned Ram Singh, knowing his servant would not sleep as long as he was awake. As the Hindu came into the room, Zarnak handed him a liter bottle he had pulled from a shelf.

"Go to Father Flynn, have this filled directly from the baptismal font. Return as soon as you can. I will be in the work room."

* * *

The next morning, after Llewellyn awoke, Zarnak explained his plan.

"Are you sure it will work, Doctor?"

"Nothing is certain, my friend, but it is probably our best hope. If we fail, the city will be at this fiend's mercy, and we will be either dead or his slaves in darkness."

The two men left number Thirteen, Llewellyn carrying a double-edged sword wrapped in cloth, and Zarnak a small glass jar containing a clear liquid. They made their way to the front of a derelict house. Llewellyn had identified it as Durant's current lair. Like the first, it had been abandoned by all but the most desperate of the poor. And it was unlikely that any but the vampire remained.

"Are you sure that this is his lair?"

"He hasn't made any secret of it, Doctor. I tracked him down as easily as I did the last time. It's as if he wants us to come after him."

"No doubt he does, Sergeant. As you said before, we are mere diversions to him, games with which to pass a small part of eternity."

As Zarnak removed the lid from the jar, Llewellyn unwrapped the sword and let its covering fall to the ground. "I'd still feel better if Ram Singh were here, carrying this."

"You've earned the right to wield it. Besides, if we fail, it's best if someone were left behind to continue the fight, however desperate it might be. Ram Singh will know who to call for help."

Uncapping the jar, Zarnak lead the way into the house.

With sufficient light streaming in through broken windows, the pair did nothing but stand by the front door and wait in what had once been a parlor. They did not wait long.

Llewellyn later said that Durant appeared in less than the blink of an eye. One moment the two men were standing in an empty room, and the next the vampire was there, standing across from them.

Paradise Denied

"Again, Officer? You do not learn fast in this country, do you?" Durant made a show of sniffing the air. "And you have been to church again. Communion with Him will not save you this time, or your friend."

Neither man offered a reply. As arranged, Zarnak approached first with the jar, closely followed by Llewellyn.

"Did you not tell him that such things as that weak tea he carries will not stop me?"

At that taunt, Zarnak hurled the contents of the jar into the vampire's face. Durant waited for it, prepared to shrug it off and then turn on his attacker. Instead, he fell to the floor, screaming.

"Now!" Zarnak shouted, and Llewellyn came forward with the sword, and brought it down upon the monster's neck. As he swung, he caught a glimpse of the now helpless creature. Its face was being eaten away, the flesh falling off to reveal the skull beneath. Some of the liquid had missed Durant's face and was instead eating its way through his clothing and into the body beneath it. There came the smell of rotting eggs, of sulphur, of Hell itself.

Llewellyn paused for just a moment. This creature had claimed his city as its hunting ground, had killed without mercy. This thing had murdered his men, fed off of one them and had threatened to do the same to Llewellyn. It was with no small satisfaction that he let the sword fall and sever the head. Without hesitation, he brought it up again, reversed it, and, remembering how Durant had staked two of his men to the floor, thrust the sword down into the body and through Durant's heart.

The two men stood back from the smoldering body. The sword, its point pinning Durant to the floor, stood straight, its hilt and guard forming a cross over the corpse. Truly dead, the body now began its long delayed process of decomposition.

Zarnak and Llewellyn waited until the last of the body had rotted away. Only the skull and a few bones were left when Zarnak motioned to the detective to withdraw the sword. The doctor put on heavy gloves, drew a sack out from beneath his coat, and gathered up the bones.

"We'll have Trapp burn these in the crematorium," said Zarnak, pulling off the gloves once he had the sack tied tightly.

"Doctor, I really wasn't sure it would work. I prayed that it would, but I wasn't sure until I saw his face going."

"Perhaps, Sergeant, it was your prayers that did it."

"That, and your 'solution' to our problem."

"Yes, well, it came to me in my office. I asked myself what the solution to this problem could be. Then I remembered. Holy water, in addition to being blessed, is still water. It retains all the physical properties of water. And one of those properties is that you can combine it with other chemicals to make solutions of various kinds."

"Like sulphuric acid."

"Yes, like sulphuric acid. Holy water affects most vampires as if it were acid. With this monster, we needed something stronger. I reasoned that an acid made from holy water might affect him as it would us, possibly more so."

"Thank God you were right, Doctor."

"Yes indeed, Sergeant, let us thank God, and pray that in our struggle against evil, we'll always be led to the best solution."

The Pelgimbly Institute for the Advanced Sciences was created by my good friend and sometimes collaborator C. J. Henderson, who generously invited me to play along. When he did, I could not resist offering my answer to an age-old question.

EFFECT AND CAUSE

The cause is hidden; the effect is visible to all.
Ovid, Metamorphoses, 4. 287

It's the age-old paradox—what if you went back in time, back to before you were conceived, and killed your father? What then would become of you? Already in existence, would you become an orphan in time, with no past and an uncertain future? Or, having deleted your reason to be, would you simply fade into oblivion?

It was not a knowable answer. At least, not according to all those in the know at the Pelgimbly Center for Advanced Sciences. Ginderhoff, Morvently, Jones, Brodsky—even Brodsky's prize simian, Cheeta von Graystoke—all agreed that the paradox was unsolvable.

Dr. Wendel Q. Wezleski, PhD, inventor of the insta-warm bathroom slipper and discoverer of the first practical theories of time travel, did not agree or disagree with his colleagues. I was there, just one of several newly hired Pelgimblian research assistants, when Drs. Wezleski and Jones were giving us newbies a mandatory orientation lecture on the dos and don'ts of time travel when someone asked "the question".

A smile crossed both their faces at mention of the paradox, ones so perfectly natural they made it clear both had been asked this particular question many times, and that, indeed, they would've been disappointed had someone not asked it then. Looking one to the other, Wezleski stepped back, allowing his colleague to take the question. Running a hand through his already unruly hair, Jones simply shrugged and said:

"Who knows?"

From what I'd heard of these men, this was not a phrase either of them used very often. Between the two of them, it was said they knew just about everything worth knowing, and a lot that wasn't. In this case, Jones explained their collective lack of knowledge.

"To know this would require that someone go back in time and kill his own father then return to tell us about it. Murder, however, is something frowned upon here at the Pelgimbly Center, by most of us anyway—especially if there's no profit in it." Those of us who had already met Director Aikana chuckled.

"One day it might happen, and if the patricide makes it back and does not disappear into a time stream that never was, then we'll know, but not before. I suspect, however, that time behaves much like running water. When it comes to an obstacle, it flows around it and continues on its way. But enough of that. Let me show you what you've no doubt been waiting for."

At that point, Wezleski left for who knew what while Jones led us from the lecture hall into an adjoining room, empty but for a control panel along one wall. He sat down and began to fiddle with dials and levers. "Atomic energies to power," I heard him mutter, "turbines to speed." As he did, a door appeared in the center of the room.

"Any requests?"

People began to shout out dates and events—the Beatles' first concert, the manned Mars landing, the sinking of the Titanic, the launch of the airship Clinton. Through the doorway Jones showed us all this and more as he tried to answer every request.

I didn't see much of it. Rather than watching random history unfold, I watched the man at the switch, what he did and how he did it. I wanted to learn how it was done, and then I wanted to do it myself. To make history, or rather, to unmake it—and possibly, me. I was going to answer the question that neither the great Wezleski nor Aristotle Jones could.

My father was a son of a bitch, and that's the nicest thing I've ever called him. My childhood wasn't Hell, but it was a long, sustained Purgatory that burned not sin, but every ounce of joy from my life. He wasn't abusive, not physically, not to my brother and me. That he saved for my mom. Once or twice a week, Davy and I heard the slaps and the yells and the cries coming from downstairs or their bedroom. Sometimes more often, if things didn't go well at work, or if his team lost, or if he dropped a roll at poker, or if he just felt like it.

No, he didn't beat us; us, he just ignored us. We were mouths to feed and bodies to clothe. He never played catch, or took us to a game, or asked how we were doing. Never a kind word. Christmas? Just another day. Vacations? Those were for other families, not ours. Birthdays—that just made it a year closer until we were on our own.

My father never let us forget what a burden we were to him—how much we tied him down, what we cost him in terms of time, trouble, and money. Davy and I often wondered why he didn't just leave, and finally figured out that he had no place else to go. He was as trapped as we were. No one else would have him, and without someone to cook and clean for him, he'd never survive.

Paradise Denied

School was my sanctuary. At first it was just some place other than home. I tried sports, but that didn't work out. Uniforms cost money, money my father wouldn't give me. And it wasn't like he was the kind of dad (actually, he wasn't any kind of a dad) to come pick me up at the ball field after a long day at work.

So I hit the books, stayed after for special tutoring, did extra credit work. It turned out I had a special aptitude for math. This lead me to take some advanced physics courses in high school, which led to a college scholarship. In my final year I qualified for a grant from the Rufus T. Pelgimbly Foundation, which combined a Master of Chronal/Dimensional Science program with an internship at the Pelgimbly Center.

I had long since left home, my only contact with my family being the occasional phone call to my mom. Things were worse for her. An injury at work had put my father on permanent disability. His government check not enough, my mom now had to work full time as well as cook, clean, and take care of a husband who wouldn't lift a hand to help her.

All her life, it had been my mother who suffered most. She did the best she could with what little my father gave her, and it was never enough. I often wondered what her life could have been like if she'd never met my father, if I had never been born, if she'd had different chances. Would her life have been happier?

Six months after starting at Pelgimbly, I was willing to bet my existence on the chance of giving her just one moment of happiness.

I spent as much time as I could in the Chronal Chamber, volunteering when I could, switching assignments and work details with anyone who was willing. Soon I had learned enough to operate it on my own, and was ready to put my plan into effect.

I couldn't lose. Late at night, no one except Janitor Swenson would be about, and his schedule would have him checking the pens of formerly extinct animals at that time. And even if otherwise, the return mode on the time machine I had selected brought the user back just ten seconds after his departure time. Assuming, of course, that I even came back. If I did, great. If not, well, I would never have been born, leaving nothing for anyone to worry about.

When the moment came, I'm glad to say I didn't hesitate. I fiddled with all the proper dials and levels, set the necessary parameters, opened my Doorway, and then stepped through, into the past. Of course, being unable to learn all the niceties of Jones's toy, I had only traveled in time, not space. Hitchhiking from the Pelgimbly Center, it took me two days to get to what may or may not have become my hometown later on.

My father had worked all his life for the same company. It was quitting time at the plant, and I was waiting for him. When he left I followed him, along the way picking up a rock large enough to do the job. He was almost home when he turned into an alley. Then it was just the two of us on the street. I walked faster, got up close, and spoke his name. He stopped and turned around.

"Yeah?"

I said his name again.

"What the hell do you want?" he asked.

I was close enough. I hit him with the rock. He went down. When he tried to get up I kicked him in the face, then bent low enough to hit him again. And I kept hitting him—for what he'd done (or would do) to my mother, for what he'd never done for Davy and me, for the childhood and the joys we'd never had. For all that, I kept hitting him.

And then it was over—too soon, it seemed. It was over and I was still there. Maybe, I thought, my actions wouldn't have any effect until I returned to my own time. Time. It was time to return to the Center some twenty-odd years away. If I could. I looked down at the broken form of what would never be my father and hit the retrieval switch attached to my belt. A Doorway opened, and I stepped back to my present.

A present that was still there; a present with me in it. Had anything changed? I thought for a moment. I still had memories of growing up, of my mother's suffering, my father's indifference, of Davy and of…of…

An intense feeling much like *deja vu* hit. A rush of new memories flooded in, not replacing but paralleling the old ones. A lifetime of memories, new memories, a new lifetime, all at once. A mother—my mother—the same as before. A brother—not Davy, but Frank. A sister—Betty. And my father—a different person, but as much my father as the man I had left dead in the past. No indifference, not this time.

My first conscious memory was of getting slapped. I don't remember what for. My entire childhood was this time a memory of getting beaten and slapped for anything I did that didn't please this man. A dislocated shoulder, a broken arm. Both the result of falling down the stairs, or at least that's what the hospital was told.

My brother, Dav…no, Frank, he got it, too, although as the oldest I tried to shield him from most of it, taking the worst on myself. Betty, though—in my father's eyes she could do no wrong. Whatever she wanted, whatever she needed was hers, even if the rest of us had to do without. My father never laid a hand on her, not when she was growing up, anyway.

He began going into her room at night when she was twelve, just as the girl she was had started becoming the woman she would be. Frank and I didn't find out about it until it had gone on for about a month. One night, while I was still trying to decide what to do, Frank waited in my sister's room. He had a knife, and when my father came in, he used it, and ended the abuse for good. He spent three years in juvenile custody before being sent to the State Pen.

The pain of my new life staggered me. In trying to escape my Purgatory I had destroyed one brother and sentenced another brother and a sister to their own Hells. I don't remember the next minute or two—I might have blacked out—but I do remember the moment of clarity that followed. I had changed time once and survived. I could do it again, and again, and as often as I needed. As many times as it took. My new father deserved to die as much as—*no*, more so than the old one.

And the sooner, the better.

I turned to the control panel, wondering how many sets of disparate memories I could handle without going mad. Before I could activate it, however, two things happened. Dr. Jones walked in, followed by Janitor Swenson.

"I tolt you someone vus in here," the janitor was saying as they entered the room. And then a Doorway opened, two men in mostly blue uniforms walking through it. I seemed to be the only one surprised to see them.

The two men walked toward me, the air around them shimmering with their before and after images. By the time they reached me, this effect had stopped. The taller of them put his hand on my shoulder.

"You'll have to come with us," he said quietly.

"What for?" I asked, though a part of me had already reasoned it out.

"Unauthorized time travel," came the soft reply.

"Since when is that a crime?"

"Since forever," the smaller one said, a bored smile on his face.

I looked to Jones. There was a sadness in his usually bright eyes. Running his hands through his hair, he shook his head, saying, "They're from the Time Patrol, son. Really, someone as smart as you should have seen it coming."

"You'll have to come with us," the tall officer repeated. "We'll need you to debrief us on just what you did in the past so we'll know how to fix any problems you caused."

"And after that?" I asked.

"You'll serve time," the smaller one told me.

They started moving me toward the still open Doorway. Beyond it I could see drab, grey walls, a shade of grey I remembered from visiting Frank in prison.

"Wait," I cried, stopping but not pulling away from them. I turned to Jones.

"I know the answer," I told him.

"To what question?" His eyes brightened at the possibility of new knowledge to be obtained.

Quickly I told him what I had done, why I had done it, and of my resulting double memory. When I was done, Jones slowly shook his head. "Go with the officers. We'll talk later."

Later? Did that mean I'd be coming back? As I was led through the Doorway the smaller said to his companion, "This poor bastard just doesn't get it, does he?"

"He will."

From the Chronal Chamber I was taken to an interview room. There, to my surprise, sat Jones. He looked older. There were streaks of grey running through his chestnut blonde hair. There were a few lines on his face, but his hair was just as unruly as it had always been, and the brightness in his eyes hadn't faded.

"How?" I asked foolishly.

"We are both time travelers. My journey, however, was one day at a time. I have been waiting quite a while for this interview." At his gesture I sat down. The two Time Patrol Officers stood behind me.

"After you left," Jones began, "I thought about what you said, what you had told me you'd done. There was, of course, only one possible explanation. To be sure, I researched the current timestream, as well as the alternate one you abandoned when you murdered…your father." And then, with pity and sorrow in his eyes, he told me. Told me how I never had a chance.

"Your mother, in both of your realities, had an affair. Each time, you were the result. A necessary effect, I believe, to account for your existence."

"I don't understand."

"Time flows—backwards, forwards, sideways. A disturbance in the stream sends out ripples in all directions. You killed your father before you could be conceived, a clear impossibility, since clearly you were. And so time adjusted, flowed around the obstacle of your birth so that you killed only your mother's husband. Of course, it might have been the knowledge of the affair that caused your father—the one you killed—to behave as he did."

"And his behavior," I labored to put the segments of my folly together, "caused me to do what I did, which in turn caused what had already happened."

Jones nodded his head.

"Sadly, yes."

After that, he left me there, caught in the loop, charged with crimes both old and new, in a time lost limbo that would forever be of my own making, the voices of the dead screaming their hatred and confusion at me.

How long, I wondered as they took me away, would it be before my own screams could drown theirs out?

My second Pelgimbly story, this one written with C. J. It addresses a question that, as a crime scene investigator, I had often wondered about. All of the Pelgimbly stories have been collected in C. J.'s book, STEAM POWERED LOVE.

PI IN THE SKY
John L. French and C.J. Henderson

> *"'Tis a lesson you should heed, Try, try again.*
> *If at first you don't succeed, Try, try again."*
> W.E. Hickson

"Hey, where's the gate? Where'd the fence go?"

Sergeant Dale Nigrone asked his questions of the security man sent to escort him inside as they passed through the front gates of the esteemed and feared Pelgimbly Institute for the Advanced Sciences. As he always did whenever a new officer came out to the most feared duty on the city's call list, Murphy had his answer ready.

"It's still there, just not on this side." He waited for Nigrone's not very creative, and certainly not original, but nonetheless inevitable response of "What?" and went on.

"It's a Moebius fence. Try climbing it and you wind up on the same side you started out. Ideal for keeping out intruders, and for low impact aerobics, or so I'm told."

Sergeant Nigrone had no idea who or what a 'Moebius' was, but he decided that rather than display his ignorance and ask, he would instead get some use out of the encyclopedias his children never bothered with and look it up when he got home. In place of the question he would like to have asked, he said, "Sounds like it'd be hard to break into this place."

"Only one person ever has."

"What happened to him?"

"They made me head of security."

* * *

"Mr. Murphy tells us you have a request, Sergeant." From his quite exposed position in front of the long table, Nigrone looked at the committee behind it.

"Don't be nervous," Murphy had told him. "They're just regular folk, like you and me. Just because their IQs top out around five or six hundred apiece doesn't mean they don't put their pants on one leg at a time. Ahhhhhhh, all except Brodsky, but he's a special case." When Nigrone had simply stared, Murphy had added:

"Besides, remember, they owe you for helping to cover up that incident with the Yeti. And the Liverwurst Pirates."

The sergeant tried hard to heed Murphy's advice, but all he could remember was the last time he'd been in a similar situation. He had been trying to make Lieutenant and, with his exemplary records in hand, had gone up before his department's standard three-man interview board. That he was still a sergeant was an indication of how well he had done.

This was a five-person panel—which made it seem somehow worse to Nigrone—the monthly meeting of the Pelgimbly Planning Committee. It was chaired by the Institute's Director Aikana, the heart, pulse, and kidneys that kept the entire place solvent, despite the incredible expenditures racked up by her staff, the most insane collection of scientists, savants, and carnival mystics ever seen since the summer when Ben Franklin, Voltaire, and the Montgolfier Brothers joined forces with the Masonic Lodge of the Nine Sisters to stage their legendary International Festival of Practical Enlightenment and Most Ingenious Pranks.

To her left side were Associate Brodsky, simian researcher extraordinaire, and Philip Morvently, esteemed first professor of non-linear philosophy. On the other side were Professor Wendell Q. Wezleski and Doctor Linda Ginderhoff, the two of them holders of so many awards, honors, citations, and medals, it would take the paper resultant from two full grown larches to tabulate them all. Nigrone could not be certain, but his instincts told him that the latter two were holding hands under the table. Deciding this was an unimportant detail, he flushed it from his mind as he tried to respond.

"It's, er, not really a request, as such, it was more of a...an idea, I mean, a notion, like, a thought, really...um, you know, that one of our crime scene people came up with."

"Then shouldn't this crime scene person be here for its presentation?"

"Professor Morvently," snapped Brodsky, his fingers drumming the table, his entire body positively ready to fracture as he anxiously awaited his chance to get back to his lab and the heavenly pack of Camel Unfiltereds waiting for him. "It's bad enough that we've decided to allow one member of the local authorities on our grounds. Shall we give them all free access? Who knows to what ends that would lead, what new problems we might incur?" With all the charm of an African dictator-for-life, he swiveled in Nigrone's direction and said:

"No offense intended." though his tone implied otherwise.

Nigrone, who had not thought to take offense until such was suggested, looked over the panel for a friendly face. Finding two such visages atop the shoulders of Professors Wezleski and Ginderhoff, he decided to address his comments to them.

"As you know, there are two things that are unique about every human being—fingerprints and, except for twins, DNA."

"There are, of course, more than two," offered Morvently with the rote, but kindly responsive voice of a kindergarten teacher explaining the difference between letters and numbers for the ten millionth time, "but go on."

"Well, the lab tech's idea was that maybe these two things, prints and DNA, are somehow linked."

"Of course they are," barked Aikana, growing angry with every passing second she saw slip by in which she did not detect even a whiff of profit for the Institute.

"Now, now," Wezleski interposed gently, "the good sergeant will never finish if we keep interrupting him. I'm sorry, Sergeant, please continue. We'll try to be polite." There was anticipation in Wezleski's voice, a gleam in his eyes as if he might have somehow figured out what Nigrone was going to suggest and was already designing a floor model in his head.

"Thank you, sir. As I was saying, if prints and DNA are somehow linked, maybe one—now how did he put it? Oh yeah, maybe one actually codes for the other. That is, I mean, well...he was thinking that there should be some way that if you had someone's fingerprints you could use them to determine his gene code. And that if you had some blood, you could run the DNA and that would tell you what his fingerprints were."

"And this would help anyone on the face of the planet how?" Brodsky did everything but yawn.

There was a smile on Wezleski's face, however, as he answered for Nigrone. "Come on now, don't you dig, daddy-O? People leave DNA everywhere, on whatever they touch. Much more so than their fingerprints. If the police could convert a fleck of skin, a drop of blood, a single hair, et cetera, into a suspect's fingerprints, think about the number of crimes that could be solved."

"And," offered Ginderhoff, growing somewhat excited, "if the police recovered a criminal's fingerprint left at a crime scene, let's say this is someone they don't have a record of. If a correlation process could be set up, why, they could convert that single print into a complete rundown of his genetic code. And once we've fully explored the human genome, that could lead to a complete description of the person."

"I still don't see..." But this was apparently the day in which Associate Brodsky was fated not to complete a sentence. Running over his words with typical enthusiasm, Wezleski interrupted him once more, saying:

"Ol' Emil Faber is supposed to have said, 'Knowledge is Good.' Cool—I agree, especially if we assume the statement means 'any knowledge is good.' Perhaps, Madame Director, this might make an excellent research project for one of our new graduate students—yes, no?"

The Director had been spinning her usual set of numbers in her head as soon as the sergeant's idea had been made clear. In the first seconds the notion hit her brain, she had rejected it completely. It was not polite to charge the world's law enforcement agencies for such technologies—at least, not overly much, anyway. The idea of having her precious cash-generating geniuses toiling on such a low profit idea had stung her worse than a Portuguese man-of-war.

But, coupled with Wezleski's notions of getting one of their interning grad students to finally pay their own way, suddenly even the public relations benefits alone from such a coup seemed like a winning idea to her. That, along with the notion that agreeing there and then could get her highly paid staff of award-winning knuckleheads back to work, the Director said:

"Yes, an excellent idea, Professor. Will that suffice, Sergeant?" Nigrone, knowing a dismissal when he heard it, nodded in the director's direction, saying:

"I—I guess so. Thanks, ladies, and gentlemen, thank you for your time."

Murphy came forward and gave the sergeant a supportive nod, then gave him a friendly point toward the door while Aikana snapped her metaphorical whip and began herding her geniuses back to their labs. Chuckling at their antics, Murphy simply rolled his eyes and escorted Nigrone from the conference room, telling him:

"Don't take it so hard, Dale. That this bunch even stopped from trying to devise their nuclear-powered mouse traps long enough to consider your idea at all is something. And don't forget, the graduate students at Pelgimbly are the ones who rejected Johns Hopkins, Cal Tech and M.I.T. as not challenging enough. How about lunch? It's Tuesday—that means it's Bird of the World day in the cafeteria—they make a great Dodo egg omelet."

"Can I get that with liverwurst?"

Murphy smiled widely upon seeing his friend's sense of humor returning. After lunch, having seen the sergeant safely off the grounds, the security head returned to the conference room where he knew Director Aikana was waiting for him.

"I've instituted plans for those emergency measures we discussed," the security head reported. His words did not do much to alleviate the worried look in the director's eyes.

"Do you really think we need to go to such extremes? What you've proposed—it costs *so* much, er, I mean, what if something should go wrong?"

Murphy looked at her with the incredulous stare of a mother who has just entered her kitchen to find her children making molten spin art with a device jury-rigged from her blender and waffle iron. Through lips frozen by their inability to decide between a horrified blanche and the cackling of the damned, he choked out:

"Ma'am, with all due respect, when *isn't* something going wrong around here? Things I never heard about until I took this job—things the entire *world* never dreamed of—time displacements, dimensional shifts, exploding airships, extinct lizards roaming the halls, volcanoes in the basement, Brodsky's chimps and their bongo parties, not to mention...well, all right, never mind, I think the point is made."

The director merely glared, a powerful defensive and offensive weapon that the woman had perfected to a point where she could practically barbecue skin, if need be. Crossing his arms over his chest, Murphy refused to be intimidated; however, answering her high voltage look by saying:

"Just wait and see; sooner or later, what I've proposed will be needed. And most likely needed badly."

"I still think we should discuss this with the board," Aikana sniffed threateningly. "Before such an unreasonable expenditure is made."

"Remember our agreement, Madame Director," Murphy sniffed right back at her. "When it comes to security, I am the law."

"Very well," the director agreed sullenly, "as long as you remember, when it comes to signing the checks around here, I am the ultimate law."

* * *

The Graduate program at the Pelgimbly Institute, otherwise affectionately known as ISAYLI (Indentured Servitude And You'll Like It) was one of the toughest known throughout the annals of recorded history. Indeed, the only one proven tougher on its inmates was the graduate program at the Napoli Gladiatorial College, and even then only during the reign of Caligula.

It was also known to be the most freewheeling. It was during his graduate days at Pelgimbly that the great Wezleski first laid down the fundamental operating principles of Time Travel over a drunken weekend, and that Einstein, on his little-known sabbatical to America, first realized that whipped crème applied to the navel of a co-ed affected the curvature of the universe three degrees more than chocolate sauce.

Research assignments at Pelgimbly were assigned on a random basis. So it was by the luck of the draw that the one prompted by Nigrone's suggestion was given to one Wheatley Glover as his winter project. Glover did not know whether to be pleased or disappointed with having received the sergeant's proposal. On the one hand, working with fingerprints and DNA was not nearly as flashy or prestigious as taking a crack at deconstructing chronal theory or boarding a party zeppelin to set sail on an exploration of the local multiverse. Then again, neither did it carry the same element of risk.

Oh yes, Glover had indeed heard the stories of postgrads who had lost appendages working on their projects—or grown several new ones. He had seen the Don't-Let-This-Happen-To-You films, made in much the same style as WWII anti-venereal disease films, or Scare-The-Student-Driver movies, the ones featuring tales of former grad students whose genders had been changed, who had been diced and shuffled, who had been turned into pygmy mice or ended up with ears made of glass, or who had disappeared entirely except for small clouds of methane left behind, which tended to collect in the stairwells.

He was not exactly sure how much he believed in these stories, although he had been reasonably certain that the one about the exchange student who was no longer a carbon-based life form wasn't true—until, that was, the night he found a tray full of silicone tucked away in the back of the chemical storage lab, a sad slate of nodules that for all intents and purposes seemed to be crying, and was most definitely cursing God in Portuguese.

When he looked at all the facts lined up, tabulated, and color-coded, Glover decided he was more than a trifle relieved to be out of the figurative, if not literal, Pelgimblian line of fire. All in all, he decided his greatest risk in the weeks ahead would be of getting bitten while taking oral DNA swabs from someone's cheek. Given the possible alternatives, he decided he could live with that level of danger.

Working out the basic theory of his assigned project took Glover just forty-five minutes under ten days. He was done collecting the swabs and sets of inked prints from most of the staff and his fellow students by the end of January. In the month of February he set up a complicated schedule, which evenly divided his time alternately between the biology lab, the computer room, the dining hall, and his bed. After two weeks, he reworked the schedule to eliminate all those time-wasting breaks for eating and sleeping. By March he was hollow-eyed and thirty-four pounds lighter, but ready to present his results.

"It was easy, really," Glover said with true modesty, working to cover an embarrassingly long yawn. It may have taken him until he was five to tie his own shoelaces, and he never really had learned to ride a bicycle, but ever since he had gotten his mind wrapped around the idea that x really could be any number, no one had been able to present him with a conceptual problem he could not eventually solve, which was, of course, why he was a postgrad at Pelgimbly, and not pumping gas as his not-so-dear Aunt Matilda had always predicted.

"Explain, please," the lovely Linda Ginderhoff, his mentor on the project half-requested, half-ordered. Pulling himself to his full height—a not-so-impressive 5' 6"—Glover answered:

"As you know, I collected inked prints and DNA samples from the entire staff, except those with concerns about cloning. I scanned the prints and did full genome workups on the DNA. After that, I assigned a number to each of the four DNA bases—0 through 3 for adenine, cytosine, guanine, and thymine, in that order. That gave me a numerical value for each genome."

Glover paused at that point, futilely looking for some reaction from Ginderhoff. After receiving a noncommittal, "Go on," he continued, saying:

"Since all computer data is essentially a series of ones and zeros, I then took the scans of the inked prints and expressed them in their binary form."

"That must have taken up quite a bit of computer space."

"Not really, Professor; given that I had exclusive use of Main Frame 14 and a smidge of space on 15."

"So you had values for both your DNA and fingerprints. I suppose you next ran a correlation?"

"Yes, ma'am, after converting both to base 12."

"Why 12?"

"There were three sets of twins, same values for DNA, different ones for prints. Base 12 allows the assigning of more than one number to each DNA base." Ginderhoff nodded slightly. Glover took comfort in the almost imperceptible friendly pursing of her incredibly well formed lips, which he took as a good sign, just before she asked:

"And your results were?"

"An algorithm that allows one to convert the value for DNA to that for fingerprints, and vice versa. I call it the Crick Equation."

"Why Crick; why not Watson?"

"Too elementary."

"Amusing," replied Ginderhoff. She had, of course, seen Glover's all-too-transparent jest involving Francis Crick and James Watson—the legendary party boys who first charted the DNA road rally for future generations—coming a mile off. As one of the more lenient Pelgimbly student mentors, however, she had often found it useful to allow those ISAYLIs assigned to her a moment or two of unscheduled hilarity to break the tension. Having allowed Glover his allotted share, she got things back on track by asking:

"So, have you prepared a demonstration?"

"Yes, ma'am. Ready when you are."

The two spent the rest of that afternoon entering DNA codes into the computer and watching the loops and whorls of fingerprint patterns appear on the computer monitor. When they tired of that, they scanned in fingerprints and caused double helices to appear.

"Not bad," Doctor Ginderhoff admitted as they finished. "Now all that's left is the final test. Do have Mr. Murphy call that police sergeant and have him bring over samples of unidentified DNA and latent prints. We'll run them, give him the results, and then we'll see if his crime lab can match them to any suspects."

Ginderhoff rose from her chair, letting Glover know that she felt he had done some first rate work. The graduate student replied by practically collapsing. So deprived of feminine companionship had he been while working on his research project, the effect of female praise nearly incapacitated the young man. Ginderhoff found the whole thing amusing, in the way that devastatingly beautiful women often do, and thought nothing more of it.

And that was, when all things were considered, honestly and truly, the monumentally biggest mistake the professor ever made in all her life.

* * *

The sight of Linda Ginderhoff's fabulous mouth tossing him a few crumbs of praise still in his head, Glover found Security Chief Murphy and had him contact Sergeant Nigrone. Now, to be fair, the horrendously costly, and mostly likely blasphemous incident barreling toward the Pelgimbly Institute—as if the venerable institution had not suffered enough such moments already that month—was not entirely Glover's fault.

The professor herself should have taken the upcoming calendar into consideration, as should have Murphy. Seeing the grad student's clouded eyes and listening to his dream-like stammer, the security chief should have remembered that such dazes had caused trouble in the past, such as when Aristotle Jones's momentary daydream of his collegiate tryst with one of the original Ziegfeld girls caused him to lock in a series of reactor cores' steam generators' temperatures on Fahrenheit rather than Centigrade settings. He did not, however; simply chuckling to himself at the inherent goofiness of the average North American male geek, forgetting his watchdog duties momentarily for the sake of a trivial amusement.

"Sergeant Nigrone," he said into the phone, ignoring the rampaging significance of what he was about to set into motion, "yes; it's Murphy, from Pelgimbly. No, nothing's escaped. No, nothing's exploded or disappeared. Or appeared, for that matter." The humor to be found in the immediate red alert response on the sergeant's part was probably the last bit of whimsy that the most mischievous gremlin, Fate, threw into the mix that day. Smiling, shaking his head at the silliness of the situation, the Security Chief tried to calm Nigrone, telling him:

"No, honestly—I'm just calling to let you know that apparently the project you suggested has been finished. Yes, so soon. Would it be possible for you to bring over some suspect samples? Yes, DNA and prints both…No, March 12th is not a good day, how about the next…No, I understand, black cats, mirrors, and all that. How about the 14th? Okay, see you then."

And with that most worst of all possible days set for Nigrone's return, the die was cast, and the conductor on the express train to disaster began gleefully punching the tickets of all involved.

* * *

Like most of the world, Dale Nigrone had not the slightest idea of what to expect when he traversed the halls of the Pelgimbly Institute. But whatever he had prepared himself for on the morning of March 14th, it certainly had not included the slightest anticipation of walking into a room where most everyone in sight would be wearing what looked to be white shock wigs.

Indeed, when he had met the sergeant at the front gate, Murphy had been wearing one. Nigrone had decided not to comment, far more interested in seeing if the Institute was going to be able to help him put faces to the bits and pieces of forensic evidence he had tucked under his arm. But once he found four out of every five warm bodies he passed to be wearing the wigs, many of them sporting white, paste-on moustaches as well, he found it impossible to resist asking what was going on.

"It's a tradition around here," Murphy told him. "We wear them every March 14." When he asked why, the security chief told him:

"Einstein's birthday. What else?"

"What else, indeed, Mr. Murphy."

Wezleski came over to the pair at that moment, a fork in one hand, and a plate in the other, one covered with some sixteen slivers of different types of pie. "You forget, though: it's a double celebration. Make sure the good sergeant gets some pie."

Murphy led Nigrone over to a table laden with all manner of baked goods. There were peach, cherry, blueberry, banana crème, apple crunch, lemon meringue, rhubarb, boysenberry, coconut crème and every other kind of pie you could mention spread out across the staggering run of tables, as well as cupcakes, cannoli, tarts, tortes, cookies, waffles, puddings, flan, Twinkies, sweet breads, and even a teetering tower composed of Little Debbie and Drake's snack cakes. That the institute would be celebrating some sort of Dentist's Delight Day did not bother Nigrone overly much. What did catch his attention, however, was the odd fact that none of the pies were baked in the usual round shape.

"Square...?" The word slipped out. The sergeant had not meant it say it aloud. Noting, but not caring about, Nigrone's embarrassment, Murphy told him:

"Of course. In addition to it being Einstein's birthday, March 14th is also International Pi Day." The security chief waited for Nigrone to get it. When the police sergeant did not, he explained further.

"That's 'p-i'...as in 3.14159, et cetera, et cetera. And so, on 'Pi Day'...?" As Murphy dragged his words out slowly, giving Nigrone a chance to dredge up the remnants of his high school geometry knowledge, the sergeant suddenly responded, saying:

"Pies are square."

"Now you're on it. So dig in, and when you've had your fill, we'll find Mr. Glover and see if we can't help you put away some bad guys."

Now, there are those few rugged individualists who will argue quite convincingly that policemen are not born hungry, that the astonishing corollary between baked goods consumption and law enforcement is but a happy accident. They would find no proof to reinforce their conclusion in the good sergeant that day, however, who was quite pleased to sample more than his share of the bountiful feast laid out in celebration of both genius and infinity. Eventually, though, the lawman reached the point where the thought of even one more strawberry-filled, cherry-glazed, sugar-encrusted cruller was too much. Making his way through the endless sea of wigs, a Huckleberry Hound coffee cup firmly in hand, Nigrone reluctantly turned his back on the myriad mounds of munchies and allowed Murphy to lead him off to where Wheatley Glover and Main Frames 14 and 15 waited.

Noting the fact that the two were leaving the room, Ginderhoff made a sad set of eyes to Wezleski, telling him with a sigh:

"I should go with them, Wendell. I am Glover's advisor, after all."

"And on what are you advising him," the scientist asked, "that he needs both Security and the police?"

Ginderhoff was not surprised Wezleski had forgotten the sergeant's request and Glover's subsequent research. He had been taking so many side trips off to other dimensions since the pair of them had cracked the steam barrier it was a wonder he remembered to put a tie on in the morning (of course, there was the morning that a tie had been all he had put on, but as it had been an exceedingly long and wide one, no official reprimand had been made). Still, she was worried about how distracted he was becoming and so explained what had happened in great detail.

"And," Wezleski asked absently, his mind still more focused on the wondrous combined tastes of coconut and kiwi in his mouth than it was on preventing disasters, "he was invited to do the blind testing today?"

"Yes, Wendell, it was the only day everyone could manage."

"Today...of all days?"

"Yes."

"Oh, dear."

Now, there was no one who has ever worked, taught, studied at or run screaming from the Pelgimbly Institute who had ever heard Professor Wezleski utter the words "Oh, dear" and then failed to take immediate shelter against the apocalypse about to come. It took no genius to recognize that whenever those two fateful words passed Wezleski's lips, anything could happen; the dead might walk, inert chemicals could very well explode, dogs and cats would not be unlikely to come together in spiritual harmony, or, in short, reality as we know it could simply wink out of existence.

Linda Ginderhoff knew this all too well. To her credit, showing an intestinal fortitude matched only by the 300 Spartans, the British during the London Blitz, and the American public when they went to vote last election day, she stood her ground and asked simply:

"What's wrong?"

"The Pi Day tradition," Wezleski reminded her, "that doesn't require baking in square pans."

As memories flooded her brain, the lovely Ginderhoff's two-word retort of dismay was composed of language much stronger than Wezleski's. Nearly all thoughts of pie forgotten, the pair rushed to stop the trial run before it was too late. Everyone else in the room, having heard the great Wezleski say "Oh, dear," had waited only to see in which direction he would finally leave. Observing him exit in a roughly northeasterly direction, the remainder quickly fled in as southwesterly a line as the Institute's hallways would permit.

* * *

At his station, Glover was worried.

"I don't get it," he thought. "This thing should have completed its run by now." Checking the program's status, he found;

"What? The damn thing's drawing resources from the other mainframes."

Knowing that this was in no way correct, the grad student decided to shut things down and start over. A quite practical solution; but when he typed in the code that would end the program, he was dismayed to find that nothing happened. He attempted again only to encounter the same result all the way down to his now heightened sense of dismay. He tried hitting Ctrl-Alt-Delete to no avail. Finally, he decided to do a cold reboot, but he gained no results that way, either. Nothing he did seemed to affect what was happening.

The program would not end.

The computer would not shut off.

"They've already begun," a breathless Ginderhoff shouted, her eyes wide with horror as she and Wezleski ran into the room. Seeing the looks on both of the scientist's faces, Security Chief Murphy shouted:

"My God—what is it?"

"It's Pi Day tradition," Wezleski explained as he desperately tried to catch his own breath, "for the senior students to introduce any number of viruses into all the computers within the Institute—viruses that automatically change any number entered on this day for any reason to the ultimate value of pi. I know," he raised his hand to forestall Murphy's objections, "virus definitions are updated on the quarter hour here, but our wily seniors merely accept that as a minor challenge."

"And," added Ginderhoff, her breathing practically back to normal, "you know what a challenge means around here."

Although he knew he probably should not, Murphy began to relax. Moving his hand away from a switch he had been considering pulling, he asked, "So what's the big deal? For one day, none of the computers work right. The sergeant just has to come back tomorrow—right?"

"Oh, no." This interjection, coming from Glover, indicated he had just realized the full extent of the problem. Even in the midst of approaching disaster, Ginderhoff took a measure of pride in the quickness of her student.

Remembering Director Aikana's recent memorandum encouraging the new talent, she said:

"Explain it, won't you, please, Mr. Glover?"

"Pi as a number has been calculated to over a trillion digits, and the thought is that it may well be infinite. When I hit the 'Enter' key, due to the virus's invasion of my program, I, in effect, instructed the computer to take pi's ultimate value and determine its DNA."

Still failing to fully grasp the situation, Murphy answered:

"Yeah—so?"

"What Mr. Glover is attempting to communicate," Wezleski explained, "is that we are right now, Mr. Murphy, in the process of defining the DNA of an infinite entity. Now, as a good Catholic boy, can you think of any being, fact or fantasy, who might be considered infinite?" As circuits around the room began to audibly hum, and lights started to flicker on their own, the security chief cried out:

"Oh, God!"

"Exactly who I had in mind," answered Wezleski. As the floor started trembling and small tiles began shaking themselves loose from the wall, he added rapidly, "Now, with no way to predict what may come, can anyone here say that at some point the Definition won't become Reality?"

The idea shook all of them. Even though most in the room had put the notion together abstractly, it was in those seconds that it crashed home to them in its most concrete aspect. If Glover's program actually worked—and given the evidence all around them there was no doubting it was working—then soon they would have the image of the Divine there before them. But, since God was theoretically unknowable, He could not be reduced thusly. So, if He was…

"There's just one problem, Dr. Wezleski," said Glover in a small, strangled voice, "I can't shut it off." As the grad student's eyes began to overflow with tears, his fingers still unconsciously, desperately, hitting Ctrl-Alt-Delete over and over without success, Wezleski answered calmly:

"Of course you can't. The program's already taken over—one trillion digits—that should take another hour or so, after which it will begin to calculate pi on its own. Another few hours, another trillion digits. So, our only question is, if God actually has nine billion names, how many base pairs might there be in His DNA?"

Wezleski might not have been fazed about having a front row seat for the Second Coming, but Murphy was, and to the Nth Degree. Charged with the safety and security of Pelgimbly and all those within its grounds, he was in no mood to discover what might be contained in the wrath of a God pulled from His Olympian tasks of the day merely to join a party-load of Earthly wig-wearing sugar eaters.

Murphy shuddered at the idea, his hand returning to the switch he had been about to pull a moment earlier. As he did, his mind flashed back to the last time he had spoken to Director Aikana about his emergency measures—he had not expected to be using them so soon, but he was glad he had made the arrangements. As the smell of burning ozone began to flood the chamber, the security chief quickly inserted the series 6 Grenaldine punch key he had received only a few months earlier into the wall panel. This lit up a keyboard into which he punched a code known only to him.

"We have one minute to leave this room," he shouted, "before it leaves us. Anyone anxious to meet his or her God is welcome to stay, but don't say I didn't warn you!"

Sergeant Nigrone was the first to leave, followed closely by Glover. Murphy, with the desperately needed help of Dr. Ginderhoff, dragged Wezleski from the room. And, the instant they were all outside, he locked down the chamber. Once safely in the hall, the group watched the monitor, showing them what was happening inside the room. As they did, the security chief explained what he had done, but when the minute finally passed, nothing happened.

"What the..."

The security man did not understand; if the system he had ordered installed had been working properly, by this time massive machines should have come to life. Sixty seconds after he set the controls in motion, all within the targeted area should have disappeared and been transported to a previously empty universe at the far end of Reality—one specially selected for just such an emergency.

But nothing like that happened. Instead, the vibrations grew stronger, the rumbling louder, and the feeling that one should be getting on their knees, or at least genuflecting, was becoming increasingly difficult to ignore.

"I don't get it," Murphy cried out over the din. "The room should disappear. It should be gone!"

"Why should it be gone?" Murphy turned at the sound of Director Aikana's voice. Suddenly, all was clear to him.

"You!" Pointing at Aikana, he shouted the pronoun over again, louder, with more force. "*You*—you did this! You didn't sign the check for the Mark 9 Secure-O-Matic!"

"It was so expensive," she sniffed automatically. "We've never gotten ourselves into a situation in which we needed such a thing before. Now, you tell me what's going on now that is so bad that we need one now."

As frogs began to fall from the ceiling, Murphy did just that. Outside, lightning was shattering the ground around the Institute. Inside, as the security chief finished explaining the latest Pelgimblian pickle to the director, he had the satisfaction of watching her skin turn a deathly white. As her eyes glazed over, he caught the stunned woman and poured her onto a nearby bench. And, since Murphy could not watch the door and do that at the same time, Wezleski took that opportunity to go back inside.

* * *

"And then what happened?"

"Well," said a still steaming Wezleski, his hair softly glowing, his glasses remarkably clean, "He asked how things were going."

"With you?"

Wezleski chuckled indulgently at the limited scope of Aikana's question. Understandingly, he answered:

"I got the feeling He was after something on a larger scale."

"What did you tell Him?" Looking into his dear Linda's eyes, loving her more in that moment than ever before—as it was every time he looked into her eyes—he said:

"I told Him I was doing all right, but that generally things seemed to be in a mess. He asked what I meant by 'a mess,' and I told Him. I mentioned war and serial killers, communism, smoking bans, Republicans, the dieting craze, fossil fuels, reality television, global warming, Democrats, race hatred, fast food chains, crime syndicates...actually, when I mentioned crime syndicates, He said I was repeating myself..."

"Repeating yourself?"

"Democrats, Republicans...He had a point. Anyway, He asked if there was anything bad going on He hadn't already given us the answer to; I told him 'no,' and He just sort of thanked us for checking in. Then He looked around the room, saw what the mainframes were doing, and He got this kind of twinkle in His eyes. After that, He just snapped His fingers and—*poof*—that was that."

Indeed, with Mainframe 14 and a smidge of 15 removed from the Institute through the merciful intervention of the Almighty, the crisis seemed to have been averted. Dr. Aikana shook her head softly, cursed Murphy gently for almost convincing her to allocate funds unnecessarily, then stormed off to find other ways she could cut costs. Wheatley Glover followed after her, wondering how hard it would be to transfer to a safer place of higher learning, like Princeton, or the Marines.

Helping Wezleski to his feet, Ginderhoff asked him, "Wendell, what did you mean before? When did God ever give us the answers to all our problems?"

Wezleski smiled kindly through tired eyes, and whispered:

"Atop Mt. Sinai—the Decalogue, two tablets, some tips on better living...ring any bells, sweetheart?"

"But," she began, backpedaling in the manner of all who want something for nothing, "I mean...the Ten Commandments...but that's just...you know..."

"Yeah," answered Wezleski wearily, understanding everything, finally. "I do, now, I guess."

And, as the young lovers left, Murphy and Nigrone stood in the extremely empty room.

"So what happened?"

"Glover lost his research; you lost your DNA/fingerprint converter. What didn't happen was the end of the world." An Irish Catholic pragmatist, Murphy slapped his hands together and said, "I count it as a win, or at least a tie. Come on; let's see if any pie is left."

"Well, if it's all the same to you, Murphy," answered the sergeant, wondering if he still had time to stop off at church on his way home, "I've had enough pie for one day."

* * *

At the same time, in a previously empty universe, with the sound of omnipotent chuckling in the background, a room suddenly winked into existence. Inside it, a program ran as designed, calculating a trillion digits, once, twice, twice again, and so on and so forth. And then, within that which was once merely machine, a final connection was made, final base pairs matched up.

And then, unheard except by a single pair of ears, there was a great noise—one heard only once before.

And then, where darkness was upon the face of the deep, words were spoken anew, and there was light.

Having read comic books almost all my life, I could not resist creating my own superhero. As a crime scene investigator, I could not help but think of what might happen to that hero when she finally went public.

THE RIGHT BETRAYAL

Paul really didn't know what had woken him up. It might have been the cool breeze blowing in from the now opened bedroom window. It might have been the fact that he was suddenly alone in a strange bed, his companion of the evening momentarily absent. It was, however, probably the noise coming from outside.

Now that he was awake, Paul could hear the approaching sirens coming from all directions at once. They got louder and louder, then suddenly stopped just outside the window.

Paul got out of bed and went over to the window. His first thought was to turn on the light. He thought better of it when he realized that he wasn't quite sure where it was. Turning the light on would also frame him when he looked out the window, and he did not remember where he had left his pants.

By now red and blue flashing lights were putting on a show outside. Paul looked out the window and saw police cars, fire trucks, and at least one ambulance. Looking past them, he saw the reason for their presence.

A passenger van had apparently misjudged the sharp turn at the north end of the street. The driver had lost control and struck two parked cars. It then ricocheted off them and crashed into a third car, pushing it up on to the curb, through a fence, and into the yard across the street. The van followed it and both cars were now on fire.

Trees in the yard caught the flames from the burning vehicles and were alight. These flames, in turn, spread from the trees to the house. Firefighters were rushing to fight against the multiple blazes while police tried to rescue the occupants of both the van and the house.

Paul was fascinated by the tragedy playing out across the street. Even here in the city, one did not see something like this every day. He wanted to share in it.

"Michelle, hurry up in there. You're missing all of the excitement." No answer. *She must really be busy*, Paul thought. He had warned her against ordering the fish at that steakhouse. Now she was paying the price. He turned back to the drama outside.

Paul could see that the rescuers were not going to make it in time. The occupants of the van—visible only as panicked shadows against the light of the fire—had only seconds left before the flames totally engulfed the vehicle. If the noise had awakened them, the people in the house might get out in time, but the steel doors and barred windows designed to frustrate all but the most determined of home invaders and burglars also thwarted police efforts to gain entry.

And then a comet streaked down from the night sky. The wind from its passing blew out some the fire. As if that wasn't enough, it stopped in mid-air, turned, and landed.

The figure the comet became could best be described as a blur of blue and green. The two vehicles in the yard suddenly came apart. The doors of the van came off and the blur disappeared, reappearing a second later, only to streak across the street to where the ambulance was parked. Two people—a mother and child, badly burned but alive—, were left in the care of the surprised paramedics.

"Michelle, whatever you're doing in there, stop right now. It's her—it's Turquoise!"

When Paul turned back to the window after calling Michelle the second time, it was all over. The front door was off the house, everyone was safe, and the fires were out. As usual, Turquoise was nowhere to be seen.

Paul shut the window and went back to the bed, ready to tell Michelle all that she had missed. Then, in the quiet that had replaced all the noise and excitement, he began to put some pieces together. An open window, Michelle's sudden absence, Turquoise's just as sudden timely appearance, the lack of any reply from the bathroom. Could it be that he had just spent several extremely pleasant hours with a supergirl?

The loud flush that came from the bathroom put an end to that adolescent fantasy. Paul sighed as he got into bed to wait for the woman who was now not quite as exciting as she had been a few moments ago.

Michelle came back into the room wearing almost as little as he was.

"You missed all the fun," Paul said.

"A girl does have to freshen up, doesn't she?" Michelle said from the doorway. "Besides, I don't think I missed all the fun. You're still awake, aren't you?"

* * *

Darryl Larkins was the best detective on the city's homicide squad. His clearance rate was generally over 90%. There were few murders he could not close. In addition, he was frequently asked by his fellow detectives to assist with their cases, and his suggestions usually led to quick solutions and solid arrests that stood up in court. He was the best cop in the city, and one of the best in the state.

In recognition of his ability, dedication and hard work, Larkins was rewarded by being given the dirtiest job there was.

Every detective knew it was coming; the rumors had been brewing for weeks. The only question was which of them would get it. Then, last Monday, the Chief of Detectives reassigned all of Larkins's cases, and ordered him to report to the colonel's office for a special detail. After Larkins left, each man silently thanked whatever god he worshiped that he wasn't the one to have to tackle the riddle of Turquoise.

When Larkins got to Colonel Bishop's office, the secretary waved him right in. Bishop told Larkins to take a seat and got right to the point.

"Darryl, you are, of course, familiar with our resident hero, Turquoise?"

Larkins responded with a terse "Yes, sir." Of course he was familiar with her. Everyone in the city was.

"The mayor wants to know who she is. He told Commissioner Crain to put our best detective on the case. The Commissioner told me, and right away I thought of you." Bishop picked up a file that was on his desk and handed it to Larkins.

The detective briefly looked at the file. It was the standard one kept on a suspect under investigation. This one had the name 'Turquoise' printed on the front. Larkins carefully put the file back on the desk, halfway between himself and the colonel.

"With respect, sir, why does the mayor want to know? Turquoise has done nothing but good for the city. She's asked for nothing in return. She's never been accused of a crime." Larkins paused. He wanted to make his concern clear. "She's entitled to her privacy. What right do we have to investigate her?"

The colonel had his answer ready. "A fair question, Darryl, one that I asked the Commissioner, and one that he asked the mayor. As I understand it, one day it might become necessary to contact Turquoise, in the event of an emergency she might not be aware of. She may be injured during one of her rescue operations, and we would need to know as much about her as possible in order to provide proper treatment. Then, too, she has tremendous power. She may get tired of helping the city and turn against us. We have to be ready."

One of the reasons Larkins had risen to the top of his profession was an innate sense of when he was being lied to. His internal crap detector had gone off as soon as the colonel started talking. This had to have something to do with the billboards.

"Colonel, I am very sure that the mayor fully understands power and all the ways it can be abused. Just as I am sure that one other reason for him wanting to find Turquoise is to have some hold over her. If it's just the same to you, sir, I'd rather be tracking down the bad guys, not the good guys."

Bishop let the insubordination slide. He fully agreed with Larkins. As a commander, however, he could not let his agreement show. Instead, he raised his voice just a little and lowered its tone just a bit.

"It's not the same to me, Detective. You have been given a job, and you will do it. Once it's done, you can go back to catching killers."

Larkins met Bishop's eyes. Slowly, deliberately, in a manner that made his meaning clear, he asked, "And what if I don't find out who she is? I'm good, but not even I can solve every case."

Bishop again picked up the file, held it out for Larkins to take. "You'll solve this one, Detective. I don't think you want to go back to uniform patrol."

Larkins had taken it as far as he dared. He had asked as best he could if this investigation was just a show, something to keep the mayor happy. Told that it was for real, Larkins would do the job. It was either that or pay the price. He'd pay a price, anyway. Turquoise was the city's hero and it was his job to unmask her. She was to be thrown into a spotlight she did not seek, used by men who cared more for themselves than they did for their city. Than she did for their city. Than they did for anything except power. And he would be the one to hand her over to them.

Larkins almost refused to take the file. He almost asked for a new set of blues and a beat assignment. Then he thought about patrol. He remembered what it was like for the new guy on a squad, working too many nights and weekends. He'd hardly see his family, and the overtime money from weeklong trials and working cases would dry up. He had two daughters, and there was college to think about. He would need that money.

Larkins reached out and took the folder from Bishop. "I'll need a place to work, sir. Preferably someplace quiet, away from the other detectives."

"An office has been assigned, Darryl," Bishop said, handing him a set of keys. "We'll expect a progress report by next week."

Once settled in his office, Larkins reviewed what he knew about Turquoise.

She had appeared just over a year ago. A bridge over the interstate had collapsed, trapping dozens of people in their cars. The now-familiar blue-green had been seen everywhere, moving heavy pieces of road bed as if they were building blocks, and tearing open car doors like paper. Lives were still lost, but not as many as there would have been if she had not been there.

Too many people were saved that day; too many saw her for there to be any doubt. The city, and the world, had its first superhero.

During the next year, if there was a fire, a major accident, severe weather of any kind or a natural disaster, she was there. She moved too fast for anyone to take a clear photograph of her. Once, a lucky—and now rich—tourist accidentally caught her blurred image on videotape. Advanced computer enhancement revealed only the feminine outline of the city's new hero, nothing more.

She never stayed to be thanked. She did not give interviews. She did not issue press releases. Nothing more was known about her, not even her name.

Needing to call her something, the city's various television stations and its newspapers held a meeting. After much discussion, and many warnings from comic book publishers, the new hero was dubbed "Turquoise," for the blue-green combination of her costume. That, and because all of the good names were protected by copyright laws.

Naturally, the city went crazy. After repeated denials, city government admitted to an "extra-normal" force in the city that was protecting its citizens. The mayor tried to take the credit for arranging her presence, but no one really believed him. Tourism grew, and Turquoise-oriented businesses sprung up over night. The city put "Home of Heroes" on all its letterheads, stationary, and correspondence. The sports team changed their uniforms to a blue, green and—of course—turquoise color scheme. The sale of comic books increased by 200%, and everyone owned at least one Turquoise t-shirt.

The crime rate dropped, too, for a while. The police were closedmouthed about how much help, if any, they were receiving from Turquoise. There were those who claimed that she had saved them from muggers, rapists, and killers, but most of these claims proved false. It soon became apparent that, however much she involved herself with saving people from fires and accidents, Turquoise had no interest in fighting crime, a fact that the newspapers and television stations were quick to reveal. Thus assured, the criminals took to the streets again; their main targets the flood of tourists coming into the city hoping for a glimpse of the hero.

Everyone was talking about Turquoise. There was endless speculation as to who she was and from where she had come. Several women, and a few men, stepped forward to reveal that they were Turquoise, and were available for private interviews, book deals, and movie contracts. Most quickly recanted after being taken to a high rooftop and asked to fly away. One or two did try, but were restrained by security guards hired for just that purpose.

What the real Turquoise thought of this no one knew. Keeping true to her original pattern, she remained silent, with one exception.

A few months ago, there had been an election. The campaign for the city district attorney's office had been close. The polls called the race a toss-up. Then the billboards appeared. "Harper and Turquoise—a Winning Team," they announced, displaying the face of one of the candidates next to an artist's conception of Turquoise. The night after the last billboard went up, they were all painted over. No one saw the vandal, but a blue-green streak was reported passing by several of the signs. Harper lost by a wide margin.

And the mayor belongs to the same party, thought Larkins. *Which probably explains this move to unmask her.* Flying was one thing, ripping open doors was another, but being able to influence an election—that was real power.

The mayor wanted—no, he needed—a hold over Turquoise. Larkins would discover who she was. The mayor would pay her a quiet visit. A deal would be struck. Turquoise would be given a choice: cooperation in exchange for silence, collaboration, or an end to a private life. Larkins hoped that when he found her, she'd be stronger or smarter than he was; that she'd show the courage he lacked.

And he would find her. He knew that. He was not a vain man, but he did not suffer from false modesty. He was one of the best detectives there was. Given any kind of a lead, he'd track his man—or woman. He always had, and he would this time as well.

The file that Bishop had given him was of little help. All the reports of any accidents or other events in which Turquoise had been involved had been provided. There were media accounts of Turquoise's exploits. Newspaper clippings and magazine articles were included. There were transcripts of local and national television broadcasts. There was a listing of available videotapes of these broadcasts.

When she had first appeared, both the print and video media had tried to find out who Turquoise really was. News footage and amateur videos were studied frame by frame. Anyone who had any contact with her had been extensively interviewed. The best description that had been developed from all sources was that Turquoise was blond, of average height, with an average figure. No one had ever gotten a clear look at her face.

The effort to discover Turquoise's secret was soon halted. Not only had no progress been made, but it quickly became clear that the public was against it. Everyone knew that in order to be most effective, a hero needed a secret identity. They also knew that only the bad guys had an interest in unmasking the hero.

Larkins wondered what that made him. "Just a guy doing his job and providing for his family," he said to himself. He almost believed it.

Looking over the file, Larkins realized that something was missing. It took him a while to realize that there was no mention of any federal involvement in the hunt for Turquoise. The Feds had to be interested. But there was no record of anyone from Washington showing up before, during, or after any Turquoise-related incident. It couldn't be that Washington was not interested. Either the Feds were taking great care not to be noticed, or else they were the ones behind Turquoise. In either case, Larkins did not expect any help from any federal agency. He also did not expect any interference, unless he got too close to their secrets.

Larkins spent the rest of the day going over the file. When he finished, he had no idea where to start. Two weeks later, he was still at a loss.

He had gone back and re-interviewed all the witnesses. He had watched all the videos and read all the reports and newspaper clippings. He had explored and abandoned over a dozen theories, from secret government projects to rich, bored heiresses. Still, he had nothing to satisfy the calls coming from Bishop's office demanding progress.

In his office, Larkins picked up Turquoise's photograph—the one made from the now famous videotape. "You're out there somewhere," he said to her picture. He tried to focus through the photo, as if to make clear the fuzzy figure and indistinct features.

"If you were a crook, it would be easy. There would be a crime scene, evidence of some kind, something to provide a clue. But you're one of the good guys." Larkins thought about this for a moment.

"So let's start treating you like a bad guy." He stared at the photo again, then looked through his desk drawers for something. Remembering that he had had a different desk somewhere else, he went back downstairs to the homicide office. Grabbing a magnifying glass, he returned to his office and studied Turquoise's picture yet again. His guess had been right. He picked up the telephone and called Max.

Max Hammond was one of the reasons that Larkins was as good a detective as he was. Max had been the crime scene technician on Larkins's first murder case. Larkins had heard about Max from other detectives, and had been told that Max was one of the best evidence techs around. Larkins had taken Max aside, confessed that it was his first murder, and asked Max for any help or advice that he could give.

The civilian with twenty years experience took a liking to the rookie detective. He took the time to explain to Larkins just what he was doing and why he was doing it. Larkins was smart enough to listen, and the two formed an almost unbeatable team.

That was ten years ago. Now, with thirty years in the department, Max was eligible for retirement. Larkins had not too long ago asked him when he was going to pull the plug.

"Trying to get rid of me, Kid?" Max replied. Max had been calling Larkins "Kid" since that first murder, and was not about to stop just because Larkins had two children of his own.

"No, Max. I'm just worried about what I'm going to do without you."

"Well, don't start worrying yet. I'll quit when I can't do the job any longer."

"Then you're good for another ten years. We'll retire together, and let the place go to hell without us."

When Max came to the phone, Larkins asked him to meet for lunch. He tried to keep his voice even, to make it sound like a casual date between friends. Max put him off, claiming that the Lab was too busy for him to take a break. He finally agreed to meet the detective for coffee after their shifts were over.

By the time Larkins got to the coffee shop, Max was already waiting. However busy the Lab had been, the crime scene man had gotten off early.

"How's it going, Max?"

Larkins's greeting was met with a gruff hello. The detective put that off to one of Max's moods, signaled the waitress, and ordered coffee. After she had brought his cup and refilled Max's, Larkins started to explain what he wanted to do.

"No."

Larkins hadn't been ready for Max's interruption. "What was that, Max?"

"I said 'No.' I'm not going to help. It's not right, and I won't be a part of it."

"Look, Max…"

"No, Kid, you look. Ten minutes after you were called into Bishop's office, the word went around that you had drawn the Turquoise case. When you called today, I knew what you wanted; that's why I put you off. I had to have time to decide how I felt about it."

Max picked up his cup and took a sip of his coffee, giving Larkins a chance to comment. The detective stayed quiet, waiting to hear his mentor out.

"Turquoise has been good to this city, and good for it. She's saved a lot of lives and brought us quite a bit of fame and prestige, not to mention tourist money. All she's asked is to be left alone, that we respect her privacy."

"She's never really asked that, Max." challenged Larkins.

"By her actions, she has," Max snapped, waiting for the younger man to argue the point. When Larkins did not reply, he went on.

"That's all she's asked…to just be left alone, and now, His 'Honor,' the mayor, would deny her that. I'm telling you it's not right."

"You know what's right, Max? What's right is that I have a job to do, one that I'm good at. I find her, I stay a detective. If I don't, it's back to patrol, and you know what that means."

Max nodded, he knew what the loss of hours and overtime would mean to Larkins.

"So this is not about right and wrong. It's about following orders. Whatever we owe Turquoise, whatever I owe her, it doesn't match what I owe my family."

The older man thought for a moment. "I see your point, Kid, but think about this. When you do find Turquoise, and the mayor puts pressure on her, or her identity is exposed, what if she just up and leaves the city? Who's going to catch the blame? The mayor? The commissioner? Bishop?"

Max shook his head and pointed a finger across the table. "You, Detective Darryl Larkins—you'll be the man who exposed the hero and caused her to abandon our town. The papers, TV, the same men who gave you the assignment—they'll crucify you.

"Speaking of which, you know, Darryl, there's a very good reason nobody names their kids 'Judas' anymore."

"I'll take that chance, Max, and their silver if it comes to that. For my family, yes. But also because I know that whatever happens, I'll keep my mouth shut. I'll find Turquoise, and when I do, I'll give her up. What the mayor does with the knowledge is up to him. If I turn this job down, they'll just give it to someone else. I can't be sure that whoever it is won't sell out to the press at the first opportunity. My silence, that's all that I owe her."

"That's all you're willing to pay. You owe her a lot more."

"Max, I need your help. If I can't have it, fine, no hard feelings. But I'm asking you for the last time because I know you'll keep your mouth shut, as well. Can you say the same for anyone else in the Lab? Will they stay quiet, or will they tell what they find out to a wife, or husband, or friend? How soon before something leaks out if we leave this to others?"

Max finished his coffee. He stared past Larkins at some unknown point in the distance. Finally, he said, "Good point. Maybe it is just that simple. We are the only ones that we can trust." He stood up to leave. "Let me think about this, Kid. I'll let you know tomorrow."

The next day, Max called just before noon.

"I'm in, Kid, but let's keep that between ourselves. I'd hate to be the last person ever to be named Max."

They met that night at Max's apartment. Larkins showed Max the picture of Turquoise.

"So? I've seen that picture a hundred times. What about it?"

"Look at it again, oh highly trained observer."

Larkins held up a magnifying glass to the part of the photo that had drawn his attention. Max stared at it for a moment, then realized what had interested Larkins.

"Turquoise, darling," he said to her photo, "Didn't your mother ever tell you that a proper lady always wears gloves when she appears in public?"

To Larkins he said, "So where do we start?"

The detective pulled out the file he had on the hero.

"Last week there was an accident. Two vehicles collided; one caught fire. The flames spread to a nearby house. Turquoise showed up just before everybody got barbecued. She ripped a van apart to save the driver and passengers."

Larkins handed the file over to Max. "It's the only thing we've got. Everything else she's touched is either not suitable for prints or else is long gone to the junkyard or cut up for collectibles. Tomorrow, head out to the city impound lot and see what you can do with it."

"If it's still there, you mean."

"It's there. The report says that the car was totaled. The owner hasn't bothered with it, and we're waiting for the insurance company to pay the fees before we release it."

"And you expect me to find prints on a car that's been burned, ripped apart, and hosed down by a fire truck."

"Max, if anyone can do it, you can."

"True, and if not on this one, then the next one, or the one after that. Sooner or later she'll leave me a print. I just hope nobody buys her gloves for her birthday."

After Max reported for work the next day, he checked the recovered stolen vehicle log. He found two that had been taken in carjackings. He then advised dispatch that he'd be at the impound lot checking those two for prints. He gave the dispatcher the makes, models, and tags of the cars. If anybody asked, he could now justify his trip to the lot.

Once at the lot, he did process the two cars for fingerprints. After he had finished searching the second one, he looked around the lot. The van that Larkins had described was two rows over. Not seeing anyone paying any special attention to him, Max drove over to it.

The initial accident had damaged it more than the fire had. Max could see the front-end damage, the right side crushed and the two passenger side doors folded in so that they could not be opened. He knew from the report that the driver had been unconscious so, had Turquoise not rescued them, the driver and her passengers would have roasted. Max had had an image in his mind of her swooping down and peeling the roof back like a food tin, freeing the passengers. Instead, he found that she had just ripped off the driver's side door. He found it lying in the back seat.

Unable to open the side cargo door, Max had trouble getting the driver's side door out of the van. Normally he'd have called for help, but this was not a normal case. He finally thought to open the rear hatch, and then muscled the door over the back seat. The door fell with a *thud* into the rear storage area, barely missing Max's left foot.

"And how would you have explained breaking two of your toes while working on a car you had no right to be in?" he asked himself. After a pause to give thanks that he didn't have to explain, he eased the door out of the van, and leaned it against the rear quarter panel.

He found what he was looking for right away. On the inside right doorframe were four oval impressions. He found a matching set on the left frame. Two slightly larger impressions were on either side of the outer frame. Taking out his magnifier, Max could make out the lines of the friction ridges that made up Turquoise's fingerprints.

"Just as I had hoped. Like fingers into window putty," he said out loud, remembering the time when he had reglazed the windows of his old house. "Turquoise, when you grabbed this door, your fingers betrayed you. You left your mark as surely as if you had signed your name. Now, if your prints are on file, you belong to me."

Max got his portable power tools out of his station wagon, and removed the sections of the door that bore Turquoise's prints. Back at the lab, he'd make rubber impressions. Then he'd roll them in ink, and then on to clean white paper. The computer would do the rest. If Turquoise was on record, he'd know who she was by nightfall.

Later, Max sat in the darkness, holding a computer printout in his hands, He had waited until everyone in the Lab had either left for the day or had gone out on a call. Then he had let himself into the Latent Print Unit. Max had worked there for a time. He had taken a promotion that had promised regular hours, no night shift, and every weekend free. It was two months before the boredom of doing the same thing every day drove him back onto the street. But in that time, he had learned to use the identification computer.

Working in the dark seemed appropriate. Guided by the light from the terminal, Max entered the inked pints into the system. Fifteen minutes later, there was a match.

Max held the printout for a moment before reaching for a light. Until he read what was printed on the paper, the secret was still safe. At least, that was the lie he told himself. Turquoise's secret had been doomed as soon as someone in authority had decided it would be. No one can hide these days, not for long—not unless she shuts herself off from the world. And who could do that anymore?

Max reached over and turned on the light. He looked down and learned who she was and where she lived. He sat there for a long time before deciding what to do with his knowledge.

When Larkins came into work the next morning, he found an envelope on his desk. It had been sealed with red evidence tape, the kind the Crime Lab used to warn the handler that there was something potentially hazardous about the package's contents. "Meet me tonight at the coffee shop," read the note clipped to the outside. It was unsigned.

Inside the envelope was an arrest record. It was from two years ago. It indicated that Donna Cahill had been arrested for trespassing during the protests against the city's new power plant. She had received a fine and had been cautioned that further offenses might lead to jail time. Other documents from the envelope indicated that that had been her only encounter with the law and that she had a remarkably clean driving record.

"If I could fly, I wouldn't have any speeding tickets, either," Larkins said out loud to no one in particular.

Without hesitation Larkins wrote his own report, one stating that the individual known as "Turquoise" had been identified through fingerprints as Donna Cahill. He purposely left Max's name off the report. If asked, he would give the colonel the details, but Larkins knew that his friend would prefer not to be linked to the unmasking.

His report complete, he called Bishop's office and asked for the earliest appointment. He mentioned that he wanted to discuss closing out the mayor's special detail. In fifteen minutes, he was presenting his report to Bishop. Thirty minutes after that, he was driving the colonel to the address listed on the arrest report. There, the colonel was to extend to Ms. Cahill the mayor's personal invitation to a very private lunch.

When Larkins and Bishop arrived at the house, they found the front door open. The house was empty. As the two walked though the house, Larkins noted rings and squares in the dust that had settled on the furniture, indicating to him that various items had recently been removed. Nothing large appeared to be missing. The stereo and television were both still there. Just small things seemed to be gone, the kind of personal items that people take with them from house to house, to make them homes. With this in mind, he checked the rest of the house.

"She's gone," Larkins said to the colonel.

"You mean she's out; we'll wait."

"No sir, I mean she's gone, as in not coming back. Look in her closets; there are gaps where clothes were hanging. Look in the bathroom: no toothbrush or other personal items. There are no photos or any mementos lying about. Everything here is just stuff. There's nothing left that was of any value to her."

Larkins walked into the kitchen. "Finally, there's this." He handed an envelope to Bishop. They had missed it during their first walkthrough. It was green, with the mayor's name written on it in blue ink.

"One guess as to who it's from."

Bishop took the envelope from Larkins's hand and started to tear it open.

"That's addressed to the mayor, sir."

"I have to check it out to make sure it's not booby-trapped," Bishop said with a smile.

"Very brave of you, sir."

"Mr. Mayor," Bishop read aloud, "I had thought my service to our city meant something to you. I was wrong. You have instead chosen to risk my leaving it. For the good of our city, I will overlook your actions this time. Any further attempts to hunt me down or expose me will cause me to relocate. Before I do, however, I will break my public silence. I will hold a press conference and name you as the cause of my departure."

"It's signed 'Turquoise.'" Bishop held it out for Larkins to read, then folded the letter and put it back in the envelope.

"Who did you say identified her prints?"

"I didn't say, Colonel."

"Who was it, Detective?"

Oh, Max, what have you done? thought Larkins, as he tried to think of a way not to answer. Not finding any, he said in a whisper, "Hammond, sir."

"When you see him, tell him I want to talk to him."

"Yes, sir. Will you be giving that letter to the mayor, or do you want me to do it?"

"I think, Darryl, that I'll make copies for the mayor and the Commissioner. This letter is too valuable—or rather, too important—to the case. I'll take it with me and keep it in a secure spot."

"Like the vault in Evidence Control?"

"Someplace like that, yes," Bishop said, thinking more of the safe in his office.

On the way back, Larkins wondered if Bishop realized just how valuable the letter was. The colonel no doubt saw it as a hold over the mayor. He now had proof that the mayor had risked losing the city's hero in trying to advance a personal agenda. Larkins wondered if Bishop knew that with that letter, he could retire several times over. It was the world's rarest collectible, the only known sample of a superhero's handwriting. It was worth millions, but Bishop no doubt saw it only as a tool to use in his power games.

That evening at the coffee shop, Larkins found Max waiting. The crime lab man was grinning broadly, as if he wasn't going to be facing a host of trumped up departmental charges.

"Was it really her, or did you set the whole thing up?"

"It was really her, Kid, and a very nice lady she is." Max held up a photo taken with an instant camera. He gave it to Larkins. "That one's yours. I've got another."

Max waited until Larkins had gotten his first clear look at Turquoise. "She's not at all what I expected, Kid. She's a little older than what I thought she'd be. And she doesn't look a thing like what you'd expect from some of the comic books out today."

"Why'd you do it, Max?"

"Kid, last night, when I had her future in my hand, holding a secret that only I knew, I was torn. I was going to betray somebody—either Turquoise or you. And there was no way I could avoid betraying myself. I had to choose between selling out a friend or a hero."

"And so?"

"And so I decided to betray everybody: Turquoise by giving her up, you and the department by warning her, myself by trashing my career. It was the best choice out of a bad lot, and I'll be able to sleep nights." Max gave Larkins another wide grin. "And so will you, now that you're off the hook."

The waitress had brought his coffee. Larkins raised it to Max. "Saved my butt again, buddy."

Max nodded his "you're welcome" as Larkins asked, "The note, was that your idea?"

"No, that was hers. I brought her the warning and suggested that she clear out. As you might imagine, she packed very fast, taking with her some clothing, personal items, and my gift."

"Your gift?"

"I stopped at the mall and picked up a pair of gloves. Got the style, color, and size just right."

"Bishop wants to see you first thing tomorrow."

"Tell the colonel to take a flying...No, don't tell him anything. He'll find out soon enough."

"What have you done now, Max?"

"While you and Bishop were trespassing on private property, I paid the Personnel Division a visit. As of today, I'm a real civilian."

"You retired?"

Max nodded. "I once told you that I'd quit as soon as I couldn't do the job anymore. After this week, I just can't do it, not for this department. What they asked us to do was the ultimate betrayal. I don't have to work for them, and I won't."

"For the record, Max, where is she?"

"For the record, Kid—go to Hell. She's somewhere you'll never find her, even if you were fool enough to look."

* * *

Sister Mary Fatima led the newcomer to one of the larger cells. She was a bit puzzled. Not that she wasn't glad that the cloister had a new member, but it was odd of Mother Superior to show a novice such special treatment. She was getting a cell that was normally assigned to an older nun, one that looked toward the distant city lights. She had been allowed to bring in a radio and a bag of what were probably personal items. In addition, Fatima had distinctly heard Mother tell the novice to attend services "when she could." Oh well, Fatima had long ago chosen to obey and not question.

"Will there be anything else, Sister…?"

"Please, call me 'Donna.'"

Ever wonder how Time Cops are recruited? I did. Here's my answer.

A SECOND AWAY

They come for you in the last seconds of your life. As the bullet is fired, but before it strikes your heart, as you fall from the roof, but before that sudden stop, as you light the match and smell the gas, but before you can say "Oh shit!" they come for you.

They come for me on Northern Parkway. I've got the green. The woman in the Crown Vic station wagon with the cell phone in her hand and a crying kid in the backseat has the red but doesn't see it. One second several tons of Ford is slamming into my side door, and the next...

I wake up. Wherever I am, it isn't Shock Trauma. No machines, no tubes, no nurses in grey scrubs making book on my chances. I sit up. Two uniformed men are standing in front of me.

"This isn't Heaven," the taller one says.

"It's not Hell, either," says the other one.

"It's Limbo, and we're the Chronal League."

Their names are on their uniform shirts: Hester and Plato. Plato's the small one. The patches on their arms show the scales of Justice, with the supporting post being an hourglass. Maybe they are the Chronal League, whatever that is. More likely this is a pre-death hallucination.

"He doesn't believe us," Hester says.

"They never do."

And Plato lays it out for me.

"Jacob Duffy, a minute ago you were involved in a fatal automobile accident. A minute from now you'll be dead, your body crushed and beyond any medical treatment. Right now we're between those two minutes."

"This is how we recruit agents," Hester continues. There's a flatness that tells me he's given this speech far too many times. "We take suitable candidates whose lives are about to end and we offer them what we have in abundance and what they've run out of—time. If you agree, we'll test you, train you, and soon you'll be helping to maintain the chronal order against the growing entropy of the future."

While most of me doesn't believe Hester—either his story or that he exists at all—for some reason, there's a part of me that does. I hear myself asking, "What if I don't agree?"

My answer comes as a video image appears. Hanging in the air in front of me, it shows my accident in graphic 3-D—my Toyota driving along, getting T-boned by the Crown Vic. There's a close-up of what's left of me being cut from the wreckage and being put in a body bag.

"You die."

"And what if I go along? I'm immortal?"

"No," Plato explains, "you still die in that wreckage. You just get to chose when. A minute from now, a month from now, ten years from now. When we're done with you or you're done with us, we put you back. Until then, consider this a second chance."

"I have questions—why me, why this way of recruiting agents, why at the end do I have to go back?"

"All part of the training. Now we need to know," Plato again shows me my death, "are you in or out?"

I wasn't ready to die when I got in my car this morning. I'm still not. I tell them I'm in.

They take me to an area that's part workroom, part lab, and part Star Trek. In the near corner is a desk. They hand me over to the guy in civilian dress sitting behind it. He's about twenty years older than me and looks as if he carries the weight of all the years he's trying to protect.

"Good luck, Jake," says Hester.

"Yeah, good luck," adds Plato.

"Thanks," the man and I say in unison.

"Sit down." I do what he tells me. There's something familiar about him—somewhere, sometime, we've met before. I wait for him to introduce himself. He doesn't.

"You have questions; forget the big one. Nobody on this level knows why anyone's picked. They got scientists and experts for that. It has something to do with what they call 'Gauger's Fifth Theorem'. But I can tell you why they recruit from those who are about to die."

His voice is weary. There's a sadness in it and behind his eyes. Maybe that's what knowing the future and reliving the past does to you. As I wonder if I'll be like that in twenty years, he goes on.

"The universe is done with you, Jake. For good or ill, you've made your mark. Any further effect you might have on the time stream is minimal." He pauses, shrugs. "That's the official answer. The real reason is that right now you're a second away from death. You'll always be a second away from death. We know it and you know it. You get out of line, you cause any problems, you piss us off in any way, someone presses the button on the stopwatch, your last second ticks away, and you're not a problem anymore. That gives us more control over you than we'd have over the Citizenry."

"Is that why you won't go back and prevent my accident? To keep me in line?"

It's obvious he's heard this question hundreds of times. "Your accident's already happened. It's a matter of fact and record. If we wanted to stop it, we would have. But we didn't. If you don't like that, say so now. There's a toe tag with your name on it just a second away."

"Let's keep it a second away. What's next?"

He points to a far wall. Something shimmers behind a control panel. "That's a chronal port, what you'd call a time machine. I'm going to send you back to do a job. See what you got. You do it right, you're in. If not..." He mimes a stopwatch. "Click."

"What's the job?"

"At the where and when I'm sending you, there's an old house that's been converted to apartments. The wiring's faulty. The house is going to burn."

"And I'm supposed to stop it?"

"No, it's meant to burn. So are all the people in it. Your job is to make sure they do, that no one gets out."

"But why? I thought..."

"Don't think," the man snaps. "Don't ask why. Just do the job and you get to keep on doing it." His voice softens. "I forgot this is new to you. Serving Time requires sacrifice. Sometimes from us, most of the time from others. The greater good and all that."

He looks down at his desk, lost in his own thoughts. Without looking up he says, "Someone in that house is what we call a 'nexus'. Around him or her, great and terrible events will flow. Great and terrible events are not good for the time stream. It's best that they don't occur."

"And if no one survives the fire..."

"Whatever disaster is looming will be delayed or prevented."

"Until the next time."

"There's always a next time. That's why we're here."

With a "Let's go," he stands up and leads me toward the shimmering port. I step through and find myself on a city street. It's dark and quiet, maybe two a.m. Row homes run up and down the block, most of them vacant and boarded up. Lights shine in the windows of some of them. I wonder which one of them will start burning, and how soon.

I also start wondering why they would send an untrained, untested rookie into such a critical situation. Then I remember that this is a test and I start to think that maybe there is no nexus, and that a vacant house will burn and that the sole purpose is to see if I can follow orders.

As I think this, I notice that the light in one of the houses is flickering. It grows brighter and now the flames come from the upstairs windows. And so the test begins.

I step into the shadows and think of all the things I could do but won't. Bang on doors and wake up neighbors. There's a gas station up the street;

surely there's a payphone. I could run there and call 9-1-1. Or I could break in through the front door and see if there are any lives to save. Instead I do nothing, except watch the fire burn.

As the flames grow I remember I'm supposed to do more than watch. "Make sure no one gets out," were the instructions. Since I'm probably being watched, I decide to go around back and make a show of doing my job.

The alley is not as dark as I thought it would be. Surprisingly, the three lights that the city put there years ago are all still working. I pick my way through the trash, scaring rats and crushing roaches, until I get to the rear of the burning house.

The top floor is now fully engulfed. The flames that were at the front are now licking at the back. There are bars on the rear first floor windows and maybe a deadbolt on the back door.

I'm about to return to the street when I see her—a small girl, maybe nine or ten. She's pressed against the first floor back window of the burning house, beating at the glass, trying to escape the flames.

I'm under a light. She notices me, sees me as her salvation. I can't hear her, but I know what she's saying—"Help me, help me!"—screaming it over and over.

I forget everything but the girl. I rush to the house, planning on kicking open the back door and carrying her to safety. Then something holds me back. I see the future crumbling because this girl was pulled to safety. But if she's the one, surely there'll be another time to stop her. They can't mean for me to let a little girl burn.

Of course they do, those were my orders. Or am I supposed to go beyond what I was told and do what I think is right?

The flames take her before I decide. That's what I tell myself. But my feet were moving away from the gate, into the alley, and towards the street. And my thoughts were not of the future, or of the girl, but of a stopwatch and a fatal car crash only a second away.

And then I'm back in Limbo, or whenever is it where the Chronal League meets. And the same sad man is waiting for me by a console. In the time I was gone, he'd changed into his own uniform. I look at his name, and suddenly I understand it all.

"I passed, didn't I?"

There is regret and anguish in his voice. "Yes, you did—again."

He flips a switch on his control panel, and I'm back in my Toyota as several tons of Ford slams into my side door and...

* * *

For the fifth time, I send myself back to the accident, this time five seconds before I was first recruited. Hester and Plato come into the room.

"How did it go, Jake?" Hester knows the answer, but asks anyway.

"Same as always."

"Jake, there was only one decision you could have made. It will always be the only decision you could have made. How often do you have to pull yourself out of Time before you realize that?"

I think of the future, and of a car crash that's still only a second away. And then of a little girl who is still silently screaming for help.

"Until I get it right. Until I save the girl."

The Bad Ass Faeries series was created and is edited by Danielle Ackley-McPhail. As I'm writing this there are three books in the series, a fourth planned, and hopefully many more to come. I finally broke into the series in book three, IN ALL THEIR GLORY. I submitted two stories. Danielle took them both and combined them into one. This is the first.

NOT WRONG AT ALL

There was a new drug on the streets of Baltimore. That was the word at any rate. Fairy dust, Super Juice, Red Angel, Tinkerbelle—those were the names it went by. No one in the department had seen it or had anything solid as to where and by whom it was sold. It was still just a story and a rumor.

The usual dealers were no help.

"That rich boy shit," said one.

"Ain't none of my peoples can pay two for a hit of that stuff," said another.

"Wish I had some," said a third, "Supposed be a bad ass high."

The Feds didn't know or care about the drug, and nobody was getting killed over it. At two hundred a hit, it likely was some designer drug that wasn't illegal yet. So that was as far as it went. With all the real dope out on the street, nobody worried about something that may not even exist.

* * *

And it's things that aren't supposed to exist that are going to kill me, Steele *thought as she looked at the door that stood by itself in the back of the basement and wondered if the shimmering was getting brighter.*

* * *

Detective Bethany Steele was working dayshift when the body was found. DOA in Patterson Park. Just another Sunday morning. "Stop at Hohn's, bring back donuts," McLarney yelled as she left to look at the dead body.

They'd seen it before: at the bottom of elevator shafts, beneath the JFX, and on sidewalks below open windows fourteen floors above. Sudden impact trauma, gravity at work, that sudden stop at the end—whatever one called it, the body about five hundred feet from the Pulaski Monument bore all the marks of a fall from a great height. The only problem was that there was no great height anywhere around.

"Where did he fall from?" Steele asked the assembled uniforms and crime lab techs.

"Small plane?" offered one Southeast officer. "Maybe he jumped and forgot his chute?"

"Catapult?" suggested another. "I know these seniors over at Mount St. Joe built one as a class project. Ever hear the expression 'When pigs fly?' They did that year. 'Course, the landing was kinda hard on them."

"That was a trebuchet," Dolan from the crime lab added. "And it wasn't used to launch this guy. I got the animal cruelty call last year. Those pigs came in at an angle." She took another look at the body. "This guy dropped straight down."

Photographs were taken, reports written, evidence collected. They put the death down as 'one of those things.' Steele made a note to check with the Helicopter Unit for sightings of small aircraft over the city.

The ME's examination only deepened the mystery.

"Look at these." Dominic Jones pointed to long parallel gashes on the victim's back.

"Something from the landing?" Steele didn't remember seeing any jagged rocks on the scene. "They don't look like knife wounds."

"They are not," the pathologist replied, "As best as I can determine, with the body in the condition it is in, both wounds are of equal length and seem to have been made from the outside in. But that may just be damage from the fall. I can tell you that they match..." Jones displayed a shirt. "...the tears on this guy's upper clothing. And these were found in the jacket lining."

He held up a plastic bag containing several large white feathers.

"Any very big birds seen in the area, Detective?"

* * *

Two days later, Jones called with the blood results.

"Tox screen is back. There was something strange in his blood."

"Drugs?" was Steele's obvious guess. It was a rare day when a homicide victim did not come back with something in his system.

"I do not know, Detective. If it is, it is unlike any drug I have ever seen. It appears to be something like DNA."

"Something like? You mean animal DNA?"

"No, I mean it has the appearance of DNA, but it has a left-hand spiral and its base pairs are switched."

"Is that possible?"

"Not in this world."

* * *

Right there is where I should have dumped this case on Special Investigations, *Steele thought as she realized that the shimmering was getting brighter and that there were shadows of movement behind it. Told them that a giant Roc was carrying people off. They love weird shit like that. But no, I had to keep the case on my desk.*

* * *

Jones's results were verified when a chemist from the Lab handed her the report on the feathers. It showed the same combination of human DNA and "other similar nucleotides." The only good news was that the Latent Print Unit had finally identified the body—Curtis Evans, a grad student at Hopkins, working on a Master's in Biochemistry.

At last, Steele thought, *something that might lead to a logical explanation.* College students mixing their own chemical pleasures was nothing new. Maybe, just maybe, when she checked out his apartment there'd be a reason for the tears in his back and clothing.

What Steele found in Evans's apartment were his three roommates floating a foot off the floor in a near unconscious state of bliss.

Three cell phones and a digital camera went off almost simultaneously as officers on the scene photographed the phenomenon. The flash of the camera was enough to wake one of the levitating students, who promptly crashed onto the foam mattress above which she had been floating.

Later, grounded and sober, the three were taken to the Homicide Unit.

"Yeah, we were flying Red Angel," the girl admitted. "It costs like anything, but the high...hell, it's better than anything, better than the best sex you could ever have. When you're flying, it's like your whole body's tingling, especially your..."

Steele didn't care what parts of the girl were tingling. "Tell me about Curtis," she prompted.

"We bought two vials; cut four to one, that would have been two hits each. But Curt couldn't wait. Wanted to know what a full dose was like. So he opened a vial in the park and downed it."

"What happened then?" A thought was forming in Steele's mind, an idea that wasn't possible, one she knew she was going to hear from the girl.

"He was shaking, then moaning, then he sorta started, I don't know, glowing, like a bright light was inside him. Then he screamed. There was this ripping and tearing sound and then we saw his wings."

"Wings?" That would explain Evans's wounds and the rips in his clothing. Still, despite seeing three people floating in air, Steele was not yet ready to believe that a man could fly.

The girl nodded her head. "Yeah, wings. Once he realized he had them, he flapped them twice and then shot straight up in the air. We got bored waiting for him to come down so we went home and flew a little ourselves. We haven't seen him since. I guess he came down somewhere."

"He did," Steele said and told the girl about her friend's landing.

Knowing it would cut off their supply, the three students were reluctant to give up the name of their dealer.

"Besides," said one of the two male students, "it's not as if Fairy Dust is illegal. So you don't even have a reason to hold us." He then proudly told Steele that he was a law student, adding, "Charge us or let us go."

Always willing to cooperate with the public, Steele accommodated the young man. She offered to charge them with murder.

"Evans was found dead with two severe wounds in his back. You were the last to see him alive after purchasing drugs. And your defense is that he grew wings and flew away. Good luck with that."

Faced with the reality of jail, the three readily gave up the name of their dealer. He, in turn, threatened with contributory homicide, gave up his supplier, who then provided the police with the address from which he had obtained his Fairy Juice.

* * *

"It's an old house in the northeast," explained Sergeant Thorndale, the man in charge of the Quick Response Team. "No attic, three or four rooms upstairs, the same on the first. Who knows what's in the basement. We go in at four. That time of the morning, everybody's thinking about sleep. Nobody expects a knock on the door and a flashbang in the face. Jennings secures the back, I'll follow the entry team, and you follow me. That clear, Detective?"

"Got it, Sergeant."

They went over the plan twice more before grabbing some rest. At four they hit the house as planned; no one expecting trouble, each officer prepared for it.

No sooner had the first swing of the ram opened the front door than Thorndale and his men were inside. Steele followed just after, feeling awkward in the ballistic armor that was twice the weight of her regular vest. There were stairs as she went in, a QRT man standing at the bottom, his weapon pointed up. The living room was clear. Everyone was quiet, listening for any sounds of movement in the house.

Steele saw it first, a thin barrel edging around the doorway leading from the kitchen.

"Gun!" she shouted a second too late to keep a QRT man from taking a slug to the neck. He went down as automatic weapons riddled the wall and the man behind it.

The firing stopped. The back door burst open and Jennings ran inside. Eyes locked, heads nodded. Northway, the officer at the foot of the stairs, checked the fallen man and shook his head.

Steele reached for her radio.

"What are you doing?" Thorndale asked.

"Calling it in."

Cold anger was in Thorndale's voice. "When it's over. Right now we finish it."

Now was not the time to argue procedure. Not with the sorrow over a fallen comrade driving the need for payback. Steele nodded.

Northway started to go up. "You're here," he told Steele. As the least trained she was lookout and back-up. Thorndale led Jennings down the basement steps.

Gunfire below. Single shots followed quickly by more automatic fire. Silence, then...

"Clear," came the sergeant's voice. "Two down. We're both good."

"Clear above," Northway yelled from the second floor.

"Detective," Thorndale shouted, "get down here. We've got...damn, I don't know what the hell we've got."

The basement was one big room. From the middle of the stairs, Steele started looking around. In the front was what even a rookie cop would recognize as a drug lab. Vials of red liquid, packaged and street-ready. A tray of a red flaky substance, something Steele had seen on countless murder scenes—dried blood. Glassine envelopes with a reddish powder were stacked next to the tray.

A bad feeling began to grow inside her as she realized that still no one had called in. Too much, too soon. Maybe it was time, she thought. Then she looked towards the back, past the bodies of the drug dealers the QRT team had put down. The feeling got worse and her radio was forgotten.

Three beds, three people strapped to them. Two of them—the men—had tubes running from their arms into plastic bags, their life's blood slowing dripping into them. They were pale, but otherwise healthy looking.

The woman was worse. She, too, had a line in her, but she was naked, and it was clear that she had been sexually abused.

They should be cut loose, Steele told herself but couldn't form the words or the will to move. Maybe it was the shock of seeing them. Maybe it was because those on the bed were three of the most beautiful creatures she had ever seen. Maybe it was the wings.

Angels, was Steele's first thought when she realized that the large feathery objects were not part of the bedding. But could one so bind an angel and would divine creatures bleed?

There is a point in a case when it all comes together. Sometimes that point comes gradually, a steady buildup of evidence and witness testimony that tells the story. And sometimes there's a sudden realization that leaps past the facts and goes right to the answer.

"Faeries," Steele whispered as it all came together for her. The floating college students, the dead boy who flew away and fell to Earth. The names for the drugs. These were faeries. Faeries who came into this world and met the worst kind of humans, humans who had somehow discovered the properties of their blood then captured, enslaved, and abused them.

Again came the thought that it was past time to call this in, to let someone know what had happened, what they had found, to report that the world was not what it was this morning.

Having put down the bad guys, Thorndale and Jennings moved to help the victims. They took off their helmets, laid aside their weapons, and moved toward the beds. Together they removed the IVs and loosened the straps binding the male faeries, then they turned to free the female.

Feeling someone behind her, Steele turned briefly and saw Northway.

"What are they doing?" he asked, removing his own helmet.

"They're freeing the…" Steele started to explain, but as she turned back towards the room, she saw what he meant.

The faeries were free. Thorndale had picked up a blanket and was offering it to the naked female. She, however, made no move to take it or cover herself. Instead she turned to her companions and said something in a harsh—yet somehow musical—language. They nodded in agreement with whatever she had said.

Three sets of wings suddenly unfurled, filling the basement and knocking the QRT men aside. One of the males made a dash to a far corner of the room, and came back with things sharp and shiny.

"Move," shouted Northway and pushed Steele aside. "Look out," he called to his fellow officers just as the faeries attacked.

Taking a long knife offered by her comrade, the female fell on Thorndale. Unarmed and taken unawares, the sergeant had no hope of defending himself. The fairy stabbed once, twice, and then a third time, the blade piercing Thorndale's ballistic armor and going deep into his chest.

At the same time, a male fairy went after Jennings. Wielding a sword, he first slashed and partly severed the officer's leg, dropping him. As the officer fell, the fairy pinned him to the floor with a thrust though his stomach.

As Northway began firing, Steele did what should have been done with the first shot.

"Signal 13!" she shouted into her radio, "Officers down, shots fired." She then drew her Glock to join the battle.

The female went down, then one of the males. The other retreated further back into the basement.

Nowhere to go, Steele thought, *down here there's no door to the outside.*

Then the darkness in the rear of the basement lit up as a bright rectangle suddenly formed. It grew to more than the size of a man and the remaining faerie stepped towards it.

"No you don't, you bastard!" Northway yelled and rushed the glowing door.

With what seemed to be a look of hatred for all things human on his face, the fairy threw a knife that caught the officer in the right eye. Then he stepped through the door and was gone.

Steele emptied half a clip into the glowing portal, expecting it to close at any minute. When it didn't, she stopped firing and asked herself why. Why was it still open?

There was only one answer. He was coming back and bringing friends.

Why? Steele asked, looking at her slaughtered companions. *Why did they do it? We rescued them; we were going to help.*

They're not that much different from us, she realized. They thought we would be like the ones who had enslaved them. And Steele had to admit that they were not that far from being wrong.

A drug that could make men fly. Who would not want that? What government would not want flying soldiers? And all that was needed was the blood from creatures that were not of this world, that were not even human. No, they were not wrong at all.

Steele knew she didn't dare leave the basement. The door could not be left unguarded. The faeries would be back, looking for vengeance. If they got loose in her world, the slaughter would be horrific.

* * *

Alone in a blood splattered basement, Detective Bethany Steele watched a door without a room and waited for it to open. When it did it would be her against who knows how many but back-up was on its way—maybe. The basement walls were thick, and Steele wasn't sure her call for help had gone out.

Again she looked around at the bodies on the floor. Cops, dealers, faeries. Soon there would be more.

She'd hold them off as best she could, dropping them one by one until her ammo ran out. After that...Steele looked at the sword on the floor beside her. After that she'd pick it up and start swinging and hope to take a few of the winged bastards with her.

Again she sent out a 13, not knowing if the radio signal would pass through the basement walls. She gathered her weapons and waited for a war to start.

When Danielle asked me for a fairie story that involved a police SWAT team, I sent her the previous one. It was only after she received it that she told me that she wanted a "fairie SWAT team." So I told the story of what was happening on the other side of the door.

SO MANY DEATHS, SO MANY LIES

This is my world, the land of eternal youth. It's called *Tirnanogue* in some languages, *Fairie* in others. I call it home. Once upon a time it was a gentle place, one of green hills and rolling valleys, where the Goddess ruled and all obeyed her quiet commands.

That changed of course, after the Folk fled here from the mortal world. No sooner did we settle then we began changing things, altering what had been an untouched world into something more to our liking. Felling trees and hewing stones, we built homes and castles that quickly grew into villages and kingdoms.

Thank the Goddess we are a slow breeding people, that there are not so many of us that we must crowd into cities like the humans do, fouling our air and poisoning the water with the closeness of each other. We are better than that, but not by much.

There is no perfect race of beings. For every angel there is a daemon, for every noble there is a baseborne. We've had peace and war, just rulers and tyrants. And while for now we've entered into a period of peace and order, there are always those who would break our Goddess-given laws.

That's where I come in. My name is Fredag. I'm part of the Guard.

I was working Midwatch in the Artisan District trying to find out who was selling a certain poison to the youths of the city. It was called White Angel, a powder that when dissolved in wine causes a momentary elation and feeling of divine bliss. Not a bad thing, one would think. But over time more and more of the potion is needed to achieve the same effect. Soon the body craves it to the point where one will do anything to acquire it. When its use was limited to the lower quarters, the City Wardens didn't care. But now Folk were being beaten and robbed so that the weak could afford to purchase what they needed.

The past night, guards of the Last Watch had brought in two purveyors of the foul mix and thrown them into a garrison cell. So far, they had refused to tell from whom they had obtained the drug. No matter; it was my case. I'd question them my way.

A mailed glove and a rod tipped with cold iron would loosen their tongues. And if that failed, they'd be offered a choice between a clean death or one by torture. One way or the other, they'd talk.

My trip to the cells was interrupted when I was called into the Watch Commander's chamber.

"The scum talk yet?" Captain Rollo was not one for small talk.

"Not yet, sir, but they will."

"That goes without saying, Fredag. How were they found?"

"Guard Conrad trained a barghest to scent the powder. He let it loose in an area where he knew it had been sold."

The Captain nodded. "And it led him to those two?"

"It led him to three. Before he could pull it off, the barghest had done for the third."

"Nasty beasts, those. Still, they have their uses. Wonderful trackers. Maybe we should train a few more on White Angel and set them loose."

"That would be one solution, sir."

But it would not be mine, I thought. The dark hounds cared not who got in their way. Still, if the poison continued to spread, the City Wardens were certainly capable of letting them loose, no matter how many innocents might fall.

"That's not why I called you in, Fredag. I need you for something else. Let Stoinef work the White Angel."

Stoinef. Of course. Now that suspects were in hand and the case almost closed, of course they would give it to Stoinef. To him would go the glory and honor of closing the case after the rest of the Guard does all the work. He was the fair-haired princeling. It was common knowledge that he was the off-blanket son of a highborne and a kitchen wench. Despite this, or maybe because of it, he was favored by his father, and by those who sought his father's grace. The bastard would be my commander one day.

I said nothing. As a lowborne, it was not my place to comment on my so-called betters. I did my job and did it well and thus was allowed to keep doing it, until a case came long that needed a staked goat. Then I'd be set out as bait for the wolves.

The look on the Captain's face told me that the "something else" was one of those cases that required skills other than a well-placed parent. It would be one with no glory at its end, but a posting to the Thieves' Quarter if I failed. I didn't like it, but I'd taken the Duke's brass, so I didn't have a say.

Rollo gave it to me straight. "Three highbornes are missing. At first it was thought that they'd flown out to their family estate. A messenger was sent but came back with the word that they had not been there."

I waited for more but that's all the Captain said. Finally I asked, "Is that all we have—three missing young nobles?"

Rollo's answer made it clear where things stood. "It's all *you* have, Fredag. If they're in the city, find them. If they left, find out when and in what direction, then find them."

"And they are?"

"Nilus, Guibert, and Roisin."

The Captain had saved the best for last. At his, "You're familiar with the names?" I nodded. The whole damned city knew those names.

All were members of the Clan Ademar, highborne flyers, and one of the city's Five Families. Nilus and Guibert were cousins. Privileged youths with too much time and too much gold. They were not unknown to the Guard. Of course their clan's influence meant that the Guard's sole role in their debauched escapades was to see them safely home and to advise the owner of whatever tavern they had destroyed to send Clan Ademar a bill for the damages, if they dared. Few did.

Roisin was another story. Sister to Nilus, her features were said to rival those of Cedric's famed sculpture of the Goddess. Whether that was true or not, I couldn't say. She was kept out of the public eye. It was not for those like me to look on beauty such as hers.

"I need not remind you, Fredag, that the family is not to be bothered in this matter."

"Of course not, sir." Far be it from me to question the only ones who might know where the missing youths had gone. "Clan Odilo?"

"What of them, Fredag?"

As if he had to ask. Clans Odilo and Ademar had been rivals since the Goddess was a girl. And it was only Her Peace that kept them from hunting each other in the streets and slaying whoever got in their way.

"I presume that I am not to bother Clan Odilo, either."

The Captain's withering glare was all the answer I needed.

Barred from interviewing the victims' family or questioning the chief suspects in their disappearance, I left Rollo's chamber to begin my investigation, wondering what the billeting in the Thieves' Quarters barracks was like.

The first step was to determine if the three might still be in the city. That meant walking the wall. Twelve towers and five gates, all manned over four watches—that's a lot of walking. Using the Captain's name I put the duty on two of the younger guards. While they were about that business, I checked the alehouses, music halls, and bordellos in case the cousins had caused any recent damage. They hadn't. Next step the cells in each District and Quarter, just in case the two had been locked up by someone who didn't know or care who they were. If that were the case, that "someone" would no doubt take their place in lockup with no hope of release this side of the ground.

Without using her name, I also asked about Roisin. It was possible, although just barely, that she had joined her kinfolk in their carousing. It was rumored to be a fashion among the gentler young ladies to frequent those places from which they would be barred by good breeding and common sense. Some were even said to take a turn on the harlot's couch. True or not, there was no sign of the one I sought.

The guards who had walked the wall had no better luck. There were no reports of anyone answering the young Ademars' description leaving through the gates or over them.

With no evidence that the three had left the city, I proceeded on the theory that they were still within its walls, held somewhere against their will. Or that they were dead and their bodies carefully hidden.

There was a third possibility. It was one I did not wish to consider. The unsanctioned opening of a portal was a serious offense, one over which no amount of gold or influence had any power. For such a crime there was no forgiveness, only punishment. Of course, neither would there be forgiveness for the guardsman who brought such a charge, provable or not. The clans have long memories and sharp knives.

I briefly considered putting out a citywide call for them, with every guard alerted to search for and detain all those who fit the descriptions. It would work, in time. It would also drag in too many innocent citizens, causing them undue embarrassment and hasten my transfer to less enjoyable duties. I settled for sending their descriptions to the Necropolis and the Healers' District, just in case.

Without much of a home to go to, I stayed late at the Garrison, trying to come up with a viable approach that would not offend anyone of rank or influence. Failing that, I gathered my files on the White Angel case so as to be able to turn the report over to Stoinef in the morning.

White Angel. Confined still to the Lower Quarters, it was the one vice that the jaded gentry had yet to try. So far. But soon one of the younger winged nobles would wander into a tavern where it was available. He'd drink it down or sniff it up and soon it would be all the fashion, until one of them took too much. One or two dead highbornes, and no doubt the City Wardens would set the barghests on the dealers.

Barghests. What was it the Captain had said? "Wonderful trackers." Late as it was, I went to the barracks and woke up Conrad.

"Those hell hounds of yours, can they track anything?" I asked once he was awake.

"Given a scent, yes. Fredag, is that why you woke me up, because a prisoner has escaped?"

"Not a prisoner, Conrad, at least not one of ours. I'll need three of your best, with competent handlers, by Midwatch tomorrow."

"Why, what do you have?"

"An idea, one that might solve my case and help me keep my job and position."

I spent the next morning at the Ademar Estate. Not to visit or bother the family, but to convince the servants to break the law. It took a combination of pleas, bribes, threats of prison, and promises of rewards, but I managed to talk two valets and one lady's maid into obtaining items of clothing worn by my missing victims but not yet washed. Putting each in a separate sack, I took my booty to Conrad.

"I need each hound to track the owner of one of these items." I handed him the sacks.

"And what are you looking for?"

"Job security. I'm looking for three missing highbornes. So just make sure those beasts of yours don't eat whoever they find, or you and I will be their next meal."

Conrad took me to the stable where his barghests were waiting. For once I agreed with Rollo: nasty creatures they were—tall as a pony, black as the night; shadows given legs, teeth, and appetite. I could well believe the legend that they had originally been bred in a realm with magic darker than our own.

The hounds were separated then given the scent. Dragging their handlers behind them, each took off in a different direction. I stayed in the stable, praying to the Goddess that I was right.

Conrad stayed as well, keeping track of his beasts. With an affinity that led me to suspect that maybe he, too, was from a different realm, he seemed to know exactly where each one was. Random streets at first, as each barghest worked to find the scent he'd been given. Then more purposeful, as they hit on the smell and began to work.

"That's odd," Conrad muttered, more in a trance than awake. "They are...converging. Drogo from Thieves' Quarters, Dash from this District. Now Bruno. All into the Merchants' Quarters. Back into the storehouses."

Conrad awakened suddenly. "They're together. Let's go!"

He ran out of the stable, moving as fast as one of his hounds after a hare. I followed as best I could, struggling to keep up with him.

The city is mostly a labyrinth, having grown around its citizens with no plan or reason. The Folk built homes and shops where they would, leaving only enough room for a cart to pass, sometimes not even that. The Merchants' Quarter is the exception. Built near the docks, its storehouses are laid out in straight rows separated by wide passages so as to make shipments and deliveries, both legal and otherwise, that much easier. Oddly enough, for one used to the maze of the city, its grid-like layout was somehow confusing.

So it was that it took me some time to catch up with Conrad and his hounds, all three of which were baying and scratching at the door of an extra-sized storehouse toward the rear of the Quarter.

"Thought we'd wait for you before going in," Conrad said. He looked at the crest above the doors.

I followed his gaze and cursed. The storehouse belonged to the Clan Odilo.

Somewhere gods were laughing. Whatever game they were playing had me as both pawn and jester. There was no way this was going to end well—not for me, nor for the missing Ademar youths. Right then I was more concerned about myself. Even the right decision would land me in the Thieves' Quarters. I did not want to think what a wrong choice would bring.

Even as four men and three hounds waited on me, I knew there was only one path to take. Politics and influence be as damned as I was likely to be. If the barghests were right, inside there were three young people in need of aid or vengeance, and as a member of the Guard, it was my duty to see that it was provided them.

Still, it would not do to rush in. In the past, haste in these situations has lead to Guardsmen passing into the Grey Mist.

I had Conrad take one of the hounds, freeing up a man. "Go to the barracks," I told him. "Tell Rollo I need the Duke's Own—flyers for the roof, rammers for entry, swords and slings for those inside."

I had another thought. "Also send a runner to the Clan Odilo. Tell them that the Guard has found evidence of thieves and intruders in their storehouse and is moving to protect their property. If Stoinef is free, send him." The guard ran off.

"Intruders, Fredag?"

"Of course, Conrad. Surely you don't believe that the noble Clan Odilo is behind the disappearance of members of their close friends and allies the Clan Ademar?"

Whatever Conrad believed, he wisely kept to himself.

While most folk in the Guard come from every walk of life, the Duke's Own are an elite breed. To a man they are all ex-military, having served their time on the outer edge of Fairie, in the Twilight Realm, where the light merges with the darkness. These are the men who stand against the stuff of nightmares and make our petty games of politics possible. They are both a joy and a terror to watch.

They responded quickly to my summons: four on the ground, plus two flyers. Six men seem to be a small force, but there are tales of how just two once subdued a town that rebelled against the Duke. That town no longer stands, and of its few survivors, none are believed to be whole.

The sergeant in charge came up to me. "Your orders, sir?" As the Guard who summoned them, I was nominally their commander. That meant I told them what needed to be done and let them do it. It also meant that the responsibility for failure rested on me.

I explained the situation and what—or rather who—I hope to find inside.

"And those other than the hostages?"

"Meet force with force, Sergeant." They would anyway, but it had to be said.

"Very good, sir."

"One other thing: I'm going in with you."

It was my case, my responsibility. The Sergeant nodded in understanding.

"With me then, sir. Once the way is open."

They began. The flyers, their crossbows armed with iron-tipped quarrels, would take down any who tried to escape by air. They would also watch the rear and sides. In the unlikely event that someone got past the raiding party, the flyers would hunt them down.

The sergeant drew his sword, as did one of his men. I had my long knife. The rammers did their job and forced the main door in three blows. We went in. The rammers followed, backing us with slings and iron pellets to take out snipers and other distant threats.

It was messy, brutal work. The baying of the hounds had given those inside ample warning and the pounding of the ram told them just what they faced. They fought to save their lives and to take ours.

As we expected, a few tried to escape through the roof hatch. Iron pellets took down one of them, leaving the others as sport for our flyers.

There were nine inside. I engaged one, and by the time I wiped his blood from my knife it was over. Seven men dead, two wounded, and that was not counting what happened to the flyers.

We checked to make sure no one was hiding amidst the stores. It was a quick search, as there was precious little product for a building of its size. What we did find were tables of what at first appeared to be alchemical equipment—scales, balances and weights, glass vials to be used as packaging, and a strange, transparent material full of a whitish powder.

The latter I recognized immediately. I had lived with it for several fortnights. I knew its effects and the tragedies it caused. It was White Angel.

Any joy I felt about the fact that this was one case that Stoinef was not going to be solving was tempered by the reality of where I was. Thanks to me, the source of a plague devastating the city had been found. And thanks to me, one of the major clans was implicated.

I was wondering if I'd be allowed to take my medal to the Thieves' Quarters with me when the Sergeant came over.

"The storehouse is secure, sir. The prisoners have been bound. One, while injured, is in no immediate danger of dying. The other won't last the hour. Any further orders?"

I was just about to dismiss him and his troops with thanks when there came the sound of a thousand buzzing hornets. Outside the barghests let out howls that could not only wake every sleeping monster in the city, but drive them from our midst, never to return. Knowing what to expect, the sergeant and I turned toward an empty blank spot along the rear wall and watched as a portal opened.

"To me!" shouted the Sergeant and the Duke's Own gathered, weapons drawn, ready to meet and repel whatever threat might emerge.

Portals are magic, a way of travelling from one realm to another. There is no way to tell what land is on the other side, or who—or what—might be coming through.

The buzzing stopped and a shape appeared in the doorway. Seconds later, a man bleeding from several small holes fell dead on the storehouse floor.

"I recognize those wounds," the Sergeant said as we stood over the body. "Only one realm can slaughter a man like that—Earth."

Earth. Earth was the homeworld, the place from which we had fled when the God of the Tree supplanted our Goddess. The humans who dwell there are a short-lived, violent people with a tremendous talent for developing new and imaginative ways of destroying each other.

We turned the corpse and a face familiar to me stared up with dead eyes. The Lady's luck was not with me in this case. It was not one of the Angel dealers I'd been tracking. Rather, it was one of three for whom I'd been looking—Nilus Ademar. And if the body on the floor was Nilus, his sister and cousin were no doubt on the other side of the door. I looked into the shimmer of the portal as if trying to see through into the world beyond, wondering if they were alive or dead. Dead, probably, considering Nilus's fate. Either way it was not my problem anymore. The investigation was over—my part in it, anyway.

"Sir?" The Sergeant interrupted my thinking. His men were gathered around him and they all had the attitude of soldiers who had finished their duty and just wanted to go home. I dismissed him with thanks and a promise of a glowing report to his command.

"Thank you, Guardsman." The job done, I was no longer his commander. "What of the captives?"

"Leave them with me, Sergeant. We're almost done here. If we can, we'll take them to a Healer. Otherwise the ghouls at the Necropolis can have them."

The Duke's Own departed, leaving me alone with just the dead, the dying, and my thoughts.

Two highborne clans, one engaged in selling poison to the folk of the city, the other involved in unauthorized travel to a dangerous world. Both capital offenses, and each carrying the potential for scandal great enough to cost the Ademars and the Odilos much of their influence. If it came out.

That was not likely. The highbornes knew how to protect themselves. What *was* likely was a cover-up that included silencing those in the know. The Duke's Own? They were soldiers doing their job. They were unaware of the parties involved. Conrad and his handlers? They had stayed outside and knew nothing of what had happened in the storehouse. That left—me.

They would need my silence. A transfer to better duty might earn it, so might a promotion or higher pay. However nice that sounded, I knew there was only one way they could be certain that the story never came out.

I looked towards the still shimmering portal and, for a moment, considered taking my chances with whatever waited on the other side. A glance at Nilus told me what that would bring me, but maybe it would be a quicker fate than the one that awaited me in this world.

The thought of taking the quick path to the Grey Mist repelled me. So did making my report and calmly awaiting the inevitable decision. There had to be a third option.

I started thinking like a guardsman and quickly found it. Why, I asked, would an Ademar open a portal in an Odilo storehouse? There were two people who might have the answer, and one of them was near death.

I checked on my prisoners. At least one of them might make it to a healer. Then I called in Conrad.

"About time, Fredag. Can we go back now, the hounds are getting hun…" The sight of the battle inside stopped him cold. "By the Lady!" Then Conrad noticed the open portal. "What's that over there?"

"Best you don't know. We're almost through here. Just one more thing." I hesitated, needing but not wanting to take the next step. I consoled myself with the thought that it was my life against one who would soon be making his final journey no matter what I did. What was a small piece of my soul against my overall survival?

"Conrad, bring in one of the hounds, preferably the hungriest one."

"Fredag, what are you…"

"Like I said, Conrad, best you don't know."

It was my case, so Conrad did what he was told and quickly brought in the largest of his hounds, the creature called Drogo. While he was doing that I dragged my two captives closer to the center of the storehouse. I had just finished when Conrad came in with his barghest.

Neither man could take his eyes off the snarling blackness that was the hound. It was all shadow, excepting the red of its eyes and the white of its teeth. Seeing the men, sensing their weakness, it strained at its leash. Conrad was barely able to hold it back.

A foul stench filled the air; my captives had soiled themselves. This only served to excite the beast more.

I again asked myself how far I was willing to take this, what my life was worth. I decided its value was far in excess of the two men at my feet.

"The thing before you, gentlemen, is hungry. It has worked hard all day and has missed several meals. Right now it sees you as food. Should I order it released? Or will you tell me for whom you work and how are the Ademars involved?"

The one nearest the hound was close to death, but he would have spoken, had not the severity of his wounds coupled by the shock I had just given him left him unable to speak. His partner, somehow sensing that Drogo would go for his weaker friend, shook his head.

"Don't know. The one who hired us is over there, dead in the corner."

"Too bad."

I walked over to Conrad, "That one," I said and pointed to the one near death. Conrad let out the lead slowly. "You're next," I told the other.

The hound was inches away from his friend's feet when the healthier one shouted, "It was Ekbert—Ekbert Odilo. He was behind it."

I nodded and Conrad backed the hound off, using all his strength to pull it away from its would-be meal.

"And what, my friend, was Ekbert behind?"

Never taking his eyes off the barghest, he answered. "Where that portal leads, that's where he sent the three he had us snatch off the street one night. Sent them right through, he did. Said he'd made a deal on the other side. Said that the blood of the Folk does things to mortals, makes them like us. Traded the three for a mortal drug, something he called 'hero wine.'"

"Hero wine." Funny name for a white powder that was anything but heroic. "White Angel" did sound better.

The man was babbling now, his eyes still on Drogo, repeating what he'd told me over and over in an effort to earn my mercy.

It was late and I was tired. With what I now knew, I could safely make my report. It wouldn't earn me any honors, but neither would it get me knifed in the dark. Just a feud between clans—happens all the time. The Odilos would pay the clangeld, Ekbert would be banished, and all would be as it was.

Except for the young highborne lying dead in the place of his enemy. Except for his sister and cousin, no doubt dead in a foreign land, their lost spirits far from the Grey Mist. Except for those whose lives had been destroyed by a mortal poison. All might return to what it was, but that did not make things right.

The small piece of my soul I had traded for information found its way back to me as I remembered that it was the duty of the Guard to make things right. At least it was the duty of one of the Guard, at least for one night.

Drogo's growl told me how I could accomplish this.

"Can we go now," Conrad all but whined. "He really is hungry."

"Go with my thanks, Conrad, and buy your pets a steak each. I'll pay."

"After tonight you owe them each a cow."

"And after tomorrow I'll owe them a herd. I've more work for them."

Conrad gave me an odd look. "You're not thinking of going after Ekbert Odilo, are you?"

"Of course not. I'm thinking of going after the thieving, murderous lowborne who invaded the storehouse of the Clan Odilo and dared to impersonate one of its noble scions."

I said this as if I meant it. I'd need the practice when I made my report to Captain Rollo.

"Go home, Conrad. Go back to your stables, feed and rest your hounds. Come Daywatch, send me fresh ones, and someone to carry a message."

"It is Daywatch, Fredag."

"Go home anyway. I'll be here. I've business to finish up."

If Conrad suspected what my business was, he didn't say, just nodded and left, leaving me alone in the storehouse.

Not quite alone. There was the dead, and there were my captives. There was also whoever was on the other side of the still-open portal. Had they left, or were they still there waiting for us?

If what little I knew of Earth and its humans were true, I knew the answer to that question. At least I hoped I did.

I checked my prisoners. One had joined his fellows in death. The other was still alive, still hoping for mercy. That hope faded when I put my knife to his eye.

"This boss of yours, the one who calls himself Ekbert. What of his is here?"

Without the threat of the barghest, he was less willing to talk.

"I can send you to the healers blind, or with two good eyes. Or to the Mist right now. Your choice."

I moved the knife closer; let him feel its point.

"Ekbert, he kept a cloak on a hook in back. It gets cold in here sometimes."

"A black cloak?"

"No, deep red, lined and with a hood."

I checked, there was such a garment, and of a quality that an Odilo might own.

There was nothing more to do but wait for the hounds, that and take care of my prisoner. He was not badly wounded and was likely to survive. As the sole survivor of this criminal enterprise, the full weight of the Duke's Law would rest on him. That, after much torture and suffering, he would not survive.

No doubt the man still hoped for a mercy he did not deserve. Yet he was fated for the Inquisitors' chambers, and that no one deserved. I used my knife and showed him the only mercy I could.

The messenger arrived before the hounds. To my surprise, it was Stoinef.

"Fredag, all is well?"

"With me, Stoinef, but the others here have had better days." As he looked past me at last night's slaughter, I added, "You have apprised the Clan Odilo of the situation?"

He nodded. "They were deeply troubled by the news and trust in the Guard to protect their name and reputation and to bring those responsible to justice."

"Of course they do. If you would, please go back to them. Tell them that, as you can plainly see, all responsible are now facing the Lady's Justice, all but one. And that one will be brought to bay this very morning. I'm setting the barghests on him, and their justice will be less merciful than the Lady's."

Stoinef left and shortly after, Conrad's beasts arrived with two handlers. I gave Stoinef time to arrive at the Odilo Estate with my message, sure that Ekbert was paying close attention to what was transpiring.

When enough time had passed, I gave the handlers pieces I had cut from Ekbert's cloak. "Take these to the First and Third Gates, then give the hounds the scent. If they find the one we seek, hold them back as best you can."

"Why those two gates?" asked the taller of Conrad's men.

I could have told them the truth and said, "Because they are the farthest from here." Instead I shrugged. "We have to start somewhere."

They accepted this and were off. And again I was left in the company of the dead and a still-glowing portal. I spent my time picking up useful things from the floor and the table with the alchemical equipment on it.

My wait was short. In the time it would have taken the barghests to reach the gates and be set to work, a highborne wearing the colors of Clan Odilo joined me in the storehouse. He was tall, with a proud set of wings, and carried himself with a noble bearing. In the right circumstances most would have considered him handsome, but today his pale skin and worried countenance stole whatever looks he might claim.

"You are Fredag of the Guard?"

I admitted that I was.

"You set the hounds on me." It was more of statement than a question, but I answered anyway.

"Perhaps I did. Who are you?"

"You know damn well that I am Ekbert of the Clan Odilo."

"Then you are mistaken, Noble Sir. I set the hounds on the vile lowborne who has claimed to be you; on the villain who abducted, debased, and caused the death of three of your honored allies of the Clan Ademar; on the purveyor of poison who spread a plague through this city. Surely such a one deserves his fate?"

Ekbert, to his credit, did not gainsay my words. "Call them off," he begged in a now quaking voice. "Call off the hounds and name your price. I swear by the honor of my Clan I will pay it."

"My price?" I walked over to where lay the body of Nilus Ademar. "Bring him back. Bring back his sister and cousin." I went over to the equipment table. "Undo the damage your 'hero wine' has caused. That is my price."

Ekbert had no answer. He just stood there, no longer a noble flyer lording over the common folk of the city. Now he was just a man without power, without influence, without hope.

In the distance came the sound of baying hounds. By the Lady, those beasts were fast.

"Hear that, Ekbert, that is the sound of your fate, the sound of justice rushing toward you. And when those monsters from Hell burst through the door, I will step aside and let them have you. They will feed, consuming not only your body, but also your soul. No judgment after death, no voyage to the Grey Mist, only eternal suffering as a wraith in whatever daemon realm they were spawned."

Whether that was true or not, Ekbert believed me. As the baying came closer, he began searching for a way out. He glanced first at the roof hatches, thought about taking flight.

"Barred from the outside," I lied. It was then that he saw the portal.

A drowning man will clutch at the thinnest thread to try to stay afloat. Ekbert saw the glowing doorway as his only escape and ran toward it. I made no move to stop him. Instead, I used the glove I'd taken from the alchemical bench to pick up three of the pellets used the night before. These I tossed into the doorway just as Ekbert entered. The cold iron disrupted the portal's magic and it closed behind him.

It may have been my imagining, but as the portal faded, I thought I heard the sound of thunder come from within it. Three times I heard the thunder, and it was followed by the sound of a man crying out in pain and death. Maybe it was my imagination, or maybe the humans were welcoming Ekbert in their own unique way.

I had cut three pieces from Ekbert's cloak, one for each of the hounds, and a third I placed in the pocket of one of last night's dead. When the hounds finally did burst through the door, they ravaged the corpse beyond recognition. So it was, to my surprise, revealed that the leader of the criminal gang had been dead all along. My informant must not have seen him die. Or so I surmised in my report to the Captain.

My version of the events was accepted by all. A gang of lowbornes had somehow opened a portal, conducted illegal trade with another realm and caused the death of three nobles. It wasn't the whole truth, but it was as close as I could come.

Ekbert's been reported missing. Stoinef has the case.

I often wonder if it's over. If there were other so-called nobles allied with Ekbert who knew of this hero wine and the gold that can be made from it. So many deaths, so many lies, and possibly more of each to come.

The wise men tell us that we live in a land of eternal youth. Why then, at times, do I feel so damned old?

My first published story featured Matthew Grace, a crime scene investigator who had become a private eye. The collection "Past Sins" chronicles all his cases but one. This one. For some reason, the publisher did not feel that it was as believable as the others.

SURPRISE PACKAGE
A Matthew Grace Fantasy

"Boss"
"Not now, Christopher, I have to check this list."
"You did that already."
"I like to do it twice."
"Boss, forget the list. We got a big problem."

* * *

I do not know what woke me up—the clatter from out on the lawn, or the noise coming from the fireplace. Once awake, I do remember that my first conscious thought was that I did not have a fireplace. My next thought was that it was too early in November for a fat man in a red suit to be standing in my bedroom.

"The tree is in the basement, next to the trains. Feel free to get it out."

"Please pardon the intrusion, Matthew, but I need your help. Please get dressed and meet me outside."

"Why, where are we going?"

"The North Pole, of course." He scratched his nose and was gone. So was the fireplace.

"Weird dream," I thought as I pulled up the covers and started to drift back to sleep. Just then a car horn insisted that I stay awake. I went to the window. The street lamps were, as usual, out, but in the light from the moon I could see that the driver of the red Jeep making all the noise was that same fat man.

"Get dressed and get down here, Matthew. We have a long trip ahead of us. And do please hurry."

Dream or not, I know when to give up. I put on clothing suitable for a cold climate and went down to find out why Santa Claus needed a private detective.

I do not remember much of the trip. I do remember asking, as I got into the Jeep, "Where are the reindeer?"

"Home, asleep." Where I should have been, or was.

I remember asking, "So, Santa, what's the problem?"

"You'll see when we get there." He was not as jolly as I had always pictured him. He reminded me of other clients I had had, clients powerful enough in their own domains, but who had suddenly been faced with a situation not within that power's control. He looked worried, and sad.

I remember traveling north on Interstate 83 into Pennsylvania. The next thing I remember is Santa shaking me awake.

"We're here."

"Where, the North Pole? Already?"

"Already, and it is not exactly the North Pole. We shifted operations a bit when we heard Peary was coming. Since then, we've...Well, never mind that. Let's go."

It was not that cold. I was comfortable in what I was wearing. I got the feeling that had I stayed in my pajamas, I would have been comfortable in what I was wearing. It was that kind of place.

What kind of place was it? I would like to tell you, I really would, but I promised not to give too much away. Let me just say that it looked like any other small village supported by a single industry, only nicer.

We were met by his helpers—his elves, if you will. They were what you would expect. Shorter than me, but otherwise they looked like regular folk. They were all dressed in brightly colored "traditional" outfits, but they wore them as we would regular clothing, and on them it seemed natural.

It was their faces that were really different. Most of them, in their eyes and smiles, showed a wonder and trust one only sees in children who have yet to have their innocence shattered. There was the satisfaction that comes from doing a good job for a good cause, their faces far from the deceits and betrayals with which we live.

I said most of them. Whatever the problem for which I had been brought here, I could tell which elves were in on the secret. They looked worried, an overlay of fear on their childlike faces. There was relief at Santa's return, an absolute trust that their boss would set things right.

After greeting their boss, most of the helpers went back to whatever they had been doing. Three stayed behind, the ones I had figured to be in the know.

"Robert's on guard?" Santa asked. Assured that Robert was, he addressed his men. "Gentlemen, this is Matthew Grace. He has agreed to help us with our problem." (I do not remember being asked.) "Matthew, may I present Frederick, Christopher, and, finally, Gregory, my general manager."

As we shook hands, my face must have revealed my thoughts, as Gregory said, "No, we are not all named Skippy or Merry, and, no, we do not know Snow White or anyone named Bilbo, and, yes, we have heard every elf joke ever told, so please don't try. Thank you, pleased to meet you." Just what I needed: a pixie with an attitude.

As Santa glowered at his ill-mannered aide, I finally got to ask the big question. "Santa, just what is this problem I'm to help you with? After all, I'm a PI, I don't know anything about toys, just about…"

"Exactly," he interrupted, "please come this way."

He led the way into a building marked "Product Testing."

We walked past offices that were now closed for the night, past what appeared to be very modern laboratories, and finally up to a room labeled "Play Area #3."

Santa introduced the elf standing in front of the door as "Robert" then turned to me. "Here is our problem."

With that he opened the door and gestured me in. In the middle of the room, surrounded by toys, was a dead elf.

I stood in the doorway, for a moment not sure what to do. Finally, I slowly walked into the room, working my way around the toys, being careful not to step on anything that might be evidence.

Elf blood is red, just like ours. I know this because there was a pool of it around what used to be the top of his head. More of it was on the wall behind him, mixed with brain matter and other such stuff. *No sugarplums*, was the first thought that came into my head, and I hoped that Santa could not read minds.

What had happened was obvious. Someone had rigged a shotgun shell to go off inside a jack-in-the-box. The dead elf—I later learned that his name was Richard—had been testing it and set it off. A few turns of the crank, a few bars of "All Around the Mulberry Bush" and *pop* went the elf.

No one had followed me in. Robert had stationed himself in the doorway and was keeping everyone, including Santa, out of the scene.

Any witnesses, suspects, etcetera had by now had enough time to compare and coordinate stories and alibis. I wondered how many besides these five knew what had happened. The important thing now was the crime scene.

"Santa," I shouted, "I'm going to need some equipment."

"Got it all ready for you."

I walked back to the doorway and Santa handed me a "Little Sherlock Junior Detective Kit." In it was a print kit along with evidence envelopes, a magnifying glass, tweezers, and a camera fully loaded with film. Trust Santa to give good little PIs just what they wanted.

"We also have extra film, bags, and whatever protective clothing you might need." I nodded thanks, said not a word, and went straight to my work.

An hour or so later I was finished. What few prints I could find—mostly off of the jack-in-the-box and the room door—were in my pocket, along with inked prints from Richard's hands. The jack-in-the-box itself, the shot shell, and other items that might prove interesting were all in a big bag, each separately wrapped. Carrying it out of the building I looked like, well, you know who.

Richard's body was taken to what served as a hospital, Gregory accompanying him so as to impress upon the receiving doctor the need for an autopsy and secrecy.

Santa gave his other helpers the job of cleaning up the play area. He then personally showed me to the cottage that would be mine for the duration of my stay.

"I hate secrets," he said as we walked through the village in the quiet of the night, "but Robert tells me that the fewer who know about this, the better for the investigation."

"Robert's right, but how does he know so much about police procedure?"

"Maybe you should ask him."

"I will." We walked some more in silence. Then something occurred to me. "I suppose this will be a shock to your community."

"What will?"

"Richard's death. I mean, that must not be usual up here."

Santa stopped briefly and just looked at me, somewhat puzzled. He finally said, "Matthew, regardless of what we do up here, we are all living creatures. People up here get sick, sometimes they die—not often, but it happens. There have been accidents, sometimes serious, occasionally fatal. Last month we had some reindeer fall from the sky."

"What do you do when that happens?"

"Venison." After a pause he went on, "No, death is not a stranger up here. It is an infrequent visitor, but not a stranger. Violence is, however. Any crime is. Richard's death saddens me; the manner of it saddens me more. Well, here we are." We had arrived at my cottage. "Get some sleep, Matthew, we'll start fresh in the morning."

"One question, Santa."

"Yes?"

"Why me?"

"Because you are honest, moral in your own way, you have the skills and are capable of doing the job, and most of all…"

"Yes?"

"Most of all, because deep down, you never stopped believing."

"In you?"

"In me, in Christmas, in what it stands for. Good night, Matthew."

"Good night, Santa."

Despite the lateness of the hour, I somehow got a full night's sleep and still woke up in the early morning. When I went down to the kitchen, breakfast, and Santa, were waiting for me. I suppose after decades of surreptitious entry, he has gotten out of the habit of knocking.

"Good morning, Matthew. I thought that we'd get an early start."

"Good morning, Santa. I'm glad you're here. We have a few things to discuss."

"Like what?"

"I have a suspect." Just before nodding off, an obvious suspect had occurred to me. I did not want to, but I had to ask. I was worried, big time.

"Who?"

"You."

There was an Arctic quiet. Up until now I had been dealing with a somber, somewhat sad Santa. That had not bothered me. Now I was face to face with a Santa on the very edge of anger. It was not pretty. Imagine the first time that you really knew that your mother was really, really mad at you. This was worse.

"What?"

There went my Christmas presents for the rest of my life. "You did it—or, more likely, you know who did it."

"Why?" It just got worse. There went all my Christmas presents in any future lives I might have, one of which could start any minute.

"You are said to know who has been bad or good, naughty or nice. Therefore you know who did it and you are covering it up. You brought me up here to help in that cover-up."

His face changed in an instant, and I felt the fool I had just proven myself. There followed a "Ho! Ho! Ho!" I had previously only heard in my childhood dreams. It was everything I had imagined.

"Oh, Matthew, do forgive me, but I needed that. Oh, don't apologize. You're the detective, you had to ask." Santa took a moment to compose himself.

"For the record, I don't keep track. Children are children. I don't judge. I just give to whomever I can. Now, what else is bothering you?"

I had gotten the answer for which I had hoped. Still, I would not have been doing my job if I had not asked. I trusted him—who would not—but part of my mind was busy trying to figure out how to verify his story.

"There is something else. Have you considered that Richard's death was an indirect attack on you and Christmas?"

"How so?"

"If one toy went 'boom,' how many more will? Can you, in good conscience, deliver any toys this year, not knowing if they are booby-trapped or not?"

Santa rushed out, leaving me to finish my breakfast. He came back in about an hour. I was examining the evidence when he returned.

"Done," he said. "I have all available helpers working to check everything we've done. Nothing gets shipped until we're sure it's safe."

"Will you be done before Christmas?"

"There's always time before Christmas. Time has a different meaning up here. You just need to find out who did this before he does it again. What are your plans?"

"First, I need to ask you some questions."

"Will I need a lawyer?" he joked. (I hope.)

"Ah, no." Santa forgives, but does he forget?

"Good, because we don't have any up here."

"Do you have any enemies?"

"Hundreds, maybe thousands or more. Fortunately, none of them believe in me."

"I am going to have to talk with Robert and the others. Can that be arranged?"

"Already done. You can meet with three of them this morning. Gregory will be busy—you can talk to him this evening after dinner."

"I may need to have everyone fingerprinted. Elves do have fingerprints, don't they?"

"Of course."

"Are they all different?"

"I don't know, we've never had to worry about it."

"After talking with Robert and the others, I'll want to check out Richard's room, and then I'll have to try and trace the shotgun shell."

"The shell probably came from the armory."

If Santa had told me that Christmas had been canceled, I would have been less surprised.

"The armory!" I shouted. "What the hell does Santa Claus need with an armory? Are polar bears that big a problem? Is the Easter Bunny going to attack?"

"Calm down, Matthew. Remember when you were a boy. What toys did you play with? Up until a few years ago, what toys did every little boy play with?"

"Guns."

"Exactly. They wanted guns; I gave them guns. As I said, I don't judge. Before we made the toys, we studied the real things, hence the armory."

"Who has access?"

"Everyone, it's not locked. Nothing's locked up here."

"Why not?" I asked, then answered my own question. I had forgotten where I was.

Santa told me how to find the armory and Richard's room. Then I asked, "How did you find out about the death?"

"Christopher came to get me. I believe that Robert sent him."

"Santa, assuming for the moment that this was an attack on Richard and not on you or the children, we have to fall back on some basic motives—jealousy, greed, lust…"

"Lust?"

"Lust. There are girl elves, aren't there?"

"Of course." (There went that "Ho! Ho! Ho!" again.) "Where do you think new elves come from?"

"It was just that I haven't seen any."

"You wouldn't. They're all at home, taking care of their families."

He said this so matter of factly that I had no reply. They really were cut off from the real world up here. I made a mental note to look for signs of a radical feminist elf underground.

Santa could not help me with Richard's private life. I would have to ask around to find out if he had any enemies, or if he had been too close a friend with another elf's wife.

Santa excused himself for other business. I set out for a long day's work.

I found Robert in the candy factory, painting stripes on candy canes. He told the foreman that he had to take a break. "Santa's business," he said, and that explained everything. He took me to a break room and shut the door.

"Tell me, Robert," I said as we sat down with cups of hot chocolate he had poured for us, "How do you know so much about police procedure?"

"I knew you'd ask me that question. That is what detectives do, isn't it—ask questions. That's what I'm going to do when Santa lets me be a detective. I wanted to be the detective this time, but Santa said we needed a...a *professional*, Santa said. If I work with you and help you be a detective, will that make me a professional, too?"

I considered letting him go on just to see how long he could talk without breathing, but I wanted to get home before Christmas. Besides, there were stripeless candy canes backing up.

"Robert, be quiet for a minute." He shut up right away. "Robert, tell me how you know about police procedure."

"From these. I read them all the time. Gregory orders them for me. I love them. After I become a detective, I'm going to write about my adventures just like Frank White does. Why does he call himself a different name in the books?"

I let him talk. The book he handed me, JOE MARTIN AND THE CASE OF THE NOISY SPY (by Frank White, number 72 in the series), was a juvenile detective novel. I interrupted again. "These books explain all about being a detective?" He nodded and I quickly continued, "And this is how you knew to protect the scene and keep everyone quiet?" He nodded again.

"Robert, did you find the body?"

"Yes, I was walking past the testing place when I heard a noise and I went in and I found Richard. I knew he was dead because no one can live without a head and he didn't have the top of his anymore. I wanted to get Santa, but I knew that I had to guard the scene. I waited until Christopher came by and told him what had happened. Maybe I shouldn't have, he may have been the killer, coming back to the scene of the crime, but I did and I told him to get Santa. Was that right?"

His sudden stop took me by surprise. After a second I replied, "Yes, you did fine. Christopher probably would have found out when he returned with Santa. How did Gregory and Frederick find out?"

"I don't know about Gregory. Frederick came by and told me he had seen Christopher and Christopher told him that there had been an accident and I needed help. He asked what happened and did I need help and I told him and then said to wait for Santa. Do you think Frederick did it?"

Robert could not add anything after that. Santa had filled me in on what had happened after he had arrived. Neither did Robert know much about Richard's private life. I took his inked prints (twice, I had to give him a copy) and thanked him for his cooperation. He left beaming when I told him that he had been a big help.

He really had. I have known police officers who would not have preserved a scene as well. This got me wondering if Robert, who really wanted to be a detective, had not created his own crime to solve.

I thought about this on my way to the stables. Even if he had the technical ability, he seemed more the type to stage a "missing toy" caper than kill someone, and he would still have to "solve" the crime. A missing toy caper could be solved by finding the missing toys. Solving a homicide that you committed meant framing someone. Out of his league, I think.

I found the stables more by smell than Robert's directions. Frederick was there mucking out the reindeer stalls. The reindeer were out being exercised. When Frederick told me this, I thought about what birds do when they fly. From there on in, I kept an eye to the sky and was always ready to duck.

Frederick knew Richard a little better than Robert had.

"He was kind of a quiet guy. Kept to himself. Didn't know him well, just from here."

"He worked with you?"

"No, I took over from him when he went to accounting. Santa has us change jobs every few years or so, except for the big shots like Gregory and Happy." (I knew there had to be at least one.)

"What did you do before this?"

"Toymaker. We're all toymakers. It's what we do. It's just that other jobs need doing, too."

"How did you get involved in all of this?"

"Saw Christopher running like a bear was chasing him. Didn't see a bear, so I asked him what the problem was. He shouted 'Test building, accident, Robert needs help, gotta get Santa,' and kept running."

That was all he could tell me. Christopher was not much more help. His account agreed with the others. All he could add was that he understood that Richard liked to listen to jazz, which Christopher used to pick up for him when he was in shipping and receiving.

"That's how you get supplies up here?"

"Yeah, you need something, you put your order in to Gregory. It comes off your account. Once a month, somebody goes south and picks stuff up."

I was not in the best of moods as I made my way to Richard's cottage. I had inked prints from Santa, three live elves, and one dead one. After collecting the sixth in the set, tonight I would compare them and hope to get lucky. Otherwise, I had no clues, no motives, and no real suspects. I had checked the armory and all I found there was an open box of shells with one missing. No prints on the box. I could always frame Robert and let him enjoy trying to clear himself, just like real fictional PIs always have to do.

Things changed when I got to Richard's cottage.

The ground floor kitchen and small sitting room held no surprises. Neither did the upstairs bathroom or storage area. Richard's bedroom held the Christmas surprise.

The bed was neatly made. On the nightstand by the bed was a book, A CAREFUL DEPARTURE. I had heard of it. It was a how-to book on suicide. It explained the pros and cons of various methods and discussed the responsibilities of the soon-to-be-departed toward those they would be leaving behind.

I checked his bookshelf. There were several other new volumes on death and dying stacked on top of the others. There was a slim volume of verse by a death-obsessed poet from some time ago. There was a hardbound comic collection which humanized death, making her an attractive woman. Another how-to book and some novels with death as a theme completed the collection. I supposed that a toymaker would not need a book on how to build a lethal jack-in-the-box, but I was looking for one anyway when I found one more surprise by the stereo.

There was an empty CD case on top of the small rack system. In the player was the latest—make that the last—release by a hard rock star who had recently used a shotgun to take the short way home.

That was that. Santa had not needed me. He had just had to have someone, preferably junior detective Robert, come over to Richard's house and look around. Case closed.

All that was left now was to figure out why. Why Richard had done it, why he had used the method he had…and why a jazz aficionado was listening to hard rock?

The two are not mutually exclusive. I have both in my collection. But would a jazz fan choose hard rock as the last music he would ever hear?

I went back to A CAREFUL DEPARTURE to see if a shotgun blast was a recommned method. I opened the book and there was a crack like winter ice. The other books made the same noise. Books will do that the first time they are opened.

I sat on the bed and let my thoughts float. Something was coming and I did not want to block it. Finally, it drifted down the mind stream. Someone had ordered those books and that disk and planted them in Richard's room, someone who could do that without suspicion or question, someone whose knowledge of the crime had not yet been explained.

I waylaid a passing helper and had him deliver a message to Santa. He was to have everyone involved meet in Play Area #3 as soon as possible and wait until I got there. Then I went to do what Santa and I did best.

Sometime later I walked into the playroom. "About time," complained Gregory.

"Sorry about that, but burglary takes time."

"Burglary?" asked Santa.

"It's what I do best. And it's so easy up here, no locks on anything." I reached into my pocket and took out some requisition forms. From another pocket I took out a vial with white powder and a yellow envelope with a leafy substance, both of which I'm sure were not made by elves.

"Look what I found in your room, Gregory."

Santa's head elf made a break for the door. I was ready for that and tripped him as he passed. By the time he picked himself up, Robert was once again guarding the door. Christopher and Frederick were helping.

"You know, Gregory, if you had just killed him in his room with a real gun instead of being clever, you probably would have gotten away with it." I love this part, telling the bad guy how he screwed up. "Oh, and the next time you sign someone else's name, take forgery lessons first."

I did not expect him to confess, or even verify my guesses, but I made a stab at a motive based on papers I found in his office. "Let me guess. Some time ago some businessmen with not-so-sterling connections made you a proposition. You order certain supplies exclusively from them and you'll be nicely rewarded. Now, what would they have to offer that you can't get, or make, up here?" I held up the dope. (The drugs, not the elf.) "They gave you a taste, didn't they? You were tempted and you fell. It happens." The look on Gregory's face told me that I was on the right track, and so I went on.

"Richard learned something about it when he was in accounting. Probably not enough to make him suspicious, but enough to worry you, and maybe your partners. You transferred him to Product Testing to keep him from learning more—either that, or to set him up for your trap. Whose idea was it to kill him—yours or your partners?"

What he called me was descriptive if not imaginative. I did not know that elves used that kind of language. It was enough of a confession for me, and for Santa.

Later, in Santa's cottage, he and I were finally able to relax. Mrs. Claus was there, too, a very nice lady. Over something a bit stronger than cookies and milk, I explained it all to Santa.

When I was done, I asked him, "What will you do with Gregory?"

"He's gone."

"I know, but how…"

"He's gone as in not here anymore. I banished him from the Pole." In answer to my look he said, "What would you have me do? I don't have a jail, and I'm not going to build one. Execution is out of the question. Banishment is the only way."

"Thank you, Santa. That is just what I wanted for Christmas—a homicidal elf with a talent for making lethal toys. He's got a drug habit and a grudge against me, and he's loose in my world."

"I'm sure he'll not be a bother to you, Matthew. Anyway, you have been a big help. There will be a little something extra in your Christmas stocking this year."

After that we just sat around and talked. Santa told me how the angel wound up on top of the Christmas tree. I explained to him why a snowman couldn't have children. To Santa's blushes, Mrs. Claus told me how he got a black eye one Christmas Eve. Soon after that, I nodded off.

I woke up back in Baltimore, in my own bed. I was, of course in my pajamas; yes—the same ones. It was the same night on which I had first gone to sleep. What was that Santa had said about time having a different meaning up there?

It could have been a dream, probably was. I guess I won't really know until Christmas when I check my stocking for that something extra Santa promised.

This story was written in Ocean City, Maryland on the porch of a rented condo across from which was the OC Convention Center. Part of the story is true. I'll leave it to you to figure out which part.

THE LAST CONVENTION

Owens was the first to wake up, which was only fair; he had been the first to pass out.

Consciousness came slowly. He heard the sounds of the ocean through the open windows, then felt the morning sun on his face. When he finally did open his eyes, he realized that he was in the wrong room.

He looked up; the ceiling was wrong. In his room it was tiled, this was stucco. The cheap picture on the wall was of the Bay Bridge, it should have been Assateauge Island. The bed was far too lumpy, there was only one pillow, and he had company.

Owens could feel the weight of the body next to him. He did not remember asking anyone to join him last night, but, then again, he did not remember much of anything last night. His last memory was of a karaoke bar on 4th Street. Jackson had been singing the wrong song to the music.

As Owens tried to push past the memory of Jackson's version of "Colour My World", the person next to him began to snore, in baritone.

"Oh, God! I could not have been that drunk." The thought forced him fully awake, and a wave of relief passed over him. He was fully clothed, nothing felt undone, and the baritone belonged to the forever off-key Jackson.

Owens sat up and looked around. Jackson was snoring next to him. Bryant had the chair nearest the balcony, feet resting on a coffee table. Face down on the floor was...Owens could not remember his name.

Checking his watch, Owens saw that it was still early. If he and the others hurried, and were not too far from their condo on 40th St., they could still get back, wash and change, and make it to the Convention Center in time for check-in.

"What's the point of renting a condo across from the convention if you're going to sleep somewhere else?" he thought as he considered getting out of bed.

Paradise Denied

It had been a good idea—Jackson's, actually. The three of them had come down from Baltimore for the Fraternal Order of Police Convention. Held once a year, the convention supposedly was for the exchange of new ideas in police work, to introduce and promote the latest advances in law enforcement technology and for the discussion of the problems facing the late 20th century cop. What it really was was an excuse for a weeklong party.

It was the convention that the Ocean City town officials feared the most. Sure, it brought in lots of money and filled every vacant room from the Inlet to the Delaware line, but the general idea of it was frightening. A city filled with conventioneers is one thing, but most of these conventioneers were armed, and did not fear the law because they were the law.

It was not that the FOP convention caused more trouble than any other; it was the nature of that trouble that bothered the Town Council. This year, for instance, there had been an impromptu shooting match on the beach between officers from Anne Arundel County and those from Montgomery County. Tired of arguing over which 9mm pistol was more accurate, the officers, at 1:30 in the morning, decided to settle the matter on the sand. Using chemical light sticks as skeet targets, one cop would yell, "Pull!" another would throw the light stick toward the ocean, and a third would empty a clip in its direction. Since all of the participants had had a little too much to drink, most of the light sticks floated back to shore undamaged, to be used over and over until the cops ran out of ammunition.

The Ocean City police, seeing that their fellow officers were shooting over the water, wisely waited until all the firing had stopped. Then they stepped in and offered their comrades in arms rides back to their lodgings, making sure to get the names of the would-be marksmen to report to their respective commands. For weeks later, old men walking the beach with their metal detectors would be digging up cartridge cases, wondering why news of the obvious shootout had not made the papers or TV.

The next night, a fight almost demolished the popular nightspot Big'uns. A Maryland State Trooper had been droning on and on about the rigors of the training that the Maryland State Police gave its cadets. After letting him talk for a good twenty minutes, a civilian assigned to the Baltimore City Police Crime Lab quietly said, "Gee, that's sure a lot of work for twenty years of writing speeding tickets." The trooper punched the crime scene tech in the mouth.

Members of the BPD who witnessed this of course felt obligated to defend one of their own, however stupid and ill timed his remarks may have been. The trooper's buddies joined in, as did most of the other cops present, and a good time was had by all. When the fighting was over, there was hardly an unbroken table in Big'uns, the crime lab tech had been hospitalized, and every uniformed member of the BPD and the MSP agreed that, no matter how useful they were on a crime scene, civilians had no place in a cop bar.

So that some kind of control could be kept over the visiting police, convention officials had decided that all participants would have to sign in at the various seminars and discussion groups for which they had registered. Miss too many events, and you would be denied your certificate of participation. This certificate was more than just another piece of paper to hang over your desk. Without it, an officer could not take the week in Ocean City as administrative leave. And without something official, at tax time the government just might decide that the trip had not really been business related and disallow its deduction as a work expense. At least, that's what the officers were told. Having been on the receiving end of bad government decisions too many times, most of them believed it.

So Andy Jackson got his good idea. A friend of his owned a condominium directly across from the Convention Center. With three people sharing the expense, the cost to rent it would be comparable to the cheap hotels where the cops usually stayed.

"It'll be great," Jackson told the other two. "In my nineteen years on the force, and in the last four going to these conventions, I ain't never seen a nicer set-up. We can sleep in a little and get over to the Center just as it opens. We sign in for the first session, duck out after the break and come back in the afternoon. Get us some beach time."

"Then after lunch we sign in for the p.m. sessions," Bryant picked up for Jackson. "And then we're one break away from having the day off."

"You guys do what you want, some of those classes may actually be interesting."

"Owens," Bryant chided, "You mean you're really here to go to the convention?"

"Well, yeah, most of it. That's the idea, isn't it?"

Owens felt embarrassed about wanting to go to hear the new ideas and see the new technology. Why was it that the ones who thought themselves "good cops" never wanted to be better policemen?

"Your choice, son. You tell us about the convention, and we'll tell you all about the babes on the beach and all the fun you missed."

"That's a deal, Andy."

Jackson's second idea had not been as good as his first. The three had been in a bar on Somerset Street, just off the Boardwalk, when Jackson had gotten his brainstorm.

"We're only a few blocks from the end of the Boardwalk. What say we start at this end, walk north until we come to the other end, and have a drink in every bar we see?"

"Great idea, Andy," voted Bryant. "But wait, do we go to just the ones on the Boardwalk, or on the side streets, too?"

"I think, Officer Bryant, that if we can see a bar from the Boardwalk, it counts, but we don't go any farther than one block down."

"I agree, Officer Jackson. You in, Owens?"

Even as he agreed, Owens asked himself why he was going along with this crazy idea. He, of course, knew the answer.

All this week, he had been the good boy in school. He had gone to most of the sessions, picked up what literature he could for both himself and his partners and had conscientiously examined every display at the Convention Center. He had seen the fingerprint computers, the new patrol cars and the latest in non-lethal weapons. He could describe all of the restraint systems that he had been shown. He had bought himself some new handcuffs, a quick release holster, and a couple of t-shirts. He had even gotten a "Crime Lab" cap for that idiot in Atlantic General Hospital. What he had not done was have a whole lot of fun. It was time to cut loose and be one of the boys.

What harm can it do? he thought. *There can't be that many bars between here and 28th Street. We'll probably run out of money long before then, anyway. We left our guns back at the place, and when we finally do collapse, the Ocean City PD will see us home. They should be used to sweeping drunken cops off the street. Worse comes to worse, we sleep on the beach.*

So Owens agreed.

They started at Charlie's, at South 2nd Street on the Boardwalk. From there, they worked their way north, having a drink at any place that would serve them. Most of these places were named for oddly colored animals or after vaguely vulgar body parts.

They were refused entry at an under-21 club on Division Street. Bryant would have forced entry but was told that the place did not serve alcohol. Hearing this, he demanded to know why the doorman was wasting the group's time, and had to be pulled back to the Boardwalk by the other two.

At Talbot Street, the trio became a quartet, joined by an officer from the Maryland Transportation Authority Police, the agency that patrols the toll roads and tunnels of Maryland.

(*Monroe, that's the name of the guy on the floor,* thought Owens as he recalled what he could of the evening.) Any discussion over whether a MdTap officer was a "real cop" was forestalled when it came out that Monroe not only made more money than the other three, but was willing to spend some of it by buying the next few rounds.

The odyssey moved north. Owens had been wrong about the number of bars. Drinking was big business in Ocean City, surpassed only by miniature golf, t-shirt shops, and the beach. Every block had its nightspot, and every side street one or two more. By 4th Street, there was talk of surrender.

"We can't give up," Monroe slurred. "I thought you Baltimore boys were tough."

"Tough as you, Tunnel Man, tough as you, but," Bryant checked his wallet, hoping that more money had somehow miraculously appeared, "I got enough for one more round, then I'm out of ammo."

"Got a question for you guys."

"You always got a question, Owens. Where's Jackson?"

"That's not the question, smart man."

"Who cares; where's Jackson? He said he was going to the can, but he's not back yet."

Monroe pointed to the stage. "I think that's him."

Bryant groaned. "I knew when we saw 'Karaoke' we should've passed on this place."

"But I got a question."

"What is your damn problem, Owens?"

"Bryant, where's your car?"

The three Baltimore cops had driven down from 40th Street and had left their car in the metered lot across from Trimper's Amusements. At fifty cents an hour, it was the cheapest they could find without waiting for an open off-street spot.

"It's parked, isn't it?"

"Sure is, and it's twelve blocks away and going to stay there. How are we getting home?"

"What's the problem; it's a nice night for a walk."

"I think what your buddy's trying to say is that you can walk it, but you can't drive it. You may not have noticed, but we've all had a little bit to drink."

"Maybe you and Owens have had too much, but I'm as sober as a judge."

"Which one—some of them drink their lunch."

"I would, too, if I had to listen to lawyers all day. Okay, Officer Bryant, assume the position. You know the drill."

"Certainly, Officer Monroe, do your worst."

As the manager of the bar tried to get Andy Jackson off the stage, Monroe gave Bryant the standard field sobriety tests.

When asked to walk a straight line, Bryant refused, saying that the line Monroe had pointed out would not stay straight.

When he tried to extend his arms and turn in a circle, Bryant had to use what was left of his money to pay for the drinks he knocked over when he fell on the table of a couple close to him.

Bryant did manage the one legged stand, but then stood there like a stork until Owens forced his leg back to the floor.

Monroe wanted to give him the horizontal gaze test, but could not focus his own eyes on Bryant's pupils. He turned to Owens for help, but found the younger officer asleep, head on the table.

"Rookie," he said to Bryant and the other shook his head in agreement.

"Let's face it, city boy, we're drunk and out of money. It's time to go home."

"Can't go home, got to sleep on the beach."

"No, you don't gotta. You drag Jackson off the stage. I'll wake Sleeping Beauty. You guys can crash at my place. I'm down on 17th Street."

Monroe shook Owens awake. "Come on, kid, it's time to go. You're staying with me tonight. Tomorrow I'll take you to your car."

So that's how I got here, thought Owens as the evening came back. *Nice of Monroe to take the floor; I could never fall asleep like that.*

Owens shook Jackson, trying to wake the older cop. All he accomplished was to change the volume of his snoring for the worse. He shouted and shook some more, but Jackson's eyes stayed shut.

"Hell with it," Owens said out loud, "I'll try Monroe, maybe he can wake this beast."

As Owens slid out of bed, Jackson suddenly sat upright. "Signal 13, officer needs assistance." Whatever dream he was having had put Jackson back on Baltimore's streets. His shout had done what Owens could not. Jackson woke up and looked around.

"Where are we, kid? Oh yeah, the tunnel cop's place. I remember him looking for his key for about ten minutes. Dimbulb had put it in his shoe so he wouldn't lose it."

"You remember the karaoke bar?"

"The what?"

"Never mind. We're running late. We got just enough time to get back to our place, wash, and change, if we're going to check in."

"What about Bryant's car?"

"Leave it. We'll catch a bus later today and pick it up, but right now we got to get moving. You wake Bryant and I'll peel Monroe off the floor."

Jackson jumped out of bed. "I'll get Monroe; I'm closer than you are. You take Bryant. He looks like he wakes up ugly."

Owens had only to touch Bryant and the latter was on his feet. As soon as he stood up, Bryant hit his shin on the coffee table and collapsed on the sofa again.

"Great, at least now I have an excuse for feeling this bad." He put one hand on his head while the other rubbed his leg. "I'm never doing anything that stupid again in my life. Whose dumb idea was that, anyway?"

"Andy's."

"Owens, you're the serious one. Why the hell didn't you stop us?"

"Because it seemed like a good idea at the time?"

"Guys." Jackson interrupted the two. "We got a problem."

"What kind of problem?"

"Well, kid, Monroe here ain't gonna wake up."

"That's not a problem. We'll put him on the bed, lock the door, hang out the 'Do Not Disturb' sign and walk back to our place." Owens turned to Bryant to see if the man was up to the walk. Bryant nodded and Owens turned back to Jackson.

"It's only 20 blocks. Maybe we'll be lucky and catch an early bus. If it gets too late, we'll go straight to the convention. I've seen worse than us there."

"Yeah," Bryant added, "We'll tell them we're modeling the latest in undercover clothes."

"You guys don't get it. He ain't gonna wake up because he ain't asleep. This guy is dead."

Bryant and Owens just stared at the other cop. Finally, Owens asked the stupid question.

"You sure?"

"Let's see, Sherlock. His skin is cool, he's not breathing, and there's no pulse. Sounds like dead to me."

"How did he die?"

"I don't know, Owens. Maybe he just went 'Ack!' and fell over."

"You'd better check."

"What do I look like, the flipping Medical Examiner? You're the one who bought the 'L.A. County Coroner' t-shirt. You check."

"The kid's right, Andy. You'd better check." Bryant pointed to the middle of the room. There on a table was a 9mm pistol. Without moving, each of the three men searched the room with his eyes. Jackson finally pointed past the other two.

"There, by the balcony door."

It was what they had been looking for and hoping not to find: a shell casing from the weapon on the table.

"You'd better check, Andy," Bryant repeated.

Jackson knelt over the body. He carefully looked it over.

"Nothing on this side. Maybe he was playing with the gun earlier, shooting seagulls from the balcony. He probably died of heart failure, or from too much booze."

"Turn him over, Andy."

"Hey, Bryant, who died and made you chief?" When he saw the odd looks on the faces of his friends, he looked down at Monroe. "Sorry, poor choice of words."

Putting one hand on his right shoulder and the other on his arm, Jackson gently levered that side of Monroe off the floor. He stared awhile at his chest and then just as gently lowered him to the floor.

"Well?" Owens asked impatiently.

"Did anyone notice if Monroe had a hole in his chest last night?"

"Damn!" Bryant had been standing next to the couch. Now he broke and stormed toward the balcony. He was about to slam his palm against its glass door when he suddenly stopped it short. He stepped away and lowered his hand as if afraid of contact with the smooth surface of the glass.

"Owens, what in the hell are you doing?" The younger cop had moved, as well, around the bed to the telephone on a table on Jackson's side. He had picked up the receiver and been about to dial when Jackson's question stopped him.

"Calling it in, of course."

Bryant walked away from the balcony. "Andy's right. 9-1-1 is not a good idea right now."

"Guys, a man's dead, shot to death. We're cops. It's our duty to report it."

"And who…" Bryant stopped, He had started to shout, but the last thing he wanted was for anyone outside the room to hear and remember an argument, however belated.

"And who," he continued in a softer tone, "do you think shot him?"

Owen's hand held on to the receiver as he thought the question over.

"We're on the fifth floor."

"Right."

"Andy, has the door been tampered with?"

"Looks okay to me, kid."

"We're in trouble."

"One of us is, kid. One of us is."

"No, Andy," Bryant corrected. "All of us are, if we're connected to it."

"How do you figure that, Bryant? Only one of us shot him."

"Did you do it, Jackson? You, Owens?" Both men quickly denied it.

"Neither did I, but one of us had to."

"Bryant, there are other possibilities."

"Like what, Owens?"

"Let me think." Owens sat on the bed, his head in one hand. "What about if someone was in here, robbing the place when we came in? We scared him, he shot Monroe, and ran out the door."

"Or," Jackson said enthusiastically, joining in as if he were playing some game, "Maybe Monroe had a roommate who wasn't all that happy about us bunking down here. They argued, then fought, and she or he picked up the gun and ended the argument."

Bryant shook his head. "And maybe the Blue Fairy flew in through the window and shot him with her wand gun, leaving that thing on the table as a decoy. Do you guys see any ransacking? Any sign of a burglar? Any sign of a roommate? And don't you think one of us might have noticed a violent quarrel and have done something about? A drunk cop is still a cop, and the training would have kicked in."

"I don't know about either of you," Owens said from the bed, "But I don't remember anything past 4th Street and Jackson singing."

"I was singing?"

"You two get it now? None of us remembers much of anything from last night. Last thing I can recall is Monroe taking off his shoes and looking for his room key. After that, the kid was waking me up."

"Unless one of us is lying."

"What was that, Owens?"

Jackson quickly got between the two as Bryant started toward Owens. Holding him back, Jackson turned toward the bed.

"You'd better explain yourself, kid, and make it good. Otherwise, I'm letting him go."

"It's like this. I know that I can't remember anything about last night. I also know that if I did remember shooting Monroe, I sure as hell wouldn't admit it. Better one third of the blame than all of it. So I got to figure that if one of you did it and remembered, you'd keep quiet, too."

Jackson nodded. "Kid's got a point. None of us is stupid enough to admit it if he did remember. The question is—what do we do now?"

Owens looked at the telephone, then at Bryant. "Not much choice. Call now or later. The later we call, the worse it looks."

"There's always a choice." Bryant sat at the table near the gun. He looked at the polished surface of the tabletop and returned to the couch.

"There are always choices," he repeated. " We could call it in. As long as we each stick to 'I was drunk and don't remember,' none of us will get charged. We just met the guy last night. No motive, except for what had to be a drunken argument or stupid accident. They'd holler for a while, won't be able to prove anything, and let us go."

"Then why don't we call it in?"

"Andy, you got what—nineteen years? We call this in and you won't see twenty. Our careers are down the toilet. You know the Commissioner. We'll be charged and fired before our kids go back to school."

"Maybe not. All they can prove is that we were drunk. That applies to most of the cops down here."

"We were drunk and a cop died. Does the phrase 'conduct unbecoming' mean anything to you, Andy?"

"So what are our choices?" Owens had gotten up from the bed and was now pacing between it and the balcony.

Bryant held up a hand and began to tick off options.

"One, we call it in. One of us gives himself up. Any volunteers? No, I didn't think so.

"Next, two of us could decide that the third one did it and put together a story that the OCPD would believe. How about it? Owens, Jackson? Ready to sell out each other, or me?"

Owens stopped pacing. Jackson just stood there. Neither man moved or spoke. Neither looked at the other. All eyes were on Bryant.

"That just leaves us with something Owens said earlier. We leave Monroe here and get on with our lives."

They all liked that. Each convinced of his own innocence, they would readily let a killer walk to ensure their own safety. Especially when the killer was a cop and a friend, and the victim a near stranger.

Jackson broke the silence. "We could do it. Wipe the place down. Leave him on the floor. Put out the 'Do Not Disturb' sign, and we were never here."

Bryant stood up. "Let's get to it. Wipe off everything that'll hold a print."

"It won't work," Owens came over from the balcony. "Try thinking like a cop instead of a suspect and you'll see why."

He stood in front of Bryant, half turned to Jackson, and made a show of holding up his hand. He ticked off his own points.

"By now the story of our 'every bar on the boards' is making the rounds. Everybody has heard it or will hear it. A lot of people saw the four of us together. When Monroe is found, somebody's going to drop the dime to the OCPD.

"Next, your car is still at the inlet. By now it's got a ticket or two for that meter that hasn't been fed since last night. That puts us on foot and a long way from home.

"We got no one but ourselves to say we were back at the condo like we'll have to tell the detectives. The OCPD won't find anyone to back us up. Think: what are the chances that no one saw or heard three drunken cops coming home?"

"No one heard the shot that killed Monroe, did they? If they had, the ocean cops would have been here and gone by now."

"Andy," Bryant said from the couch, "This town is full of cops shooting guns off at two-thirty in the morning. People have stopped paying attention."

Owens interrupted, anxious to make his final points. "Besides, with no one seeing us come home last night, someone is bound to see us coming in today. By the time we get back, the beachgoers will be heading out. One of them will see us.

"Finally," he pointed to the body on the floor. "That is a dead cop. What makes you think they won't pull out all the stops? The OCPD will bring in the State Troopers. Those guys will dust and vacuum better than the maids at the Ritz. When they're done, Internal Investigation will send our Crime Lab down to find what the State boys missed."

Owens put his hand down by his side. "Okay, let's do it. If you think we got in here without being seen, can get back without being seen, and didn't leave a single hair, fiber, or print for the Lab to find, let's go." He walked over and collapsed next to Bryant on the couch.

"Nothing else for it, then?" Bryant surrendered.

From over near where Monroe was lying, Jackson offered a slim hope.

"We could solve it ourselves."

The combined "What?" came in unison.

"Look, we're cops, not accountants. We're trained to investigate scenes, question suspects, and solve crimes. We each tell what we remember from last night. The other two will pick the stories apart. We keep at it until we're all sure who done it."

"What good would that do? It's the other cops we have to convince, not ourselves."

"It's like this, kid. Once we're agreed on who done it, that guy stays behind, calls the cops, and takes the heat. The other two walk out of here clean. Agreed?"

"Agreed." Bryant was quick with his assent. Owens was more reluctant.

"And if we make a mistake?"

"One in three chance, kid, one in three."

"We'd all have to agree?"

"One for all, all for one."

"I'm in."

"Good. Bryant, you start."

"Let Owens go first, he claims to remember the least."

The sound of the door being unlocked was as loud as a gunshot. Jackson rushed over to the door in time to stop the maid from coming in.

"Listen, hon," he said, blocking her view of the room with his body. "Can you come back later? We had a rough night, and it's not over yet."

"You don't want the room cleaned now? You should have hung the sign on the door."

"Hon, that would have been a very good idea. Wish we'd thought of it." He reached into his pocket and handed her a bill, not bothering to check its denomination. "Come back later, please."

The maid left. Too late, Jackson hung the sign on the outside doorknob. He slowly walked over to the table. Sitting down, he took out his handkerchief and carefully wiped off the 9mm pistol. Then he just as carefully placed his thumb on a smooth surface near the safety, leaving an excellent print.

"It doesn't matter now who pulled the trigger. The maid can put me in here. You guys might as well go."

"Andy…"

"Look, kid, why trash three careers? I'll tell them what I know. I don't remember how I got here or what happened when I did. I'll keep you two out of it. They'll draw their own conclusions and charge me with manslaughter.

"The FOP lawyer is pretty good. He'll be able to drag this out long enough for me to make my pension. Then I'll retire, and we'll make a deal. If I got to go away, it won't be for long."

Jackson picked the gun up, studied it for a while, and returned it to the table.

"Whatever happens, I know that my good friends will take care of my family for me. Right?"

"Yeah, Andy, we'll look after everything, won't we, Owens?"

"Andy…" Owens was stuck on the name.

"You two go, and make sure you get your stories straight."

Being careful not to look at the body lying on the floor, Bryant and Owens left. Jackson sat alone, staring at the pistol on the table.

As the door closed behind them, Owens paused and stood in front of it.

"What are you waiting for, Owens? We should have been gone from this place five minutes ago."

"The gunshot."

"It's the cop's way out. Do you really want to be here if he does it?"

"Let's go."

They snuck down the back stairs. No one noticed them leaving.

Neither man spoke until they were halfway back to 40th Street.

"Bryant."

"What?"

"Back there, you said that no one would have paid attention to a gun going off at two-thirty in the morning."

"So?"

"So, how did you know what time the gun went off?"

Bryant stopped turned toward Owens. "I didn't. I picked a time out of the air to make a point. Why? Does that make me guilty?"

"I...I don't know. One of us did it; it might have been you. 'One in three chance,' Andy said. It doesn't really matter now. One of us did it, none of us meant it, and Andy's going to pay for it."

"Yeah, listen, let's get moving before we attract attention."

They walked farther down the street.

"How's this sound, Owens? When we left the karaoke bar, Andy went with Monroe. We saw them to the door, then decided to go home. We woke up this morning and were too tired and hung over to go to the morning session."

"Sounds good to me. We'll get cleaned up and sign in this afternoon. If we don't hear anything by this evening, we call 9-1-1 and report Andy missing."

They continued to polish their story all the way home, each wondering if the other would hold up, and neither sure how he would feel if Andy picked up the gun for the last time.

An hour later, the maid passed by the room again. The 'Do Not Disturb' sign was still on the door. Try as she might, she'd never understand cops. This morning, just as she was just starting her shift, the big one had given her twenty dollars to come by and clean the room at eight. Then when she came, he gave her another twenty to go away. A good day's tips, and she hadn't done anything.

As she passed the room, she heard the sound of a man's laughter. Inside, Jackson and the formerly-dead Monroe were enjoying another laugh.

"What I want to know is what made you think of such a thing?"

"You know, Monroe, when I woke up this morning, and saw you on the floor, I thought to myself that the only way I'd sleep like that was if I was dead. Then I started thinking that maybe you were dead."

"And you woke me up when you checked."

"Sorry, I was still half asleep, and still a little bagged. But after being glad that you were alive, I started thinking about what those two would do if you really were dead, and things took off from there. I thought that kid would never wake up. Those fake snores were loud enough."

"But good enough to fool him. I tell you, Andy, I never thought I could lie still that long. I can't believe that they never checked me out for themselves."

"I don't believe that neither of those dimbulbs ever checked the gun or the casing. Your gun still had all seventeen rounds and the casing's from a .380. Where'd you get it, anyway?"

"Picked up some casings at the show, the shooting demonstration. My kid collects them. Go figure."

"I can't wait to see their faces when the two of us walk in on them tonight." Andy Jackson had another laugh, then another sip of beer. "I tell you Monroe, with my twenty coming up, this is my last convention. I'll miss coming down here with guys like you, but at least I went out in style."

This was supposed to be a Matthew Grace story. After starting it, I found that it worked better told from a different point of view.

TISSUE OF LIES

It wasn't until after she hit Mark in the nose that Susan figured out just how to get rid of him. As he went through tissue after tissue trying to stop the flow of blood, Susan thought of the special on the forensic sciences that she had watched on cable last week. She remembered the discussion on blood, and how police used DNA analysis to positively identify someone involved with a crime scene. After her husband left the room, Susan walked over and looked at the tissues in the waste can. There were enough there for her purpose, she thought. No need to take them out now; they'd be safe there. The next time Mark emptied the trash would be the first time.

Susan hit her husband just after he had admitted to an affair with a coworker. Despite her suspicions, Mark's confession had come as a surprise. She had suspected him a few times before this, but each of those times he had proven her fears groundless. "The delusions of a hopelessly jealous woman," Mark had called them. She had expected him to deny her accusation this time as well, and again explain away his working late, his absences on the weekends, the mystery phone calls with the caller hanging up. She had expected reasons for the charges to restaurants, hotels, and boutiques that had appeared on his credit card statements—statements he thought he had concealed from her. Like the other times, she had expected him to convince her that there was not and never had been anyone else. And she had been prepared to be convinced.

Instead, he had admitted everything. "I'm tired of the lying, the sneaking around," he told her. "I love you, Suzie, but I'm not a one-woman man. There's—well —there's someone else, has been for some time now."

"Those other times, I was right about them, too, wasn't I?"

He nodded, giving her a, "What can you do, boys will be boys" smile. "I need variety, and there are too many willing women out there to say no to all of them. I'm weak," he admitted, sitting down on their bed. "I'm weak and there's nothing either one of us can do about it."

She came over and stood in front of him. "Get out, take your things and leave. I want you gone tonight."

He was silent a moment. "Sorry, Suzie," he finally said, "I just can't do that. If you want to leave, fine, I'll help you pack. I'll drive you to your mother's, sister's, or wherever else you want to go, but this is my house and I'm staying. And short of a court order, there's no way you can get me to leave. And I'm not fool enough to hit you or do anything else to give you cause to get one."

His idea about hitting seemed like a good one, and so Susan put her entire 115 pounds behind a right-handed punch, and laid him back on the bed with a bloody nose.

"I guess you were entitled to that," Mark said as he came back from the bathroom. Susan looked up from contemplating the tissues in the waste can. Mark had packed his nose with gauze. His voice was nasal. "I don't think it's broken, so I won't call the police. I could, you know," he said with a smile. "Call the cops and have you charged with spousal abuse. You'd spend the night in jail, and get out to find a court order keeping you from coming home."

Mark walked up to her, and she tensed, expecting some violence on his part. Instead, he took her gently by the arms, and sat her down on the bed.

"Suzie, you have two choices. Accept me as I am, or leave me. Leave, and I'll fight you all the way—for the house, the cars, the money. The lawyers will get it all, and we'll both be left poor and miserable." Mark sat down next to her and took her hand.

"Suzie, if you think about it, nothing's really changed. It's just that, well, now you know for sure, and before you didn't. This other woman, she's special to me and I won't give her up. That's how it is. Take me as I am or leave me."

If she hadn't hit him, if she hadn't seen the blood or watched the TV show, she would have left him. She'd have packed her bags and gone to her sister's. Tomorrow, she would have called a lawyer and began to strip the bastard bare. Instead, it was her turn to lie to him, to convince him of something.

"Okay," Susan said in surrender. "It's like you said, nothing's changed. This house, I've put too much of myself into it to leave it. I'll try to accept things as they are. If I can't handle it, one day you might find me gone, that's all. Just, well, whatever you do, don't be obvious about it. Let's both pretend there's nothing wrong, and maybe we can make it work."

Mark gave Susan a hug. He seemed to believe that the combined threat of his going to the police and her losing the house had scared her into submission.

"We'll make it work; don't worry." He went back to the bathroom to take a shower. Susan picked up the waste can and took it downstairs to empty it. Before dumping it into the larger trashcan downstairs, she took out several of the bloody tissues and put them into a paper bag. Then she hid the bag under the dishtowels for when she'd need them.

The next morning, with Mark off to work, Susan briefly reconsidered. Could she do it? Could she find this woman who had stolen part of her life, and then take hers away? She'd done some wild things in her past, but she had never hurt anyone, not deliberately. But to make this work, to keep the house, to get rid of Mark, to punish him for his years of betrayal, it would be necessary.

Susan walked over to the counter where she kept her cooking tools. From the rack on the wall she chose a kitchen knife, the one she used for roasts. She felt its weight and studied its edge. She laid it flat against her arm, tested its sharpness against her wrist.

Maybe this would be the easier way. Make it look like Mark did it. No, there was no guarantee that he'd be blamed, or, if he were, that he would be convicted. And she really didn't want to die. She held the knife out away from her, pointing it a spot where she imagined him to be standing.

I should kill him, she realized. *He's the one to blame. I could kill him easily. I'd tell the police that he beat and abused me.*

No, she would not be believed. There was no history of abuse on Mark's part. He'd be dead, but she'd be in jail.

It had to be the woman. Whoever she was, she had some part of this. She should have known better than to involve herself with a married man, to let it get so far as for her to be "special" to Mark. If it had just been a fling, Mark would have denied it, like he had before. Susan could have gone on pretending that all was well with her marriage and her life. It was this woman. She would die, and Mark would be blamed. They'd both be punished, and Susan could go on.

Susan put the knife back in its rack. She wouldn't use one from her kitchen. She would buy one, or the woman would have knives at her place. Which was where? And who was she?

Two days later, Susan still did not have the answers to those questions. She accounted for all the charges on their joint card. She went through the papers Mark kept at home and looked over the receipts for his personal credit card. There had been no clues to the woman's identity. Then that night, after dinner, the telephone rang. Susan went to answer it, but it stopped after two rings. Fifteen minutes later, it rang again. Mark was next to the phone and he picked it up. He mumbled something into the receiver and hung up.

The next morning over breakfast, Mark told her, "I have a dinner meeting. I may be home late." The look he gave her dared her to question whom he was having dinner with. "Fine," she said in resignation, not rising to the bait. "I won't hold the dinner I was planning and I won't wait up."

Mark rose to leave for work, leaving the breakfast dishes on the table. "Have a nice day," he said. He went out the door without waiting for her reply.

After Mark left, Susan went to the living room phone and pressed *69. A computer voice gave her the number of the caller who had so briefly talked to Mark. She pressed 2 to decline the computer's offer to dial the number for her for only fifty cents, and hung up.

Susan went to her own computer. Using a criss-cross directory she pulled up from the Internet, she learned the name and number of the person who had called last night. Melissa Blake lived not too far away, a twenty-minute drive. Susan wrote the address down in a notebook and dropped it into her purse.

That evening, after her solitary dinner, Susan drove by Melissa Blake's house. She drove up and down the block twice, then circled the neighborhood. She finally spotted Mark's car parked the next block over. To Susan, that decided the matter of Miss Blake. As she drove past the house for a third time, Susan passed a police patrol car going in the opposite direction. *I'll have to be careful when I come back,* she thought, *especially if this block is on a regular patrol.*

Susan waited. She wanted a night that she'd know Mark would be home. It would have to be on a Monday. Mark always stayed home to watch the football game. She'd do it on a Monday.

A week went by, then two. Mark "worked late" a few more times. He seemed to believe that, from her silence, Susan had accepted the situation.

The next Monday, Susan left Mark a note. "Out shopping. Your dinner's in the fridge," it read. "Heat it up." She had to leave him specific instructions on how to do this, since he had never bothered to fully learn how to use the microwave. On her way to Melissa Blake's house, Susan pictured Mark sitting in the living room, his dinner on a TV tray, watching the game, not knowing or caring where she was.

Susan circled the block, saw no sign of the police patrol, then parked a block away, in almost the same spot where she had seen Mark's car. Not seeing anyone, she got out and quickly walked down the street, taking care to avoid the streetlights. Coming to the front walk, she took one final look around, went to the door and rang the bell.

A woman opened the door. Susan saw right away that Melissa Blake was more attractive than she was—younger by ten years, better built, and with a fashion sense that Susan would never have.

"Miss Blake," Susan said, "I think you know my husband, Mark. May I come in?"

The woman at the door turned pale. She looked past Susan as if afraid that the neighbors would see the source of scandal on her doorstep. She ushered Susan inside quickly.

Her back to Susan as she lead her into the living room, Melissa didn't see her take the knife out of her purse. She turned to take Susan's coat. She wanted to ask how Susan knew about her and Mark. She didn't get the chance.

Susan had thought about confronting this woman, this witch who stole her husband. She had imagined her confessing all, swearing to give him up, quitting her job, and moving away. When the door opened, however, Susan realized that none of it mattered. If it hadn't been Melissa Blake, it would have been someone else. And if Blake were to leave tonight, it soon would be someone else. When the woman turned to lead Susan into her home, Susan took the newly purchased knife out of her purse. And when Melissa Blake turned back to face her, Susan buried the knife in her chest.

As the woman fell, Susan was amazed at how little blood there was. *The wound must have sealed around the knife,* she thought, *and her clothes absorbed what leaked from the wound. It didn't matter,* Susan thought, *it wasn't her blood that is important.*

Susan looked down at the body on the floor. The eyes were still open. She saw no life in them. She took a tissue out of her purse, one of those stained with her husband's blood. She smeared it on the handle of the knife sticking out of the woman's chest. Nothing—the blood was too dry to be transferred.

Susan went into the kitchen. She started to turn on the tap of the sink, then suddenly stopped. She didn't want to leave fingerprints. She used a tissue from the shelf over the sink to turn on the water. She wet the one she had in her hand, then shut off the tap.

Back in the living room, Susan again smeared the knife handle, this time leaving a red stain. She left two more stains on the inside of the front door, where the police would easily find them.

Now was the hard part. Susan left the house hunched over, and walked away at a near run. If anyone saw her, she hoped that the darkness would disguise her form enough that she might be mistaken for a man, especially by witnesses trying to remember what they saw. She made it back to the next block without seeing anyone. Before getting into her car, Susan realized that she was still holding the tissues. Not wanting to be caught with them, she opened her hand and let them fall to the sidewalk to be blown away by the wind.

After this, Susan did go shopping, buying things at the mall she knew she'd return later. She did not want to return home empty-handed. She needn't have bothered. When she did get home, Mark was just as she had pictured him. He didn't even look up when she came in and called out, "I'm home." A quick "That's nice," was all she heard from him, as he was lost in the game.

Susan went to bed early. Mark was still up, watching the end of the game. As she drifted off, she wondered how long it would before the body was found, how soon the police would connect her husband to it, and how long it would take them to arrest him.

Susan knew what she would do after the arrest. As the betrayed, long suffering wife, she'd see a lawyer, get a separation, and take steps to protect her half of their property. It would make no sense to have done this only to lose it all to legal fees. Half of their property hers, and Mark in jail—she'd be happy with that.

The police came two days later, when Mark was at work and she was home alone. Yes, she told them, she had heard of the murder. It had been on last night's news. A terrible thing. Yes, she reluctantly admitted, she knew her husband was having an affair, but they were trying to work things out. No, she didn't know the dead woman, and what was all this about? Her husband, and this Melissa Black—Blake, was it? No, that was impossible. She hoped that she looked properly shocked and surprised. Oh, he admitted it at work when you questioned him? No, she couldn't say where he had been Monday night; she had gone out shopping. Was he a suspect?

"Yes, ma'am," one of the detectives, the older one, told her. "Until we get this cleared up, we have to consider the possibility."

"I...understand, officer." Susan had practiced for this. She played it hurt, confused, frightened.

"And you didn't know this woman?" the other detective repeated.

"No, I had no idea who my husband was seeing—that is, I didn't want to know. I had hopes that he would end it soon."

"And Monday night, the night she was killed, you say you were out all night?"

"Yes, shopping."

The first detective zeroed in on this. "Your husband says that he was home, watching football. Is this so?"

Susan hesitated before answering. "Yes—that is, he was when I got home." She paused, as if realizing what she had said. "I mean, I'm sure he was there all night. He never misses a game, so I'm sure he was there." She hoped that her cover-up was just obvious enough.

"So he can't say where you were, either?"

What did he mean? "I went shopping, I can show you the packages, the receipts."

"Yes, ma'am, I'm sure. We've already checked." The younger one looked at his notebook. "You paid for two blouses and a scarf with a credit card at nine fifteen, just before the stores closed. Unless you paid cash, you made no other purchases. Did you buy anything else, ma'am, and do you have those receipts?"

"No, I looked around the mall all night, but didn't find anything until just before closing. What's this about?"

"And you don't know this woman?" the older detective asked a third time.

"I've told you, no."

"Then why were you seen by a patrol officer several weeks ago driving past her house?" Before she could answer, he went on. "Neighbors called in a complaint about a car circling the block. There'd been a few break-ins and they were nervous. A patrol called drove by and took down the number of a car that was slowly driving down the street—your car, ma'am."

"And the telephone company has record of a *69 charge made to your phone," the younger one added, not giving her a chance to answer his partner. "It was made when your husband was at work. The number ID was Melissa Blake's."

"And then there's this," the older one came in. Too late did Susan recognize this as a carefully rehearsed, well-used routine between the two. The older detective put on rubber gloves. He picked a bag off the floor and took out two smaller envelopes. From the first he took a bloodstained tissue. Putting that back, from the second he took out one that wasn't stained.

"Our Crime Lab did a very thorough search of the neighborhood. Found these stuck in some bushes. Would have ignored them if it wasn't for the blood on one of them."

He put the envelopes back in the bag, and the bag back on the floor. "Ma'am, care to explain why your fingerprints are on these tissues?"

Susan hadn't thought, hadn't known. You used tissues to wipe things off, to remove your prints. Finally given a chance to talk, she had nothing to say.

The older detective saw her confusion. "The guys back at the Lab can do wonderful things these days. They have lasers and chemicals and computers and who knows what else. They can lift a print off almost anything, then match it up if the person has a record. That marijuana arrest back when you were in college? The charges may have been dropped, but we kept your prints."

He looked at his partner. "Do it, Rich."

The younger one took out a card and began reading it. He said her name, then read out the Miranda warnings so familiar to her from years of television. This wasn't happening, she wasn't supposed to be arrested. Her husband's DNA was on the scene. That was it, her husband's blood.

"But it was Mark's blood on the tissue," she shouted as soon as she had a chance, as soon as the younger one had finished reading. They had to believe that he did it.

"I guess she waives her right to silence, Alex," the younger detective commented.

"It will be interesting learning how you knew the blood was your husband's," said the older one. "And him without a scratch on him."

They handcuffed her and took her away in a wagon. "It was his blood, his blood," she kept repeating as the door to the wagon closed.

This was the first of my stories to be accepted into any kind of anthology. As you might be able to tell, it was written just after the USSR had gone back to being Russia.

CONFIDENTIAL INFORMATION

I have been in worse cells, thought Ivan Gaidar as he studied his surroundings. *At least I have a bed to sleep in, water to drink, and a real toilet. The last time there was only a foul hole in the floor, and any water you got dripped from the ceiling. If I had to be arrested, I'm glad it was in America.*

His reveries were interrupted by the guard, "Givens, your lawyer's here."

Gaidar stood up upon hearing his American name. "He will come here?"

"Shaddup and stand away from the door."

The guard entered and harshly spun Gaidar around and against the wall.

"Hands behind your head." Gaidar complied and was promptly handcuffed.

"Please, I do not understand what is happen to me. Where is lawyer?"

"That's where you're going now, so move." He was led down a row of cells to a room in the back. The guard opened the door and pushed him in.

"There's no need for that, Officer. And you can take those cuffs off. I don't think Mr. Givens is going to be any trouble."

The woman speaking was sitting at a table that, along with two chairs, was the room's only furniture. After the handcuffs had been removed, she gestured Gaidar to the chair against the back wall. When he was seated, she turned hers around to face him across the table. Gaidar noted that his chair was bolted down.

"You are lawyer?"

The woman smiled a greeting. "Hello there, I'm Deborah Jenkins. Are you John Givens?"

"I am he."

"Where are you from originally, Mr. Givens?"

"Russia. When I left, it was Soviet Union, now it is Russia. When I go back..." His shrug completed the sentence.

"*If* you go back, Mr. Givens," she paused to let him consider her statement. "You are in a lot of trouble."

"Please, what did I do? I was just on corner when police come and arrest me. They tell me to be quiet and ask for lawyer, so I ask and you come. What did I do?"

"What the police say you did was take part in a drug deal, during which…"

"No," Gaidar interrupted, "I not use drugs."

"Let me finish, please. What the police say is that while you were in the middle of a drug transaction, you and your partners were the targets of what we call a 'drive-by shooting'. One of your party was hit, two others returned fire. One of their shots struck and killed a nine-year-old girl."

"But I did nothing. I was just standing there talking to the men when the shooting started."

"In this country, that doesn't matter." Jenkins leaned across the table and looked directly at him, commanding his attention. "In this country, if you are committing a crime and someone dies, even if you did nothing, you can be charged with murder, do you understand?"

Gaidar tried to look worried, and as if he just barely understood. "Yes, but I did nothing. I was lost and asking directions."

"A nice story, but the homicide detectives have told me that you've been seen on that corner before. The man who was shot told them that you were a major player."

"I do not know, at what do I play?"

"The police say that you have bought drugs from these people before, in significant quantities. How do you answer that?"

Gaidar thought a minute. He was not worried about being charged. He knew that he would be. But he had to be released soon. He had things to do, people to see, and shipments to make. Some of the shipments were of items that would soon be missed.

"Please, Miss Jenkins, if I tell police about shooting, who had guns, who shot child, can I go?"

"It's too early to plea bargain, and the guy in the hospital has already told the police everything they need to know. They are right now arresting the others involved. The State's Attorney will take your plea, but you have nothing to bargain with."

"There is, in this country, bail for a case like this?"

"Not for murder, not for someone who helps kill a kid. You'll be in jail until your trial."

"But I did not kill anyone."

"Which will be brought up to the State's Attorney. I'm sure that you will be able to plea to manslaughter."

"Is that not murder?"

"It is, but a less serious kind of murder."

Gaidar was worried. Even if tried and convicted, he would not be in prison long. His government would see to that, but that did not solve his immediate problem. Fortunately, he was dealing with the American legal system.

"Miss Jenkins, in your country, if I tell my lawyer something, even something terrible, can she tell the police?"

Jenkins took a moment to consider her words. "As a lawyer, Mr. Givens, I would not be able to tell the police anything my client told me, even if he were to tell me that he fired the shot that killed the girl."

"Ms. Jenkins, please be assured that I would never do anything as brutally violent as that." Jenkins's eyes widened at the dropping of his peasant accent. "Perhaps I should explain."

"Perhaps you should."

"'John Givens' is not really my name, though you may as well continue to address me as such. And I am not the salesman I am supposed to be."

"You're a spy, aren't you?" Jenkins's voice was a mixture of surprise and fascination.

"I prefer the term 'intelligence gatherer'. Spy sounds too much like James Bond."

"What is an 'intelligence gatherer' doing buying drugs?"

"Because some of my contacts prefer to be paid in drugs rather than cash."

"And what do these contacts do for you?"

"They obtain for me the things which I cannot obtain for myself—sensitive and secret information, classified equipment, names and places that your government wishes to keep to itself."

"You have those kinds of contacts here in Baltimore?"

"Oh my, no! I work in Washington. I just live here in Baltimore. It's much nicer here, cheaper, too. And a much safer place to buy drugs, at least until tonight."

"So are you willing to trade some of your secret and sensitive information in exchange for a walk out of here?"

"Not in the least, Ms. Jenkins. I worked hard to learn the things that I did, and I will not just give them away."

"Then why, Mr. Givens—or whoever you are—tell me that you are a spy?"

"Ms. Jenkins, is it not true that, as my lawyer, you are obligated to do anything in your power to obtain my release?"

Deborah Jenkins again thought before answering. "That is a lawyer's responsibility, yes, as long as it is within the law."

"Is obtaining my personal property and delivering it along with a message to my employer 'within the law?'"

"I'm not sure; does this property have anything to do with your employment?"

"Would a very substantial and unofficial retainer for services answer your question?"

A few minutes went by before she answered. When she did, there was a hesitancy in her voice that had not been there previously. "That certainly answers my question, and there is nothing strictly illegal about it. But—I can't. It would be a betrayal of my country."

"Ms. Jenkins, you are a lawyer, and a lawyer's first—indeed, her only—responsibility is to her client. I assure you that as soon as my embassy hears of my arrest, I will be free in a matter of days. They will trade me for one of your agents. The information that I have will be passed on no matter how long I am delayed."

"Then why didn't you call your embassy?"

"Ms. Jenkins, if I had called the Russian embassy from a Baltimore jail cell the FBI, who listens in to all calls received there, would have learned of my presence. It would become an international incident. Think of the publicity. 'Russian Spy Held in Drug Murder.' I wished to avoid that."

Gaidar also wished to avoid telling her that as soon as his arrest became public knowledge, some, if not all, of his contacts would undoubtedly be revealed, rendering much of his work useless.

"Ms. Jenkins, if you do what I ask, you will not only be fulfilling your obligation to a client, but, when I am traded, you will be responsible for helping to free a fellow American from a Russian prison. There's also the matter of the retainer I mentioned, to be paid in cash."

Jenkins seemed convinced. "Mr. Givens, if I am to help you, I will have to know exactly what you need me to do."

To himself, Gaidar breathed a sigh of relief, quietly thanking the God he once could not believe in for the fairness of the American legal system and the cupidity of its lawyers.

To Jenkins he said, "I need you to take my personal belongings, the ones that the desk officer took from me when they brought me in, to my embassy in Washington. On my key ring, there is a key marked 'Ocean Condo'. Tell them it is to Locker 302 at the Richardson Athletic Club on Harford Road."

"And what is in the locker?"

"Do you need to know?"

"I suppose not. I guess that it's copies of files, computer disks, and other such stuff that your contacts obtained for you."

"Something like that, Ms. Jenkins, something like that. And I am sure that I need not remind you that, as my lawyer, you cannot reveal to anyone what I just told you."

"If, Mr. Gaidar, I were your lawyer, I would not."

Gaidar started at the use of his real name. Before he could speak, Jenkins continued.

"Think back. I never once said that I was your lawyer. Of course, the courts would never accept that distinction, but what you told me will never be used in court."

"FBI?"

"Right. We knew who you were fifteen minutes after you were booked. We have the prints of many Russian agents, thanks to our people in Moscow and their access to your system. The BPD has a fingerprint computer that ties into ours. When your prints didn't hit on theirs or the Maryland State Police's, they tried ours and—bingo."

"Why the ruse?"

"We had you; we would have learned the names of your contacts. What we needed to know was where you kept the information you had not yet passed on. You would not have told us, and it would have been impossible to find, as you were probably clever enough to use a different name when you obtained your hiding space."

"What made you think I would ask my lawyer to help me?"

"You're not the first criminal to try to take advantage of the lawyer/client privilege, and you won't be the last. It was worth a try."

"What will happen now? May I call my embassy to arrange my release?"

"You will be transferred to the Baltimore City Detention Center. From there, you should be able to call your embassy. They can arrange the details of your release with the Baltimore State's Attorney."

Ivan Gaidar had learned early on to accept defeat and move on. It was time to go home. He would have to spend another night or two in a cell while negotiations were conducted, but soon he would be on a flight back to Moscow. He would not get the hero's welcome for which he had hoped, but he had done a decent job. After a rest, he would be given a new assignment.

Two hours later, Deborah Jenkins watched as the Special Agent in charge of her section went over the material from Gaidar's locker.

"A nice haul, Jenkins—good job. With this we should be able to plug all the leaks caused by our friend Ivan's contacts."

"Thanks, but it's a shame that we're letting Gaidar go."

"We don't need him, and we're not letting him go."

"We're not?"

"No, we're not. About the time you and he started talking, I had the BPD issue a press release. It stated that the Russian national involved in the girl's death was cooperating fully. His partners in the drug deal were arrested shortly after the evening news. We made sure they got the word. They know all about loyalty, and all about betrayal. They'll be waiting for him."

One of the key points in this story came from my training as a crime scene investigator. The lawyer, Sharon Manchester, later wound up in a couple of Matthew Grace stories.

CAIN

They met in a dark bar. The man who wanted murder done arrived first, and took a seat in a booth near the back. The second man arrived shortly after. He got himself a drink, something soft. He was working tonight, and he never mixed business with alcohol. He looked toward the back, then walked over and sat across from the man he knew to be his client. He sat down and lit a cigarette. The match flared up and briefly illuminated the other's face.

"You're Mr. Smith?" asked the man who had arrived first. He was nervous, constantly moving back and forth in his seat, glancing around to see if anyone was looking his way.

"As far as you're concerned, I am," the man calling himself Smith spoke in a harsh whisper, his voice loud enough to be heard from across the table, but no farther. "Tell me what you want, Barnes."

"You know what I want, that's why you're here."

"Say what you want, or I walk."

"I'm not a cop, you don't have to worry about that, it's just that…" Smith cut him off. "I know what you are. You were checked out. You're a contractor, you put up office buildings and apartments. Now say it."

"My wife—I want her dead. I want you to kill her."

"That wasn't so hard, was it?" Smith smiled, enjoying Barnes's discomfort. "You have something for me?"

Barnes took an envelope out of his inside topcoat pocket. "A picture of my wife, her personal information, her schedule."

"Anything else?"

A thicker envelope came out of the topcoat. Barnes handed it over. "Twenty thousand, like I was told." Smith picked up both envelopes and made them disappear. The bar was too dark for Barnes to tell where he had put them.

"When will you, you know, do it?"

Smith didn't answer right away. He finished his cigarette and lit another one. Again he used the light from the match to study his client. Pale complexion, black hair, a slight scar to the right of his mouth forcing a half smile. He'd know the man again.

"Best you don't know," Smith finally said. "That way you won't be stupid and go out of town or try to arrange an alibi. Cops pick up on that right away. Just keep to your regular schedule. You'll know when it happens."

"It will…will it look like an accident?"

"Or a mugging gone wrong, or a burglary, something like that." Smith wished he could see Barnes's face clearly without striking another match. Barnes was a weakling, a coward. He wasn't man enough to do the job himself, and now he was worried about how it was going to be done. Smith decided to twist the knife a little more.

"Lots of crime in this city, Barnes. The cops won't look close at another street robbery, or rape."

Even in the darkness of the booth, Smith could see Barnes start at his last comment. He decided to leave him with that pleasant thought. He finished his soft drink and slid out of the booth.

"Wait for me to leave," he told Barnes. "In ten minutes, leave twenty on the table for the tab. Walk out without talking to anyone."

The man who called himself Smith left the bar. He did not stay around to see if Barnes did what he was told. He only hoped that the man would not do or say anything stupid when he talked to the cops. *Doesn't matter anyway*, Smith thought. *Even if he tells them all he knows, he doesn't know much. Not my name, or where I'm from. I do the job clean, and the next day I'm out of Baltimore and heading home. Then I can take it easy until the next job. No problems.*

Smith wanted to wait a week, but decided to move the job up a few days. He didn't want Barnes getting too edgy. He picked a night when Barnes was staying late for a company meeting. His wife went out, shopping probably. Smith went around to the back of the house. There were woods in the back, no neighbors in view, and no outside lights. Breaking in was easy.

Once inside, he went up to the bedrooms, pulling out drawers and taking what cash he could find. Downstairs, he stacked the TV, DVD, and CD players next to the back door, taking care that none of what he did could be seen by anyone coming in through the front door. Then he waited in the dark.

He sat by a window, behind a curtain, watching the street. If Barnes came home first, or if the wife brought a friend home, he'd be out the back door before they got to the front step.

Soon he saw a car pull up. Barnes's wife got out alone. She walked up with the key ready for the lock, just like all those rec center self-defense classes teach women to do. He stepped back so that he would be out of her view when she came in. He let her get inside and close the door.

He moved quickly. Before she knew he was there, he punched her once in the stomach, taking away her air. He covered her mouth and forced her against the door. Her back hit the doorknob. He pressed against her so she could not move. Then he dropped his hand to her throat and squeezed until he saw the life go out of her eyes.

Once she was dead, he let her fall. Bending over her body, he tore open her blouse just to give the cops something extra to think about. He dumped her purse, taking the cash out of her wallet. Finished with the job, he went out the way he had come.

The other side of the woods met the back of a shopping mall parking lot. His car was parked among dozens of others, in no way distinguishable. His dark clothing and the poor lighting on the lot ensured that no one noticed him get into this car and drive away.

Back in his room, he bundled up the clothing he had worn on the job, stuffed it into a trash bag, and took it out to the motel's dumpster. It would be gone the next morning. On the way back, he stopped at the ice machine and filled a bucket. Back in his room, he poured himself a drink and sat back to watch some prime time TV, satisfied with a job well done.

They came for him three days later. Men armed with shotguns broke into his apartment late at night. The sledge hitting and shattering the door woke him up, but they were in his bedroom before he could react. Even if he were the type to keep a gun close at hand, it would not have done him any good. Before he could get out of bed, he was looking up at four very determined cops. Three of them wore ID jackets that designated them as FBI. The fourth cop wore a plain jacket, but his baseball cap read 'Baltimore Police.' At least he knew why they were there.

With shotguns pointing, the cops let him put on some clothes. They read him his rights as he dressed. He'd heard them before. He wasn't going to talk to them, and would call a lawyer as soon as the time was right. So he let them talk, he nodded in the right places, and they were satisfied. As they lead him out, he idly wondered what mistake had led them to him.

Arrested by the FBI, he was in federal custody until he got to Baltimore. Once in Baltimore, papers were exchanged and he became the responsibility of the BPD. He was taken to the Central Booking Facility, charged with murder, and held without bail.

Detectives came to talk to him. They read him his rights again, then started asking him about the murder. He remained silent, but didn't ask for a lawyer. With a lawyer, the questioning would end, and he wanted to hear their questions. What they asked would tell him what they had, what their take on the crime was. When the one playing the good cop started talking about other burglaries in the neighborhood, he knew that it had been something that he had done—a mistake he had made—that put him in, that Barnes hadn't ratted him out. Knowing that, he finally asked to call an attorney.

Two days later, his lawyer came to the Baltimore Detention Center. He had been transferred there from Central Booking the day before. He was led into a small room, which was equipped only with a table and two chairs. He was loosely handcuffed to the chair farthest from the door, then his attorney was allowed to join him.

"Are they necessary?" the lawyer pointed to the cuffs. "Take them off right now," she told the guard who was about to leave.

"Sorry, ma'am. The rules are that he stay cuffed." There were no such regulations, and all three knew it. The attorney was about to protest when Smith stopped her.

"It's okay, it's loose enough." Smith held up his left hand. He took the bracelet in his right and moved it freely around his wrist. Then he lifted his arm to show the slack in the foot long chain.

"It's not uncomfortable," he told the lawyer.

It was, though. It was another reminder of the extent to which he had lost control over his actions. The guards saw him as having committed a real murder, taking down a taxpayer rather than killing someone in one of Baltimore's drug wars. For what he had done, for what they thought he had tried to do (*should never have ripped the blouse, Smith*), they made his life difficult at every chance.

So it would do him no good to have his lawyer win a minor battle. It would only lead to more grief later.

The lawyer waited until the guard left, then leaned over and offered her hand.

"John Ravenski, I'm Sharon Manchester. I'll be representing you."

Smith took her hand.

"Ms. Manchester, pleased to meet you, but call me Smith, at least in private."

"I'm not sure I understand, Mr. Ravenski...Smith."

"Not Mr. Smith, just Smith. That's who I am when I'm not at home. 'Ravenski' is a guy who lives in Philadelphia."

"But the police have arrested Ravenski, not Smith, so let's stick to that, and not give them any of your AKAs. "

Smith nodded his head in agreement. "Good idea. In that case, call me John."

"Fair enough, John, but I'm still Ms. Manchester."

Well, Smith thought, *that set the rules, didn't it?* He didn't mind, though. He had told his contact to get him the best criminal lawyer in Baltimore, and from all he had heard, there were only one or two others in this woman's league.

Manchester had opened her heavy briefcase and taken out a file with his real name on it.

"What have they got on me?"

"They can put you on the scene, in the house where the murder took place."

"Witnesses?" Smith figured that could have been the only way. One person had seen him coming out of the house, another saw him leaving the woods and getting into his car. Or maybe it was just one guy in the woods the whole time. No problem, then—witnesses could be dealt with.

"No; no witnesses. The crime lab came up with physical evidence that says you were there."

"What kind of physical evidence?" Smith knew that he hadn't left any, none that could come back to him. That left him thinking *frame*. By why him? The cops would have done a local.

Manchester paged through her folder, looking for the lab reports.

"Here they are. There were fibers found near the back door where it had been forced. More were found at the victim's throat. So far, none have been matched to any of your clothing."

And none will, Smith's internal commentary continued, *since everything I wore, I tossed. And I don't wear black in my real life.*

"What else?" he asked aloud.

"The police traced you back to the motel. The lab searched and vacuumed the room, and the FBI did your apartment in Philly. Again, nothing."

"So what have they got?" Manchester had that look of saving the best for last. A good courtroom technique, but annoying right now.

"Not much, only the fingerprint match."

Smith's mind shut down. If she had told him that there had been a video camera that had recorded the whole murder, he'd have been less surprised. "But I wore gloves the whole time," he wanted to shout at her, but he knew better than to admit guilt to anyone, even his lawyer.

The look on Manchester's face told him she enjoyed her little surprise. *Just like I enjoyed playing with Barnes and the others,* Smith thought. He could tell that she did not like him, was probably sure of his guilt. She would still do her best for him, she seemed to be too good an attorney to do otherwise, but only her mind was in it, not her heart.

When he calmed down enough to talk, Smith asked, "Where were the prints found?"

Manchester picked up and read the lab report, as if she didn't already know the answer. Reading from the report, she said, "The latent prints from the drinking glass found in the dish drainer on the kitchen counter have been identified as the right thumb and right forefinger of John Ravenski." She put down the report. "Apparently, it was a computer match from the FBI files."

That interstate bust ten years ago, that's when I stopped being myself on jobs. Smith still could not figure out where the prints had come from.

The lawyer put her reports away. "Really, John, no matter how thirsty you were, you should have waited until you were clear of the scene to get a drink."

Suddenly it hit him. "That son of a bitch set me up." His fist hit the table, hard and loud enough that the guard looked in through the window in the door. Not seeing him attacking Manchester, he turned away again.

155

Manchester had, at first, been startled by his reaction. As Smith calmed down, she saw what might be a defense building. "Who set you up, John?"

Smith ignored her. He saw it all, meeting Barnes in the Pair O'Dice Lounge, making the deal, him leaving first. Then he pictured Barnes carefully picking up the glass he had been drinking from, putting it in the pocket of that big topcoat he was wearing. After finding the body, before calling the police, Barnes put it where the lab would find it.

But why? Barnes had already paid. Guilt, maybe, or payback for the rape threat. If he thought that Smith would stay quiet, that was a bigger mistake than Smith leaving the glass behind. *If I go down, he goes with me,* Smith promised himself. Barnes had to know that if Smith were arrested, he would be, too. Still, it was his word against Barnes's, and no proof other than his word. Any accusation would look like a last ditch effort.

"John. Mr. Ravenski. Smith!" Shouting his chosen name, Manchester finally got through to Smith. He came out of his reverie.

"Ms. Manchester," he said without excusing his fugue, "what's the police take on the killing?"

"They see it as a B&E. There had been a few in the neighborhood. They figure you came down to do the crimes. This one went bad and you decided to get the hell out of Dodge. And except for that one mistake with the drink, you'd have gotten away with all of them."

Manchester let him take that in, then asked, "Now what's this about getting set up?"

Smith ignored her. He thought for a moment, then asked her, "They talking death penalty?"

Manchester nodded. "A murder done during another felony with evidence of attempted sexual assault. Add to that the political situation. Too many minorities on the Row. The State's Attorney's been waiting for an eligible white male to balance the population. You're it."

That decided him. "Tell them I want to deal."

Manchester dismissed that with a wave. "You don't really have anything to deal with, John. They got you inside the house, with no previous relationship to either the victim or her husband."

"Well, Ms. Manchester, that's not exactly true."

Smith laid it out for Manchester. He told her about meeting Barnes in the Pair O'Dice, about Barnes hiring him to do the murder, and why the BPD or FBI would not be making any fiber matches. He then told her of his theory on how his prints got on the drinking glass.

"You know how that sounds, don't you?"

"Yeah, like I'm desperate and grabbing at straws. But consider this. The glass my prints were on, it won't match any other glass in the Barnes home. However, it should have about fifty twins in the Pair O'Dice. The bartender there should be able to put Barnes and me there together. If need be, I'll take a polygraph and pick Barnes out of a line-up." Smith let out a short, bitter laugh. "Hell, work it right, Ms. Manchester, and you can present me as the innocent victim of an elaborate frame."

Manchester considered this for a moment, then shook her head. "It won't be enough, John. The police aren't stupid. They'll know it for what it was: conspiracy to commit murder. They won't see you as an innocent victim."

"They won't, but a jury might, and the State's Attorney will realize that. Give him a choice. He can have both me and Barnes, or he can take a chance on losing us both."

"He might go for that, he might not. Is there anything else you can give me?"

"Write this down." Smith gave her three names. "These guys were mobbed up. The first in Chicago, the second in Cleveland, the last in Boston. All three were turned by the Feds. None of them made it to trial."

"You killed them?"

"For now, let's just say that I can point the way to the ones who gave the orders, and supply proof as needed. I'll give the Feds these three and the BPD can have Barnes—all part of the same deal."

Suddenly dealing with much more than a simple murder, Manchester took some time to think. Smith just sat back and watched her work through the possibilities.

"John, if what you're telling me is true, then giving up the details of the other three murders would establish your, well, I don't want to use the word credibility…"

"Try credentials."

"Your credentials, then, as a hitman. The Baltimore State's Attorney would then probably accept some kind of plea for your testimony against Barnes. My question to you is: what are you willing to take?"

"Make the best deal you can; no more than twenty."

"That's a long time."

"I won't serve it. The FBI, the DEA, a few others will claim me. I'll do federal time. After some jobs, I'll be out in five."

"What do you mean, 'some jobs?'"

"Lawyer/client privilege?"

Manchester nodded, "Of course."

"Ms. Manchester, imagine an inmate serving multiple life with no chance of parole. Now, this man kills another inmate or, worse yet, a guard. Besides the death penalty, which takes too long and costs too much, what can they do? What can happen to this man?"

"I have no idea."

"Oh yes, you do. I can tell from the look in your eyes that you've figured it out. *I* happen to him, or someone just like me. A prison has a con they can't control, one who has nothing left to lose, well, the Feds send one of us in. He gets taken out, order is restored. Each job counts as so many years served. They call it 'cooperation in other matters.'"

Manchester was quiet. Smith knew he had laid a heavy burden on her, one she could talk about only to others covered by their privilege. She gathered up her papers and began to leave.

"I'll do what I can, John. No promises, but I should be able to make some kind of deal."

"I'll be waiting to hear from you."

Smith did not have to wait long. Within three days, he and Manchester were back in the interview room.

"The Feds almost beat me to the State's Attorney," she told him. "It took them a while, but they finally connected 'John Ravenski' to the 'Smith' they've been tracking for the last three years."

"They're slow but not stupid. What happened?"

"The FBI called just as I was pitching the deal to the ASA. You can forget the line-up and the polygraph. The bartender at the Pair O'Dice picked Barnes out of a photo line-up. He remembers seeing the two of you together. And the glasses match."

"So what are they offering?"

"Here's the best I could do: you take a plea on the murder, testify against Barnes; you'll get ten to twenty. After the trial, you'll be transferred to federal custody. Once there, you tell them what you can about the other three killings. Given your full cooperation with this—and 'other matters'—you can expect a significant sentence reduction."

"Where do I sign?"

Leonard Barnes was arrested the next day. His trial was well attended. The media was more than well represented, the story of murder for hire the lead item on all four of the local news broadcasts. Except for his brother, who had to take care of the family contracting business, Barnes's entire family was there. They were usually quoted on the evening news as being sure that Leonard had no part in this sordid business. The family of Lois Barnes—the deceased—was also present. In their turn, they had always been sure that Leonard would come to a bad end, although they never suspected that he was capable of murder. At least, that's what they told the TV cameras.

Maryland law did not permit cameras in the courtroom, so the day Smith testified was the first time he had seen Barnes since that night in the Pair O'Dice Lounge.

He looked smaller from the witness stand, and paler. *I guess being arrested for murder will do that to some people,* Smith thought. He still wondered why Barnes had set him up. Smith gave his testimony in a flat, toneless voice, letting the jury read whatever they wanted into his lack of expression.

Barnes's lawyer tried to make an issue of his plea bargain, but Smith could tell that to most of the jurors, twenty years did not seem like much of a deal. His arrangement with the Feds was not mentioned by either side.

As he finished his testimony, Smith again looked over at Barnes. The man had kept his head down most of the time, but as Smith left the stand, he picked up his head and looked right at him. The expression on his face was one of bewilderment, as if asking how Smith could have said the things he did. The smile Smith remembered from the bar was gone. *Wiped it right off his face, I did*, he said to himself.

It wasn't until he was back in his jail cell that he realized what Barnes's lack of a smile meant.

Frank Barnes got to work early. Ever since Leonard had been arrested, he'd had to do both his and his brother's share of the work. That meant coming in before dawn and staying late into the evening. Frank didn't mind. It would be worth it once he had the business organized the way he liked it. Then he could sit back and relax. The deals he would make with the unions and the men behind them would see to that. He'd do less work and make more money—money he would not have to share with Leonard. His brother had high legal fees. He'd already offered to sell his share of the business to Frank. The price Frank offered him was low, but Leonard believed Frank when he told him that it was the best he could do. Needing the money, Leonard was in no position to bargain.

Frank had been working for an hour when the trailer door opened and Smith walked in. Without waiting for an invitation, Smith walked over and sat down in front of Frank's desk.

"Morning, Barnes; remember me?"

Frank said nothing. In the light coming from the window, the scar on the right side of his mouth was more visible than it had been in the bar, the half smile more noticeable. Except for the scar, he was a good match for his brother. Smith saw Frank's arm drop as he started to reach for something in a lower desk drawer.

"If that's a gun, remember what I do for a living, and don't be foolish."

Frank's arm straightened and came from behind the desk. "How did you get out?"

"I've got friends, Barnes—or rather, the people I work for do. As soon as I realized that Leonard hadn't set me up, I called some of them. Arrangements were made. There was a 'mix-up' at the Detention Center, and some of the wrong people were 'accidentally' released. As soon as I was out, I came to see you."

Despite the coolness of the trailer, Frank was starting to sweat. "I don't know what you mean. I've never seen you before."

Smith's voice took on a menacing tone. "Don't play games, Barnes. You set me up. It was your brother's house. You could have planted that glass for the police to find. And if they hadn't, I'm sure you would have tipped them off in some other way."

"What do you want?"

"What I want, Barnes, is to do you like I did your sister-in-law, but that wouldn't help me any. The way I see it, I helped you get rid of your brother as well as his wife. That makes another twenty you owe me." Smith looked toward the safe behind Frank's desk. Frank caught the look.

"I've got fifteen in the safe, the week's payroll. I can give you that, and the other five when I go to the bank to replace it."

Smith pretended to think it over. Finally, he said, "I'll settle for the fifteen, and an explanation. Why use me to set up your brother, why not just have me take him out?"

Frank's explanation was reluctant and halting. He didn't want to give it, but he was afraid of what the man in front of him would do if he refused.

"I wanted the business. If Leonard were killed, his share of it would have gone to Lois. I could have bought her out, but she might have wanted to look at the books, and I couldn't afford that. Leonard and I look enough alike. Most people mistake us for each other."

"Except for the scar."

"Yeah, except for the scar." Frank reached up and ran his hand along the right side of his mouth.

"I figured if I had his wife killed, then made it look like Leonard had arranged it, he'd be forced to sell his share of the business to me to pay his legal fees. I thought the bar was dark enough so that you wouldn't notice the scar. That's why I stayed away from the trial.

"At first I was just going to phone in a tip to the cops—who you were, how they could get in touch with your contacts. Then when you left the bar and I saw that glass on the table, I got the idea to leave it in Leonard's house. If you did her in the house before anyone noticed the glass, they'd find your prints. If not, no harm done."

Smith stayed quiet long enough to make Frank afraid that he was going to forget about the fifteen thousand and take personal vengeance. Smith was thinking about it, and under other circumstances he would have, after getting the money. Instead, he just nodded slightly, as if accepting what he'd been told.

"Get the money."

Frank turned around, opened and emptied the safe. He stood back to show Smith that there was nothing left inside but papers. He took a manila envelope off his desk and put the cash inside. He handed it over. Smith took the money, stood up, and turned to go.

"This makes us even, right?" Frank asked him when he was almost at the door.

"Almost." Smith left, leaving Frank worried about what he meant.

Smith had not gone more than five feet off the site when two detectives—one local, one FBI—came up to him. He knew there were more nearby. He handed over the money and held his hands out for the cuffs.

"You get it all?" he asked the Fed.

"Clear as a bell," the detective answered. He reached into Smith's coat and took out the microphone.

Smith turned toward the site and watched as the police broke into the trailer to arrest Frank Barnes. *There'll be another trial,* he thought, *then five years or so of prison, doing the system's dirty jobs. After that, well, I'll be out, but it won't be the same. Can't go back to freelance.* He looked over at the Fed designated as his keeper. *It will be work for them or not at all, or else get an honest job.*

Smith again turned his attention to the trailer. They brought Frank Barnes out in handcuffs. Smith had wanted to be put in the same wagon as Barnes for transport, but the cops weren't being that accommodating.

Smith watched the man who had cost him five years and his life being taken away. To himself he said the words that he'd make sure Barnes would soon hear. "There's a mark on you, Barnes. Like I said, we're almost even. I'll see you again, or a friend of mine will, and you'll serve your time, the rest of your life, in pain. Then we'll be even."

Smith's ride came. He was put into the back of a caged police car and taken off to begin his own long journey.

As I mentioned before, I'm a comic book reader. I'm also a fan of old pulp characters like the Shadow and the Spider. This story is the result of my wondering what might happen if someone took these books too seriously.

HERO

Darnell grew up with heroes. He had found them in a forgotten crate in the basement of his parents' newly rented house. Exploring shortly after moving in, he discovered them in a storage area under the basement stairs. The books that contained their stories opened to him a world of flying men and dark avengers, of chaos and evil, of order and justice. At seven years old, he did not wonder why none of the heroes were black, or why none of his neighbors were white.

Over the years, his fascination with his comics and pulps lead to a love of reading in general. This lead to an increased interest in school. And as he learned history and science and math, he grew apart from the friends he had made. Although he still played ball with them after school and hung out with them on Saturday afternoons, when it grew dark, he went home to read and study. His friends stayed on the corners and when the darkness settled, they studied different things.

At night, the city became another place. Darnell's friends learned this quickly. They saw the drug deals go down and watched the dealers get rich. They saw arrests, some of them brutal affairs during which the police were more interested in their own safety than the rights of innocent men. They also saw that the ones who were arrested returned to the streets the next night. They heard of murders, although the second and third hand stories that reached their ears had by then been glorified into tales of bravery and cunning. The heroes of the street became those who could make the biggest deal, defeat and bury their rivals, and laugh at the attempts of the police to put them away.

Darnell learned none of this—not then. His heroes remained those who lived in the two dimensional worlds of his books, where justice was always certain, the law always right, and the bad guys always lost. His friends never spoke to him about the nighttime. They liked Darnell, but he was not of their world, and they would not share it with him.

But Darnell knew about drugs and crime. He knew about racism and the reported brutality of the police. He knew about the gangs and the murders. He had read about it in his newspapers, and so he was certain that he knew all about it.

In the summer of the year he started middle school, Darnell entered the world he thought he knew. As a teen he stayed out later. The long summer days that bypassed evening and went right into night found him on the streets and corners so familiar to his friends. Brought up on heroes, he could not understand a world where the criminals were successful and unpunished, where the police showed contempt for the laws they enforced, and where justice was less of an ideal and more of a bad joke.

He tried to make it right. He would call the district police station and tell them of the drug dealers and where they could be found. But when one of them disappeared for a few nights, another took his place. If he heard of a crime, he would call the detective unit he thought would be most interested and wait in vain for a return call. Once, he witnessed a police officer beat a man who had just been arrested and handcuffed. He called the department's Internal Investigation Division to offer his observations and testimony. He was assured that the matter would be investigated and resolved. The officer who took his call hung up without taking his name.

In July of that year, his father took advantage of a pay raise and bonus and the family escaped the city for a week at the ocean. They returned to their home to find the kitchen window broken, unlocked, and opened. The VCR and television were gone, and the remaining contents of the house scattered. The police officer who came to take the burglary report did just that and no more. He took their names and a list of the missing property and then, after telling them not to touch anything until the Crime Lab arrived, left without talking to any of the neighbors. Two hours later, the technician from the Lab showed up. Although she was friendlier than the officer had been, and worked hard in searching for fingerprints and other evidence, she found nothing usable. When asked, she explained that there was little chance that their property would be returned or the burglar identified.

Not much changed for Darnell in the next few years. He continued to do well in school. He still bought and read comics. Detective stories had replaced the hard-to-find pulps. There were still too few black heroes; the ones presented being merely variations on the white man's themes. It was ironic, he thought, comparing the worlds he read about to the real one he had come to know.

If anyone needs heroes, he thought, *it's us.*

He thought about the role models that were offered his people. Most of the athletes used drugs themselves. And while the ministers, activists, and politicians were important to the community and deserved to be respected and emulated, to ten and twelve year olds, their lives lacked the excitement and rewards of the outlaw culture of dealing, shootouts, and narrow escapes from the law and rival gangs.

When Darnell was a junior in high school, two of his friends wandered onto the wrong street wearing the wrong jackets. Mistaken for members of a rival gang, they were shot down from a moving car. The only evidence found were a few mutilated bullets, none of which were useful for comparison, even if a gun was found. Despite the usual public outcry and promises from officials that something would be done, the murders quickly became just two more drug killings, to be solved only if a dealer gave up a name in the hopes of making a deal.

Some people were shocked into action. Support and drug awareness groups found new lives. A neighborhood watch was re-instituted. After a few weeks, all but a few students had left the groups, and the pressures and business of daily life soon caused the watch to go back into dormancy. Darnell and the rest of the remaining group members tried to interest their fellow students in the fight against drugs, but most were too busy with sports or school, or too lazy to care, or too involved with drugs themselves. One student wrote a series of articles about the drug culture for the school newspaper. He did not name names, but the pictures he painted were clear enough to most people. The severe beating he received was more of a lesson than the articles could ever be. No more were printed. The groups soon broke up.

A hero was needed. The law had failed. Worse, it had surrendered the streets. The police were now the recorders of crime, not the avengers. The activists and ministers had failed. They could not inspire the people to rise up and expel the demons from their midst. The community itself had failed, giving up and accepting crime as the price you paid when you could not afford to move. Having grown up with heroes, Darnell knew that when everyone else has failed, only a hero could succeed.

At first, it was easy. He had come to know the streets, but had never become part of them. He was as anonymous as anyone could be. A few blocks from his home, his face was not at all familiar.

Money was not a problem. Knowing that he would need a stake, he took the best from his comic and pulp collection and sold it to the book dealers he had come to know. Instead of taking store credit or buying more books, he had other plans for the money.

He next made small purchases from several dealers so that each would recognize him when they saw him and regard him as a sometime customer. During the first several buys, he was so scared and anxious that the dealers mistook his sweat and anxiety for the onset of withdrawal. Each time he made a purchase he quickly sought solitude, disposing of the drugs as soon as he could. His one fear was that he would be stopped by a police officer out to make his quota of arrests by busting users and not pushers. Staying away from places too close to home, he soon became a semi-familiar face, a regular whom no one really knew.

His working capital started to run low. He had planned for that. Having established himself as an occasional user who bought from several dealers, he no longer had a need to buy drugs.

He bought the gun from a "regular" dealer, a small man in a dirty sweat suit who did nothing to disguise his profession. Darnell told him what he wanted, then left. An hour later he went back to the same corner and traded the last of his comic book money for a small .32 caliber semi-automatic pistol.

On the way home, Darnell could feel the weight of the pistol in the pocket of his sweatshirt. He felt different. He felt dangerous. The people he passed on the street were also different. Now, they were his. Some were his to protect—the kids running down the sidewalk, the old men sitting on their marble steps replaying last night's ball game, the young girls coming home from their honest jobs at the sub shop. Others were his prey. He could pick out the dealers, the gang members, the ones who were the reasons he had bought the gun, the ones he would hunt.

He did not use the gun that night, or that week. The gun lay where he had hidden it, behind a panel under the stairs where he had first found his heroes. Each day he would tell himself that that night he would go out, that tonight was the night he would start the hunt. Each night would be filled with reasons and excuses not to go out. His sleep was broken by disjointed dreams of discharging guns and exploding faces, of being chased through endless alleys by freshly-dead drug dealers. He would wake up afraid of the night, afraid of the gun, feeling a failure and a coward.

He would get rid of the gun, he decided, just throw it away, then he would not have to worry about it. Then he remembered why he had bought it. That night he went out.

"Just a test," he thought. "If the moment is right—a dark street, no witnesses, no police—I'll do it. And if I can't, I'll drop the gun in the dumpster and at least I tried." He expected to come home unarmed.

It was warm for April; everyone was out. Darnell felt relief that tonight it would end before it could start. He walked the streets, rejecting each dealer as he saw him, willing himself to believe that it was impossible to use the gun without being seen.

"Hey, schoolboy," he heard from a dark alley. "Still armed and dangerous?"

It was the dealer who had sold him the gun. "What you do with it? Going to hold up Leon's Lake Trout?"

Without thinking, Darnell said, "I've been looking for you. This thing doesn't work." He pulled out the gun and walked into the alley.

"You got the safety off—"

The gun went off. Darnell quickly turned around. No one was looking into the alley. No one would, in that neighborhood, look toward gunfire. He then looked at his victim. The dealer had fallen backward. The hole the bullet must have made was invisible in the man's dark clothing. His eyes were open, staring at Darnell in surprise and death. Darnell looked at the gun in his hand, the gun he had not meant to fire, the gun he had planned to give back. He ran, praying that the alley had another exit.

He made it home without being stopped. The gun hidden, he hid himself in his room. He did not sleep that night.

What if he wasn't dead? He looked dead; should I have checked? Could he identify me? Would he? Did I touch anything? These thoughts worried at him. He washed his hands several times. He told himself it was to get all the traces of gunpowder residue off of them.

That morning, having spent the night at the window waiting for the blue flashes that would signal advancing police cars, he saw the paper thrown onto his front porch. Rushing outside, he had the paper opened before he was back in the house.

He found the article on the second page of the local section. The dealer's death was one of four that evening. All of the killings were reported in one story, none given more than two paragraphs. The paper reported the discovery of the body about an hour after Darnell had gotten home. The police stated that the killing had obviously involved drugs and believed it was one of several related shootings.

As his worry was replaced by relief, Darnell felt tired. He told his parents that he had been up all night and was too sick to go to school. He went back to bed and slept until the afternoon.

Darnell knew that the police might have his description, that they may not have told the press everything, and that they probably lied to the media as a general principle. Still, the fact that he was home and not downtown at police headquarters meant that he was not an immediate suspect.

Calmer now, he reviewed what he had done. The dealer was dead and had not lived to give a description. He was not a named suspect, and too many people matched his general appearance for him to worry about anything but bad luck. He had never been fingerprinted, so even if he had left a print, it could not be identified. He was as safe as he had expected to be when he had planned this.

He killed his next man quite deliberately. Still nervous and scared, he used that feeling as he approached the dealer.

"You selling tonight?"

"Always open, what you need?"

"Not here."

"Why, you scared of the cops? I got my boys either end of the street. They see a car, you'll hear '5-0' same as me?"

"Look, I get busted again, I'm an adult. Ain't no juvy court. I got to be careful. You don't want the business, I'll go someplace else." Darnell turned toward the alley.

"Man, you buying, I'm selling." The dealer followed.

Darnell turned just as the dealer entered the darkness of the alley. He fired twice into the man's face, the bullets striking his cheek and eye. Darnell made sure that the ejected casings were in plain view, then fled the alley. His victim lay slumped against a wall, a crooked smile and a bloody wink waiting for whoever found his body.

Darnell did sleep that night—not well, but he slept. In his dreams he saw vague forms, the men he killed, future victims, the police, all staring in silent accusation.

The body was not found until the morning. Dark alleys in that neighborhood were not well traveled. It was not until a derelict stopped to relieve himself that the dead dealer was noticed. It was not until the trash men came to pick up the garbage that the police were called.

In the next few weeks, three more dealers were killed. From each scene the Crime Lab recovered .32 caliber cartridge cases. As Darnell had planned, these casings were matched in the firearms laboratory and all were found to have been fired in the same weapon. It was the only lead that the police had. There were no prints from any of the scenes, and descriptions from the few witnesses who had come forward were so varied that they could have been describing different people.

Darnell did nothing stupid. He did not return to any of the scenes, choosing a different site for each execution. He did not call in false descriptions of the assailant in the hopes of leading the police astray. And he told no one of his crusade, so there was no one to inform on him. Unless he was careless or unlucky, he was safe from arrest.

With each death, sleep came easier. He was still troubled by disturbing dreams, but the accusing faces and the chases through endless alleys were no worse than his previous fears and nightmares of what the drug problem was doing to him and his world.

The toll was higher than Darnell knew. By chance, the first two dealers had worked for the same gang leader, who decided that their deaths had been the opening moves in a war that had been developing between his and another organization. In retaliation, he ordered the deaths of several of his rival's dealers. In turn, his rival ordered out his own troops. In the resulting chaos, the deaths of three additional dealers went unnoticed by the gangs, were ignored by the press, and were merely recorded by the police.

Darnell was not surprised that there had been no mention of the killings in the papers or on TV. The police did not usually admit to—much less inform the press about—a series of related deaths, especially ones for which they had no suspects. Darnell planned to correct that after his next hunt. He would send a typed letter to both of the city's papers, all of the television stations, and to those radio stations that still regularly broadcast the news. His letter would reveal how and why the deaths were related, and announce his campaign to the city. He would invite others to join him, and together they would rid the city of the plague of drugs. He would, of course, leave the letter unsigned. He had considered using a pen name, but signing himself "The Scourge" or "The Dragon" seemed a bit silly. Besides, all the really good names had been used by the comics.

Two weeks went by before Darnell found his next target. Because of the war, dealers had been extra cautious. Police patrols had been increased and the gangs' own hit squads were out looking for rivals. Finally, he found a target.

Darnell made his connection and was told to wait on the street. The dealer turned away and went down an areaway that connected the street with the back of the vacant house where he kept his goods. Darnell waited until the dealer was halfway through the tunnel before quietly following him. It was not until the dealer was in the yard that he noticed Darnell. He was dead before he could object.

The gunshots had just finished echoing when Darnell heard the sirens. From the sound, they were heading his way.

"Damn!" he thought, "Not now."

Whether they were for him or not, he could not take the chance. He could not be stopped anywhere near the body, and not with a gun. He quickly wiped it off, dropped it by the body, and fled through the back alleys, wiping his hands as he ran.

Just as Darnell had met with the dealer and was arranging his buy, a bored patrol officer decided it would be fun to roust a group of kids on the corner, not knowing that he would be interrupting a drug transaction. One of the kids shot him three times. The officer lived just long enough to call for help.

Except for the vague description of "several black males," the officers responding to the call for help had no idea who they were looking for. They covered the area, looking for anyone suspicious. The police helicopter reported that a young black male was running through the alleys just a few blocks from the scene of the officer's murder.

The increasing sound of the sirens and the darkness of the alleys conjured up Darnell's nightmares. He ran blindly, convinced that the entire police force was hunting him. The connecting alleys through which he fled seemed endless, so it was a relief when he finally saw an exit to the street. Then he saw the police car and knew the game was over.

The rookie officer had stationed herself at the end of the alley for a purpose. Based on the helicopter's report, this was the running man's most likely exit. She was convinced that it was he who had gunned down her fellow officer. As he came out of the alley and raised his hands in surrender, she fired three times, hitting him twice. Darnell fell, and died.

The officer who had killed Darnell was assigned to administrative duties pending the hearing that would, to no one's surprise, exonerate her of any blame in his death. After the police tried and failed to connect him in some way to drug activity, a department spokesman called Darnell "a victim of a tragic accident, which at times is inevitable in our ceaseless campaign against drugs." The deceased officer whose boredom had killed two people was hailed by the mayor as "a fallen champion in the war against crime, a true hero for our times."

This last story got its start in C. J. Henderson's Brooklyn living room. Thinking about it on my way back home I had it fully plotted by the time the train pulled in to Baltimore's Pennsylvania Station. I had it written in a week, then had to write it again after my computer crashed.

WHAT GOES AROUND

Gypsy's Caravan is one of the better theme parks on the East Coast. It won't scare the Mouse or the people with the Flags but it's large enough so that the average visitor needs two days to see and do everything. During the peak season, both the park and attached motel are usually full.

I do security work for the park. Not the uniformed guard type of security, or the kind that makes sure that the employees—sorry, *park associates*—don't tap the tills of the souvenir shoppes. (Yes, it's really spelled that way on all of the stores.) Neither do I walk the grounds at night making sure no one sneaks in or stays over. I'm more the kind of security you don't see—that is, if I do my job right.

I'm the troubleshooter. When something goes wrong that might attract unwanted attention—say from the police, or worse, the press—I'm called in to take care of it. If all goes well, then no one outside the park hears about it. If it's the kind of occurrence that can't be contained, then I'm at least expected to control the situation long enough for the press agents to spin things in the right direction.

Actually, the police are not that big a problem. Winslow's a small town, and Gypsy's the only major industry. The mayor, the chief of police, the town council—they know who pays their salaries. And if they ever forget, Hamilton Winslow is usually right at their elbow to remind them.

Hamilton Winslow owns the park, and most of the town. William Winslow founded the town before the Revolution, and, in many respects, the effects of that war have yet to take hold here. Free speech, representative government, equal rights for all—not in Winslow. There is the principle of one man, one vote. Hamilton's the man, and he has the vote. Everyone else goes along. Those who don't like it are free to leave, and are frequently helped to do so by the local police.

Paradise Denied

Hamilton was the one who hired me. I was on the good end of twenty years with the Baltimore Police Department, waiting for the right job to come up before turning in my papers. Hamilton was attending a theme park owners' conference at the Baltimore Convention Center. While there, he engaged the services of a professional "escort" for the evening. When he woke up in the morning, she was gone and so was his wallet.

I answered the larceny call. To his credit, he told me the truth about what had happened, rather than give me the old "I guess I forgot to lock the door" story. After that, he told me who he was and about owning Gypsy's. We agreed that to avoid embarrassing him or the park, he had probably lost his wallet shortly after leaving the convention center, and that he had not discovered that it was lost until he had returned to the hotel—alone.

As I was writing the lost property report, Hamilton asked me how long I had been on the force. One thing led to another, and I left with a job offer. A month later, I was the newest park associate of Gypsy's Caravan.

As I said before, my job at Gypsy's is to quietly deal with situations that might lead to unfavorable mention in the press—and a dead body at the Sly Fox Motel almost always qualifies as one of those situations.

I was in the armory making sure that the newest shipment of blank cartridges used in the Wild West show were indeed all blanks when my pager went off. The message, "911—Fox," told me to finish my inventory later. Grabbing my equipment bag, I took the Cannonball Express to the main gate, then the Safari Shuttle to the motel. When I got there, the manager lead me up to room 324. He opened the door, waved me in, then left me to do my job.

The body was that of a white male, probably in his late forties. He was in the double bed nearest the window, under the covers. I pulled back the sheet and saw that he was wearing only boxer shorts. The rest of his clothing was on the other bed, no doubt thrown there as he undressed for the night. There were no signs of trauma on the body, and nothing to indicate that any struggle had taken place in the room.

So far, it was obvious. Whoever this was had gone to sleep last night with every intention of waking up today. Sometime during the night, something inside him gave out and ruined his plans.

I didn't stop being a cop when I left the BPD. And just because my new job was to protect Gypsy's interests didn't mean that I took it any less seriously. So I set about doing those things that must be done whenever a dead body is found.

Not for the same reasons, of course. The police investigate dead bodies in case they're homicides. I do a full investigation to show that the park was in no way responsible for the death. And of course, if the investigation shows that we might be responsible, we know before anyone else and can take steps to mitigate that responsibility.

Before doing any searching, I got out my digital camera and took photographs of the room and the deceased. Digital photography is perfect for what I do. Digital means that I don't have to trust any darkroom people not to tell what they see when they develop the photographs. Digital means that I can print the pictures I need when I need them. And digital means that if things in the photograph need to be "adjusted" to fit alternate versions of what happened, it can easily be done.

After taking my pictures, I got the brush and powder out of my bag and fingerprinted the obvious surfaces. Hallway doorknob, bathroom sink and toilet, the bottles in the trashcans. Someone may have been with the deceased when he passed over, and I may need to know who it was.

Just in case someone had been with my new friend, I stripped off his shorts and threw them on the other bed with the rest of his clothing. I'd run a UV light over them later to see if there were any stains that suggested he had entertained a guest. As I took off the boxers, I noticed that lividity had already set in. The body was loose, so rigor had come and gone. He must have turned in early last night. He'd been dead for a while.

I called Winslow General Hospital and told them I had a special patient at the motel. That would clue the dispatcher in to sending an unmarked van. If we timed it right, we'd be able to remove the body without any of the other guests knowing anything was wrong.

I knew from past experience that the hospital van wouldn't arrive for at least twenty minutes. While I waited, I finished my search. The room gave up nothing aside from what you'd expect a man traveling alone to bring with him. A wallet from the pants on the bed told me that the deceased was Hector Young, that he was forty five, and that he lived in Richmond, Virginia. Tucked away in his wallet was a season pass to the park. *Hector,* I thought, *why'd you have to come to Gypsy's to die when there are so many nice parks in your state?*

Before I left, I'd check with the desk to make sure that Hector Young had rented this room, and that the guy on the bed was the Hector Young who had checked in. I made sure to take a photo of his face to show around downstairs. (Another nice feature of digital—the view screen on the back lets you display the photo you just took. And if you don't like it, or if it's the least bit embarrassing to the cause, well, that's what "Delete" is for.)

Everything went smoothly. Hector was picked up and sent to the hospital with no one the wiser. And Hector was Hector; the desk clerk recognized the picture. When I asked if she was sure, she told me that few people check in alone, that it's usually either couples or families with kids. Someone checking in by himself—him, you remember.

That last bothered me. Why did Hector check in by himself? If the pictures in his wallet were to be believed, he had a wife and two kids. Why didn't he bring them? A convention? We have them all the time, but Hector had none of the usual junk that you pick up at those things—no goodie bags, no brochures, no "Hi, I'm Hector" nametag. Besides, the Sly Fox is strictly for the tourists. The convention center has its own hotel and he would have been staying there.

There was something else bothering me, too. I wasn't sure just what it was, but my cop instinct told me that something was off in that room. There was something there that shouldn't have been, or else something that should have been there (besides the wife and kids) was missing.

Back in my office, I downloaded the pictures from my camera to my PC. I reviewed them one by one, zooming in and out, looking for that something out of place. Nothing in the bedroom or bathroom. I turned to the shots of the body. And there I found it.

I spent two years in the crime lab before becoming a sworn officer. Even after that, I saw my share of dead bodies. So I really shouldn't have missed it in the first place.

When a body dies, the heart stops pumping blood. Since it's no longer in motion, the blood, like all liquids, seeks its lowest level and pools in the parts of the body closest to the ground. The pooling of blood after death is called lividity.

When Hector died in his bed, the blood in his body should have collected in his buttocks, back, and legs. Instead, only his buttocks and feet bore the redness of lividity. Had he been found in a chair, that would make sense. So it was more than likely that he had died somewhere other than his room. I was going to have to visit Doc Harris sooner than I thought.

Martin Harris is the Chief Pathologist at Winslow General. Actually, he is the only pathologist, but he says the title looks good on his resume. Like all good morgues, his is located in the basement of the hospital. I had called to tell him that I was coming, so he was expecting me.

"He died sitting up," the doc said by way of greeting. Then he bent back over whomever he was doing.

"That much I know." I tossed the bag containing his clothing on a spare gurney.

"Anything on them?"

I shook my head. "Nothing I could find." Martin stripped off his gloves and pointed toward his office.

"So what did he die of?"

"Heart failure."

This is what Martin has told me every time I've come to him about a death. It's what he tells everyone. It was almost funny the first time, but now it's just a ritual I have to go through to get the information I need.

"And what caused his heart to stop?"

"Stroke." That was odd. A heart attack, maybe, but Hector hadn't looked like any stroke victim I had ever seen. "At least, that's what's going on the autopsy report," he added. Now it made sense.

Like me, the other park associates, and every appointed position in town—and most of the other ones—Martin owes his job to the goodwill of

Hamilton Winslow. Anyone making the park, the town, or the man himself look bad would soon be looking for other work. As I understood it, Martin Harris came to Winslow after a not-too-distinguished career in forensic pathology. In fact, I once heard it said that he had only become a pathologist because his patients couldn't sue. Still, toward the end of his career, he made one mistake too many and was allowed to retire quietly. His reputation preceding him, he couldn't get work as an expert witness. Winslow General hired him in spite of this reputation, or maybe because of it. This was the only job Martin could get. He's not the type to lose it over something stupid, like the truth.

At this point, I could do one of two things: I could say "okay" and ask him to send over a copy of his report when it was finished. The family would be notified, arrangements would be made to send Hector back to Richmond and all would be right with the world, at least, with my little part of it.

But as I said, I didn't stop being a cop just because I retired. And truths left unspoken have a way of coming back around on you. So I did the other thing.

"And what caused the stroke?" I knew I wasn't going to like the answer.

"This." Doc Harris reached into a drawer and took out a small white envelope. He threw it on the desktop. Whatever was inside made a dull *thunk* when it hit the surface. A *thunk* I knew well from my time on the force.

"What caliber?" I asked, not having to look.

Martin shrugged. "Who knows; who cares? It's not like anyone's going to see it, or know that it even existed." He looked at me as if I were going to challenge him. I answered his shrug with one of my own. Idly, I picked up the envelope and shook out what was inside.

I weighed it in my hand. It was small, a .22 or .25, depending on whether it was all there. It was in good enough shape that a ballistics match might be made. But this bullet would never be put under a microscope, not for the murder of Hector Young. Hector had died of stroke, and like it or not, that was the way it was going to be.

I handed the bullet back to Martin. "Where was the hole? I didn't see it."

"Almost smack dab on the top of his head, just 10-15 degrees off center to the rear. Easy enough to disguise so that it looks like part of the autopsy."

Not so easy, really, but only if someone's looking for it. I thanked Martin and went on my way.

You might be wondering why a theme park would cover up murder. It's the message it sends. We sell illusions, the illusion that things are different here, that real life stops at the front gate, that while you're our guest, you're in a safe, fairy tale world where nothing goes wrong. There is no crime. At our parks, people can't die, and certainly can't be murdered. A park that admits to reality will soon find its guests paying someone else for their illusions.

It was too late for the truth, anyway. Whoever had moved Hector to his room made sure of that. "Park Officials Cover Up Murder" made bigger headlines than "Death at Gypsy's Caravan." And since it was my job to keep the park off the front pages, I had to work around the truth.

Back in my office, I went over all the things I didn't know. Who had killed Hector, and why? Where was he killed, and how did he wind up back in his room?

I thought about the first two questions. The 'who' wasn't that important. He was getting a free ride on this one. The 'why' worried me somewhat. If Hector's death had been personal, if someone had wanted him and him alone dead, then no problem. But if his death had been random, that meant that there might someone out there who had decided to start targeting park guests. Not wanting to think in that direction, I decided that I'd worry about that when the next "stroke" victim came along.

I called the Richmond Police Department to ask for their help in notifying Hector's next of kin, and then walked from my office over to Central Command. Maybe they would be able tell me how Hector had gotten back into his room.

People had died in the park before. Not that we'd admit it. We have an established procedure for dealing with the situation. Whenever there is a person in distress, a medical team is dispatched. When they arrive, even if the patient is DOA, they treat him as if he were still alive. An ambulance is called and the patient is rushed to Winslow General. It is there that he is declared dead, not at the park. By order of Hamilton Winslow, no one dies at Gypsy's.

At Central Command, Harry Jones had the Board. From the Board, the man on duty could watch any of twenty monitors showing different views of the park. The views changed every three minutes, just long enough for someone watching the screens to view them all once before they shifted to other parts of the park. If the security man on duty sees something worth checking out, he can then freeze that camera, maintaining the view long enough to determine if any action is needed.

Cameras cover the entire park, with the exception of inside the restrooms. Hamilton wanted to put them in there, as well, worried about what illicit activities might take place in the stalls. I managed to convince him that the bad publicity that could result from the discovery of cameras in the ladies' room far outweighed whatever mischief might occur in there.

Monitor duty is rotated among the regular security staff. It is a break from park duty and most people look forward to it. Harry had been on duty all week, and would have been watching the Board yesterday when Hector passed away.

"No, nothing unusual happened, Mr. Webster," he told me when asked. Harry's not the brightest bulb in the chandelier, but he does an adequate job when given the right instructions. That goes for most of the security staff. They're hired more for their looks, muscle, and ability to follow orders than anything else. And Hamilton is against hiring anyone with a police background for regular security work. "No offense, Jake," he told me once, "But ex-cops are nothing but trouble. Their first instinct is to confront the situation and arrest someone, not make the matter go away. And they don't usually like bosses—any bosses. Give me a hungry college kid who can't find a job any day."

The instructions for handling the "special" sick cases aren't written down, but they are explained to everyone. So are the consequences of not following that or any other procedure. Screw up and it's, "Well, goodbye. Here's a week's pay and a pass to the park. Don't use it anytime soon." Given that, it's unlikely anyone used his own initiative to move a body.

Still, I checked the log that had to be filled out whenever any Security action was taken. No entries beyond the usual—a few would-be troublemakers were ejected, there were several sick cases, but these were the more typical motion sickness, heat strokes, and too much junk food upset stomachs seen every day. I looked up at the Board and not for the first time wished for a digital system that would save every image captured to a hard drive. "Too expensive," I was told every time I brought it up. Today it would have paid for itself if I could have found just one picture of Hector.

I left Central Command and went back to think in my own chair. Except for his season pass, there was no indication that Hector had died in the park. I tried to get comfortable with the idea that he had died outside my jurisdiction, maybe somewhere in Winslow proper, shortly after leaving the park. The more I thought about it, the better I liked it, keeping my fingers crossed that my random shooter was just an idle worry. In any case, I had done all I could do. I decided it was time to get back to doing what I was doing before the 9-1-1 call had come in.

And that was checking the ammunition for the Wild West Show. Real guns are used in the show (Hamilton insists), so I've made it my job to make sure that only blanks are fired in them. And that despite how it appears on stage, that no actor ever fires a gun directly at another performer. That kind of accident we don't need.

A sudden, terrible thought hit me. Guns, possible live ammo, and a dead man with a bullet hole in his head. I had a vision of Hector in the park, sitting on a bench, just resting, watching the crowd go by. Then a stray bullet from the show sails over the crowd and takes him out of the game for good. It's happened before, in Baltimore. Two years before I retired, a shot fired in celebration of the New Year traveled over the rooftops and killed a man two blocks away.

In a rush for the armory, I was up, out of my chair, and into the hallway when I remembered two things. The first was that I had already checked the ammo being used in this week's shows. All of it blank. The second was that the guns in the show were big, .44 revolvers, and not capable of firing the bullet that had killed Hector. I slowed down and walked to the armory.

Weapons inventory, checking and counting the ammo and comparing it against new orders and known stores helped passed the time, but it really didn't get my mind off Hector. The 'how' and 'why' of Hector's death kept nagging at me. I put myself in the shooter's place. Where could I stand to be able to shoot a sitting man in the head? I mentally reviewed the layout of the park, looking for the right combination of accessible high spots and benches, and then thought of something else that put the shooting out of the park.

One of the things the security team is trained to recognize is the sound of gunfire. Anyone who has really heard a gun go off—and TV and the movies don't count—knows that it sounds nothing like a car backfiring. It has a distinctive *pop*. Security is trained to run toward that *pop* if they ever hear it. Not to confront the shooter, but to get as many guests out of the way as possible. Once the guests are clear, the few guards qualified to carry weapons would be called in to deal with the gunman.

No one reported any gunfire yesterday. And the security coverage is such that every part of the park is at least within earshot of one guard or another. That made me feel better, until I remembered where I was standing. Maybe everybody heard the gunfire, and just didn't pay it any attention.

Stepping outside the armory, I walked down the Main Street of Dodge City like a gunfighter of old. I looked south, then north, and then I knew where Hector had been sitting when the bullet took his life. I went back to the office to find out who had killed him.

The phone on my desk was beeping and blinking, telling me that there was a message waiting. I pressed 'Play'. A woman's voice told me to call Detective Haywood of the Richmond PD about Hector. I dialed the number she gave me. The same voice answered the phone.

"Juliet Haywood."

"Detective Haywood, Jake Webster here, from Gypsy's Caravan. You called about Hector Young."

"Yes, Mr. Webster. I talked to Mrs. Young. Your dead man was a used car salesman, owned a few car lots, actually, and according to his wife he was supposed to be in Maryland on a buying trip."

"'Supposed to be,' huh?" Well, now I knew why Hector had been here alone, and what the probable motive for his death was. "Did Mrs. Young give any reason for Hector taking a long detour?"

"No, and I don't think it's occurred to her yet why he did."

"Let's hope it stays a mystery to her." She made a sound of agreement and I went on. "If you would, call and tell her that the funeral home can pick up her husband's body at Winslow General. I'll make sure that the death certificate and all other papers will be ready."

"Sure thing. Anything else I can do for you?"

"Detective Haywood, you've been more than helpful. If everyone in the BPD had been like you, I'd still be working there."

Once she heard that I had been on the force, we started talking shop. By the time she decided that she had better get back to work, we were 'Jake' and

'Juliet' to each other. I told her to make sure to look me up if she ever came out this way, and promised to drop a few park passes in the mail for her.

After hanging up, I turned to the computer and looked up work schedules and personnel records. It didn't take me long to put a 'who' with the 'where' and 'why' of Hector's death. Tomorrow I'd be going to visit the Big Wheel.

If you think I mean Hamilton Winslow, you're wrong. The Big Wheel is Gypsy's ferris wheel. It's at the back of the park, right near Dodge City and the stage of the Wild West Show. There might be other places in the Caravan where you can get shot in the head while sitting down, but near the ferris wheel, no one would pay too much attention to the shot that killed you.

Gus Rodgers had been with Gypsy's since it opened. He started by sweeping up, then worked concessions, then spent some time inside the character suits. After getting tired of being punched, poked, and prodded by the kiddies, he switched to working the rides. He's been working the Big Wheel since they built it five years ago. He's grown old working for the park, and some of the first kids he put on rides are now bringing their children to the park. I suppose he's near retirement.

Gus got married a few years ago. His wife is younger than he is—much younger. In fact, she's just about Hector's age. From the changes made in Gus's personnel jacket and insurance forms, I noted that his new wife used to live in Richmond.

It was early morning when I got to the Wheel. Gypsy's wouldn't open for a few hours yet. Safety inspectors were about, making sure that all the rides were in proper working order. Morning cleaning and maintenance crews were taking care of whatever the night shift had missed.

Pulling what little rank I had, I rode the Big Wheel during the regular test runs. If anyone wondered why I stayed on for several rides, or why I kept switching cars, nobody asked.

Gus's shift didn't start until late afternoon. I came back then. The line to ride the Wheel was moderate—about a twenty-minute wait. Gus saw me approaching, relief man in tow. After his relief took over, Gus joined me on a nearby bench.

In a park this size, with everyone hurrying from one attraction to another, trying to get the most out of their admission price, no one pays too much attention to what's going on around them. Oh, they'd notice a clown or a juggler, but not two guys just sitting on a bench talking. We had more privacy there than we would in my office. Still, we kept our voices low.

"Tell me about it, Gus."

"About what, Jake?" From his tone and the look on his face, I knew that my guess about the Wheel had been right.

"The guy on the Wheel yesterday, the one who got on but didn't get off—you know, the dead guy."

"How did you figure it out?" Gus asked. I didn't answer. I had my own questions.

"How's the wife, Gus? Does she know about Hector?"

He shook his head. "If she does, she hasn't said anything." He gave a sour laugh. "Not that she would—not to me. She doesn't know that I know."

"Tell me about those two—Hector and your wife." The nice thing about not being official is that pesky little things like Miranda warnings don't apply. If I had had a badge, I would have had to warn Gus about talking to me long before this, and to offer him a lawyer would no doubt make sure he kept his mouth shut. As it was, we were just two guys talking. And for whatever reason, Gus was willing to talk. I was willing to let him.

"They were friends from way back, when both of them were in high school. I think they met again when she went home for a visit. After that, she went home on visits a lot more. He started coming to the park."

"How'd you find out about them?"

"Does that matter, Jake? I found out, I took care of it. And there's nothing you can do about it."

So that's why Gus was so willing to talk. He had been around long enough to know how things were run, and to what extent Hamilton Winslow would go to avoid bad publicity. Well, maybe so, but that didn't mean he knew Hamilton, and he sure as hell didn't know me.

"By now, Jake," Gus went on, "I'm betting that however the doctors say Young died, it wasn't from no bullet in the head. He's probably all packed up for his last trip to Richmond, with papers saying that his death was natural."

"Well, Gus, I'm not saying you're wrong. I'm just trying to get all the loose ends tied up, just to make sure that there's none to trip over later." I looked at him to make sure that he thought he understood. Then we watched the Wheel go around a few turns.

"So who helped you, Gus?"

He was too quick to answer. "Nobody!"

In barnyard terms, I told him what I thought of that, and then I added, "Gus, to kill someone on a ferris wheel takes luck, timing, a good aim, and cooperation. I rode the Wheel this morning. Rode it until I figured out the angle needed for a good shot. With all the struts and supports, the only clear unobstructed view is from one car to another seven cars away. And that matches the angle of entry of Hector's wound."

I gave Gus time to think about this, then went on. "You don't show any type of firearms training—never with the cops, never in the Army. And for the shooter to be sure that his target would be in the right car, he had to have the cooperation of the ride operator—and that's you. So tell me, Gus, how much did you pay Harry Jones to kill Hector for you?"

Gus's face dropped. Bullseye! It had been a wild shot, but it had struck home.

"You asked Harry to help because he was on the Board this week. Anyone else ran the risk of the camera catching him in the act. Harry, however, could have left his post just long enough to kill Hector, and be back before his absence was noticed. And Harry is one of the few here who is qualified with firearms. Now tell me everything, Gus, or so help me you'll be wearing a bandana and beating a tambourine in the big parade ten times a day."

Gus didn't reply right away. "After I figured it all out," he finally said, "after I knew who it was, I'd see him on the Wheel every two weeks or so. I don't know why he rode it. Maybe he got his kicks watching me at work, knowing that he'd soon be with my wife. Maybe he didn't know who I was, and just liked riding ferris wheels. I don't know. And I don't know if I'd have done what I did if I hadn't seen him regularly. It was like he was rubbing it in. So, yes, I planned the whole thing out. Got the idea when I noticed that he was always coming around during the western show. So I asked around to see who needed money, and who was likely to do what I needed to get it. I came up with Harry Jones. Told him I'd pay him two thousand dollars, and it was money well spent. After that we waited until I was sure Young would be coming. And never mind how I knew; let's just say my wife's not as subtle as she thinks she is. When I was sure, I passed the word on to Jones. He had to call in some favors, but he made sure that he was on the Board this week. After that, well, it happened how you figured it."

Gus's story rang true. I saw last night that Harry had switched work assignments to get on the Board this week. Whoever he owed a favor to was not going to collect.

There was one final question. "What did you do, Gus, after Harry pulled the trigger? Let a dead man ride all day until closing, then take him back to the Sly Fox?"

"Nope," Gus shook his head. "He only rode until the end of my shift and Harry's. Harry got a cart and we made like he was sick. Then we took him back to the motel, stripped him, and put him to bed."

"Okay, Gus, that's it. Get back to work." I stood up.

"That's it? 'Get back to work?'"

I shrugged. "Like you said, Gus, what can we do? We call you on this, we put ourselves in a bad light." I gave him my best smile. "Just don't expect a raise anytime soon."

"You going to talk to Jones?"

"I might mention it to him, just to remind him that killing guests is against company policy."

Just for fun, I did say something to Harry. He wasn't nearly as polite as Gus was.

"And what you going to do about it, old man?" Old man? I may have retired from one job, but I was nowhere near Social Security. If Harry didn't pay for the murder, he would surely pay for that crack. "Send me away, you're coming with me. Last time I checked, covering up murder was still against the law." And he was right—in most places—but this was Winslow.

"Just wanted you to know that I knew." And left it at that, for a while.

Paradise Denied

After dealing with Harry and Gus, I finally went to see Gypsy's other big wheel. I gave Hamilton the 'who', 'why', 'where' and 'how' of the murder. I also told him that Gus and Harry thought that we couldn't do anything about it.

"Jones, I can understand," Hamilton said in a calm voice. "He's only been here, what—a season?"

"Two; he worked admissions security last year."

Hamilton went on. "It's Rodgers I can't figure. He's been around since forever. He should know better."

Hamilton was still shaking his head when I suggested calling in the police—ours, the county's, the state troopers, anybody—just to keep those two from getting away with murder. Even with offering up Doc Harris as a sacrifice, he didn't like it. I didn't think he would.

"So what's your next idea, Jake?"

I told him. This one he liked.

"Sounds good," he said. "Running the Big Wheel all these years, Gus should know that what goes around, comes around. Let's do it."

The next day, I again pulled Gus off the Wheel.

"You're fired, Gus," I told him. "No retirement, no pension, not even a park pass." I held out an envelope. "Here's your week's pay. Spend it wisely, you'll need every penny."

Gus turned white, then red. "You can't do this, I'll...I'll..."

"What, Gus, turn yourself in, confess to murder just to make us look bad? Go ahead; even if anyone believes you, we were just going on information provided by Doctor Harris. And he's been wrong before. One more time's not going to matter. Part of his job description is potential scapegoat. At worst, the park is embarrassed and the doc gets fired, except that he's got a pension. You—you'll go to jail for the rest of your life." I held out the envelope again. "Take this and go, Gus, or you'll go without it." I nodded to the two security guards standing close by, neither of whom was Harry Jones. I had other plans for him. Gus took the envelope and left.

Before firing Gus, I had paid a visit to his wife. I told her just enough to let her know that Gus had had something to do with her lover's death. I made sure that she understood that a future with Gus was no future at all. I explained the value of silence and the long-term benefits of accepting a position with Gypsy's Caravan. She was not a stupid woman.

Gus got home to find the locks changed. He later found that not only had his wife cleaned out their joint accounts, but that the house was now in her name alone. All he had left was a check that no one in town would cash.

Hamilton had put the word out on Gus. No one knew why, and no one asked questions. He couldn't get a job, a room, or even a kind word. The next day he was taken in for vagrancy and given a bus ticket out of town. He left, a sad broken man with little money and no future.

Harry was just as easily dealt with. About the same time I was firing Gus, officers driving a Winslow PD police car reported that someone had taken a shot at them. A bullet was recovered nearby—a .22 or .25, depending on whether it was all there. Acting on a tip, police searched Harry's apartment. There they found a small caliber pistol. Ballistics tests showed that it matched the recovered bullet. Harry was charged with, tried for, and convicted of attempted murder.

Was any of it right? It wasn't right for Gus and Harry to have killed Hector. And you're probably thinking that it wasn't right for me to have covered up his death. Maybe so, but I managed to do my job and still get a sort of justice for Hector Young. I'll settle for that.

Publication History

Fast Eddie's Big Night Out, Futures Mystery Anthology Magazine 32 (4th Quarter, 2003)

A New House, Weird Stories 2, Nov 1996, Fading Shadows Publications

Paradise Denied, Futures Mystery Anthology Magazine Spring 2004

The Best Solution, Crypt of Cthulhu, Vol. 18, no 1, Hallowmas 1998

Effect and Cause, Futures Mystery Anthology Magazine, Mar/Apr 2006

Pi in the Sky (with C.J. Henderson), Tales of the Talisman, Volume IV, Issue 1, 2008

The Right Betrayal, Originally published as "Turquoise" (Double Danger Tales 25, Feb 1999, Fading Shadows Publications) and "Turquoise Betrayal" (Double Danger Tales 27, Apr 1999, Fading Shadows Publications)

A Second Away, Startling Stories, Winter 2010, Wildcat Books 2010

Not Wrong at All, Published as part of "So Many Deaths" in Bad-Ass Faeries: In All Their Glory, Mundania Press 2010

So Many Deaths, So Many Lies, published as part of "So Many Deaths" in Bad-Ass Faeries: In All Their Glory, Mundania Press 2010

Surprise Package, Classic Pulp Fiction Stories 31, Dec 1997, Fading Shadows Publications

The Last Convention, Mystery Buff Magazine, Vol. 1, no. 4, 1998

Tissue of Lies, Strange Worlds 7, Nov 2000, Wild Cat Books

Confidential Information, 100 Sneaky Little Sleuth Stories, Robert Weinberg et al (eds.), Barnes & Noble 1997

Cain, Strange Worlds 8, Jan 2001, Wild Cat Books

Hero, Hardboiled 31, Jan 2004, Gryphon Publications

What Goes Around, Alfred Hitchcock's Mystery Magazine, Jul/Aug 2002

About the Author

John L. French is familiar with crime and monsters. Having worked over thirty years for the Baltimore Police Department as a crime scene investigator he has witnessed more than his share of what horrors one person can inflict on another. Working with patrol officers and detectives, John has been involved in putting many of these people behind bars for very long sentences.

In 1992 John began writing stories based on his training and experiences on the streets of one of the most dangerous cities in the country. His first story "Past Sins" was published in Hardboiled Magazine and was cited as one of the best Hardboiled stories of 1993. More crime fiction followed, appearing in Alfred Hitchcock's Mystery Magazine, the Fading Shadows magazines and in collections by Barnes and Noble. Association with writers like C.J. Henderson and James Chambers led him to try horror fiction and to a still growing fascination with zombies and other undead things. His first horror story "The Right Solution" appeared in Marietta Publishing's LIN CARTER'S ANTON ZARNAK. Other horror stories followed in anthologies such as THE DEAD WALK and DARK FURIES, both published by Die Monster Die books. It was in DARK FURIES that his character Bianca Jones made her literary debut in "21 Doors," a story based on an old Baltimore legend and a creepy game his daughter used to play with her friends.

John's first book was THE DEVIL OF HARBOR CITY, a novel done in the old pulp style. This was followed by SOULS ON FIRE, the Chronicles of the Grey Monk and PAST SINS, the Casebook of Matthew Grace. John was also consulting editor for Chelsea House's CRIMINAL INVESTIGATION series. John's latest books are HERE THERE BE MONSTERS, a collection of Bianca Jones stories and BULLETS AND BRIMSTONE, which teams Bianca with Patrick Thomas's Hell's Detective. John and Pat later presented their mix of pulp fiction and the supernatural with the FROM THE SHADOWS, featuring John's pulp avenger The Nightmare along with Pat's characters Nemesis and the Pink Reaper. John is the editor of BAD COP, NO DONUT, MERMAIDS 13 and the forthcoming TO HELL IN A FAST CAR.

One of these days John may get a website and a Facebook page. Until then you can email him at jfrenchfam@aol.com.

CPSIA information can be obtained at www.ICGtesting.com
Printed in the USA
BVOW080352210113